# WITHIN MAGIC

## DAY LEITAO

SPARKLY WAVE, MONTREAL, 2019

Within Magic | Portals to Whyland Book III



Print ISBN: 978-1-7750637-9-7

# CONTENTS

1

## ICE AND DREAMS

S ian had never been in such a landscape. It might have been a river one day, but now all he saw was solid ice. Ice everywhere, and the lights of a city far away. Karina called his name, she was close, but somehow she couldn't see him. He walked to her and held her gloved hand.

"Sian?" she gasped in surprise, her voice almost breaking.

"It's me."

Her face was smile and tears, soft and lovely as always, looking at him that way only she did, as if he were something more amazing and wonderful than even he thought he was. Quite a feat.

He pulled her towards him, thinking that if only he held her tight enough this time, she wouldn't disappear from between arms. Maybe there was a right way to hold her.

There wasn't. His hands were no longer solid, or she was no longer solid, as they moved through her. He'd feared kissing her, afraid that she would disappear again, but since it was inevitable, he brushed his lips on hers. Their energy blended and electrified him. Still, she disappeared—like she'd done so many times.

A strong gust of wind blew so much powdery snow that he couldn't see anything. When it stopped, he was no longer on the frozen landscape, but in a forest by a running river. He felt hot despite the shade of the trees.

A person with a silver cloak and hood walked in his direction. A woman, as she wore a dress under the cloak and had thin, delicate hands.

"I finally found you," she said.

Her voice was soft and calming while at the same time ringing in his ears like a familiar song. This was a dream. Well, of course. Any place where there were people, not Maris, had to be a dream. Every time he saw Karina it was a dream—or maybe a nightmare, reliving their parting over and over.

"Wait," the woman said. "Hold on. Stay."

"It's not like I was planning on going anywhere."

Still, he was surprised that he remained there. The realization that he was in a dream usually pulled him awake.

The woman exhaled and smiled. Her hood covered the top of her face, but he could feel her eyes piercing him. "The fight tomorrow. Don't wear shoes."

This was quite odd advice, and unnecessary. "There won't be any fight."

"Please, don't wear shoes tomorrow."

Sian blinked. "Right. I'll consider hurting my feet on the rocky, uneven, rough ground just because you said so. Who are you again?"

"Everything is energy, Sian. Negative and positive working together, making the world you see. You can connect with the energy of the ground, separate opposites, manipulate energy. That's how you'll win."

"Miss Everything-is-Energy, that's some neat philosophy."

She chuckled. "It's who you are. It's what you can do. Ground yourself and let the energy flow or—" She sighed. A sad sight. "If you fail, everything will be lost tomorrow."

"What everything?"

"More than yourself."

"I'll think about it. Any other advice?" Not that he was planning on following it, he was just curious.

"Plenty. But what is advice but words you'd better find out for yourself? This is all I can give you now."

The woman disappeared in front of him as if she had never been there in the first place.

Sian sat up, his heart racing, short of breath. Weird. It wasn't even as if he'd been scared in the dream. It had felt so real, though. He climbed out of the nook in the cave wall he'd chosen for his bed. Only now his body was getting used to the hard floor covered with leaves. He walked down to an inner, well-hidden cave with a small entrance Maris couldn't get through. It had a pond secluded from their eyes. The weather was finally getting warmer and he wouldn't almost freeze in its water.

His reflection stared at him. His hair was now below his shoulder, split ends like flowers, but what he disliked most was the overgrown beard on his face. He'd wondered if he could ask a Maris to use his sharp claws on him, but ended up deciding that the risk outweighed the nonexistent gain. He'd better get used to this new wild, rough look, and perhaps to this new wild, rough Sian.

Appearances were still important in Marisia, but it wasn't about clothes, beard, or hairstyle, but about how he held himself. What mattered most was not giving way to fear—or worse, despair.

After one last look behind him to double-check that nobody peeked, he took off his clothes slowly. His pants skid off easily from his ribs, thinner than ever. Worms and herbs were anything but a fattening diet. He'd still been exercising, walking, training, and climbing, so at least the muscle wasn't lost. He removed his shirt last, avoiding his reflection. The clothes were not yet rags, but were getting close to there. Well, in a place where everyone was naked, it was unlikely that he would be criticized for his lack of style. Plus, nobody was going to catch her breath and look at him up and down here—at least he hoped not, as female Maris were far from his type.

As his feet felt the bottom rock, the words from the dream came back to him. Clear dreams like that usually had some meaning or some relation to something that was real, but he couldn't figure out what not wearing shoes could mean. He waded in the water, feeling it all around his skin, refreshing and purifying. A part of the small pond had mud and it sort of worked as soap. Sort of. Better than nothing.

The dream came to his mind again. Energy, positive, negative, yada, yada. It sounded like some mumbo jumbo people in some villages in the North or South of Whyland would say. Mumbo jumbo —he knew it had meaning and wasn't nonsense, but didn't understand why people with magic couldn't also work on their communication skills. If someone could take the trouble to pass a message through a dream, why not take the trouble to find a way to be intelligible? And that voice, there was something familiar to it, but he had no idea what.

He wished the part of the dream with Karina had lasted longer. It wasn't the first time he'd dreamed about her, and every time what he most felt was the agony in knowing she'd disappear. And she'd been disappearing faster and faster. Perhaps he was seriously contemplating that he'd never find a way back from Marisia.

Sian took a deep breath and dove, the clear water caressing his skin and hair. He should better focus on the day ahead, when he was going to challenge the Marisia King. His chances of beating him in combat were zero.

∼

THE FREEZING WIND felt like knives hitting Karina's face as she walked from the metro to the address she'd been given. Zoe walked with her, making them not one nutcase who ventures in extreme cold, but two. Well, she was curious, and who could blame her? Karina sometimes thought her friend also wished one day she'd venture in another dimension. Her friend's hood and tuque covered her now blue hair. Somehow she'd managed to make it look natural and elegant. Of course, she wasn't that elegant now under her thick coat and with a red nose.

When the windchill brought the sensation close to -40, Karina always felt as if her nose would fall off. Still, she had never heard news about fallen noses, so she was pretty sure hers was safe and still attached to her face, even if she could no longer feel it. Senses can be deceiving.

Sian had been in her dreams—again. They should be good dreams, but there was always the dread of parting. The taste of his brief kiss still lingered in her mouth, and that felt good. But something was off about his appearance, and with her fuzzy memory of the dream, she wasn't sure what it was. What she did know was that it gave her a horrible feeling, as if he were in danger, suffering, or both. Could he have been imprisoned for his crimes? Her chest tightened with the very real possibility. It was just a dream, though, and couldn't have anything to do with reality, only with her own fear. And that fear was nonsense. Darian—and Cayla, by consequence—wouldn't allow Sian to be mistreated, even if he were imprisoned. Still, her dread for him also pushed her forward, as she tried to find a solution, a way to reach him, a way to at least make sure he was all right.

Her heartbeat reverberated through her body as she approached the address. The sky was already black even though it was only five in the afternoon. She and Zoe walked in a deserted street until she reached a metal door in what looked like a deposit or old warehouse. The night, the location, and the ugly door gave her the creeps, but the cold made her want to enter whatever building it was.

"Are you sure this isn't dangerous?" Zoe dared voice one of Karina's fears.

She wasn't sure, no. "I've met Karl before at a cafe. He was all right. You don't have to come, though."

"I'm not going to turn around now." Zoe smiled. "For one thing, I'm freezing."

Karina laughed, nodded, then pressed the bell.

She had posted ads online asking for people who knew about interdimensional teleporting, and while she'd gotten quite a few trolls, this guy seemed legit. He was part of an association for teleporting, researching obscure texts about the topic. They'd come to Montreal after sensing intense activity in the city. The activity had been Karina. She now wondered if the high-rise where she lived worked as a teleporting tower, despite the floor divisions.

But she didn't want to try from her home. Well, in truth she'd tried more times than she could count, and nothing happened. Either way, this guy had built a tower, and this is what she'd come to see with her own eyes.

But trusting strangers and trusting people who didn't know much about advanced magic was quite a risk. Plus, her goal was to go to Whyland, and she did wonder whether trying to go there wouldn't open portals and make them vulnerable again. She also feared ending up in the wrong place, being locked away from home forever, or being lost, not to count the millions of things that could happen. She took a deep breath. The book Sian had given her was in her bag, and, if she was so good at opening portals as he'd claimed, why couldn't she find a way there? That if nothing went wrong. And if six months hadn't changed everything.

∼

DARIAN HAD BEEN in the north for two days. This was the warm north with deep forests and wide rivers of his childhood, for at the time he wasn't always in the Light Gardens; he also ventured in Whyland. Now that the communication with his city had been broken, some sources of trade were gone as well. The official explanation had been people moving out and natural catastrophes erasing villages from the map.

The north had rearranged itself, and Darian had been there overseeing a new trade port and a small military base, manned mostly by northern people, because it was important for them to have defenses there. Whyland was at peace—for now—and it allowed him to focus on different endeavors, but they couldn't forget that tides change. But then, maybe he'd been there in the faint hope that he could find his city again. This time there was nothing, though, and no sign of anyone from the Light Gardens.

Back in Siphoria, he was eager to see Cayla. Five days away from her was torture. He rushed to the council room, where she could be meeting with advisors or representatives from other kingdoms. He hated that part because he still hadn't forgotten Arlenia. As much as King Conrad's threat turned out not to be true, the thought of Cayla anywhere near him was unbearable. And yet they'd met a couple months before. Darian had to bury his jealousy.

Today there were no international representatives in the castle, though, and Cayla wasn't there. Darian knew where he'd find her.

Cayla was at the castle's small training yard with Alessa. Darian hadn't told her, but he'd gone to the criminal archives and researched all he could about the girl. She seemed to have been involved in a murder for self-defense many years before, when she'd been arrested, and then mysteriously released. The recent records implied she'd been working as a highly paid bodyguard, usually looking after big criminals' wives or companions. Blotchy past, no doubt, but she got along with Cayla and made her happy. And perhaps she'd been only trying to survive. Now, hired as an official defense teacher, the girl would have no need to go back to her life of crime.

Alessa showed knives and their use. Cayla wore a light dress, and she was so focused that she didn't notice his presence. Darian just stood watching her, sunlight reflected in her hair, dark eyes staring at the knives. Determined. Strong. Beautiful.

With a blunt knife, Alessa touched some points on Cayla's neck, and then Cayla did the same. Darian approached them.

"Funny," Cayla said. "I'm not sure I feel comfortable learning the right spot to kill a person."

Right. Leave girls to themselves and they start talking about girly stuff, like how to commit murder.

"You never know," Alessa replied. "Hopefully you'll never need it. In any case, you could use it to decide which points to avoid, or even to give someone a quick death."

Cayla sighed, a hint of worry on her face. Darian in fact hoped she'd never have to fight again, but he couldn't blame her for wanting to be prepared.

Cayla said, "Can we go back to the fighting stances?"

"Sure," Alessa replied. "Much more likely to be useful."

Cayla took two knives and held them. "Before, I never understood why two, if you usually only strike with one. Now I get it."

"You do?"

"Defense, right? It's not because it's sharp and pointy that it's attacking, it's just—"

Cayla noticed Darian and dropped her knives. She had a smile but also a look of surprise, and ran towards him. "Are you stalking me now?" Her tone was playful.

"Yes." He laughed. "No. I just got here."

Alessa was arranging her knives and looking in the other direction. With nobody else there, he lifted her, sat her on a low wall and kissed her. He'd missed this closeness, their physical connection, her warmth, her smell, her taste. He loved the softness of her skin in his hands.

Then, he felt a horrible pain in one of his fingers and pulled it away before she noticed it was bleeding.

She looked worried. "Did you cut yourself?"

"Just a little." That was a lie. The cut was deep. He tried to sound playful. "What's this? Some kind of trap?"

She shook her head. "No. I was learning how to hide knives... I didn't know... I'm so sorry. But you should watch your hand!"

"Shouldn't the knife be sheathed or something?"

"Not when you hide them like that. I'm so sorry. I didn't expect..."

Darian shook his head. "It's fine. But if you have more of those, you'd better tell me where they are."

She looked at him. *That* look. "Maybe you can find them."

His hands were behind him, one of them stanching the bleeding on the other, and he tried to focus away from the pain. "I guess you do want me to chop a finger off."

She chuckled. "That's the last thing I want."

He kissed her lips lightly. "I'll see you later. We—"

"No. I can stop training."

"No, no. Continue. You like it. Plus, I just got in Siphoria, I need a bath. I can see you tonight. We could have dinner in the city."

Cayla squinted. "I missed *you*. Not food."

Darian laughed. "You can have both. Later."

"Later, then."

He kissed her forehead and turned away, rushing towards the castle's medical office, hoping she didn't notice the blood dripping on the ground.

Four Maris carried a sturdy net where Sian lay, looking down. In any case, he certainly hoped it was sturdy enough for him to get to Marisia's castle. Not a very dignified way for a possible future king to arrive, but the alternative would be walking there. On the bright side, he wouldn't get tired from flying. The river, mountains, and plains passed below him as they approached a rockier and even drier area.

Sian laughed at himself remembering the day he realized that the reason the Maris from this tribe had picked Sian to be their champion. It wasn't because they thought he had some special talent, but rather because they didn't want to sacrifice one of their own. Every tribe had to send a challenger every year. It would have been their leader's son, as he was the only one at the right age. Instead, Sian was going. Smart move. Sian was smarter, though.

Still, he liked the leader's son, Komiak, or at least that was what he understood his name was. They'd spent some time practicing fighting together, which only convinced Sian of the pointlessness of even trying.

The thing was, in theory there was no point in a king making people challenge him. Wasn't that a huge risk? Apparently not, because the king always won. It was probably a display of his power, a reminder as to why he was their leader, and an appearance of fairness, so that nobody would dispute his leadership, since in theory he "earned" it against every tribe every year.

But not all tribes liked to send their own. With some coordination, Komiak had spoken to other leaders. The solution was simple: disobedience. If all tribes refused to send a champion at the same time, there wasn't much the king could do. He couldn't retaliate all his subjects. And if he tried, they could all attack him together. This was a decent plan, but prone to some risks, since it depended so much on everyone's cooperation.

Sian had a second plan. There was a plant that grew near the river with highly sedative properties. He'd studied the plant and learned that the seeds carried the active principle. It had taken him quite a few very sleepy nights to figure that out, but he did. With this, he concocted a powerful sedative, to be spilled on the king's fountain. Sian hoped it didn't come to that, but it was solid as far as a backup plan went, hoping that the super-powerful king wasn't that good a fighter when sleepy and groggy.

The one thing that didn't put Sian at ease was that Komiak never stopped training. The fact that the young Maris was still thinking he'd need to face the tyrant king the following year was far from reassuring. Another issue was that Sian hadn't negotiated with anyone directly. Cut off from his ability to talk to people—or creatures—needing a stone to translate what he spoke, he felt as powerless as he'd never felt in his entire life.

They landed at the front yard of Marisia's king's lair after about an hour of flying. It was a cave like a lot of the dwellings on this land. There were cave dweller Maris, and plains dwelling Maris, but the plains with few trees or ruins and shades were far from where Sian had been living.

At least one thing in common between the king and the tribe that took him. Sian calmed down his heart, reminding himself that the day he'd decided to come to Marisia he had forfeited his life. He should be glad that he was still alive, perhaps living on borrowed time, and should thank every second he still had a chance to breathe, a chance to fight, a chance to survive.

The cave was a lot more gigantic than even he could imagine. Its first chamber could fit the Siphoria castle. It had no lake or water in it, only stalagmites and stalactites and some water dripping from the ceiling. Hopefully the Marisia King would drink from a small personal fountain, or else Sian's failsafe plan would be doomed. No, he couldn't give into despair. There was a life for Sian, with much more than he had now, and he had to hope one day he'd find it back —or it would find him.

For some time he'd dreamed that maybe someone would come and try to rescue him, bring him back home. He'd watched the river and the areas by that fated tower, but no human had ever come. Perhaps all the teleporting paths had been blocked. Perhaps Sian's life was destined to be semi-starvation and loneliness forever. Maybe. But he wasn't going to give it away for nothing, he wasn't going to give it away for a tyrant king who had to kill his subjects just to make sure they knew who was the boss. Had he been the real boss, he'd never need this nonsense. The stupidity of forcing Maris to fight him and overusing his authority would be his downfall. It had to.

They crossed the gigantic chamber, Sian, Komiak, and three more Maris. Sian had hoped they'd come in a larger number, but the custom was for a small delegation, and it made sense not to act suspicious. Sian still sometimes didn't understand why they didn't just straight up have a mutiny and revolt against the king. But then, maybe, authority had been ingrained in their brains. When someone is born into a societal structure, it is hard to even conceive something different, and changes are scary. The alternative, however, would be to die one by one.

Like the cave Sian had been living, this one had a second chamber, but this was even bigger than the previous one, with a ceiling higher than even the highest tower in Whyland, and the shape of an arena. Down, on the bottom, stood the king. Sian reminded himself of his plan in order to quelch the small pang of fear almost forming in his chest. The creature was huge, like four times the size of any regular Maris. Each of his talons was thicker and longer than Sian's arms, and he thought he had pretty well-built arms—as far as humans went. His beak was so huge that he would be able to snatch off Sian's entire upper body.

So that explained why that king had been so confident in calling challengers. It had nothing to do with braveness, but with cowardice, fighting creatures who were so much smaller than him. Incredible how nobody had ever called him up on that. Then, maybe, whoever did call him up was no longer around to say anything. On second thought, it wasn't that incredible.

The purple stone was round and clumsy but Sian carried it as he didn't want to stay in the dark as to what was being said. He also wanted a chance to speak, if it came to it. Komiak took Sian in his claws and they flew to a nook in one of the cave walls. There were more nooks with other tribes, as if in an arena or theater for a spectacle.

Sian was at a great disadvantage not knowing how to fly. He could climb, though. The walls were rough enough that he could move on them, if it ever came to that. His climbing had improved a lot in the last few months. Where before he would see smooth rock, now he found fissures and cracks for his hands and feet. Feet. He stared at his very old boots and remembered the words in the dream. They made no sense, but then, how much of his logic applied to that world? How much of his logic had been trained away from magic, away from so many things that he was only now grasping?

That dream had either been his own mind telling him something he didn't know, or someone trying to give him a message or warning. Perhaps it was literal. Sian sat down and unlaced his boots.

Komiak looked at him. The Maris means of communication was very different from humans. They sent thoughts and images.

Screeching was more for show, emphasis, or distant alerts. Komiak never screeched, but he could communicate with the purple stone.

The stone spoke, "Good idea. I don't think you'll be allowed to wear those."

Neat that nobody had told him that—except the dream lady. "Right. Anything else I didn't know?"

"We'll try to allow you to wear your clothes."

Yes. That point. Sian didn't see how wearing clothes could change the result of the fight. In fact, looking at that Maris king, Sian could wear a spiked armor, and it wouldn't change anything. Unlikely that a frayed shirt and thinning leather pants would do much. No way he'd stand naked in front of an audience. But then, in theory he wasn't even supposed to fight.

A cold chill ran through his spine. "Komiak." The creature looked at him. "Did you forget our agreement?" Sian whispered, which was stupid. That stone wouldn't whisper.

Komiak just stared at him. It would be foolish to say anything about their plan.

Sian took a better look at the place where the king stood and his heart sank. He had running water behind him instead of a small pond or drinking fountain. There went any hope for his failsafe plan. Perhaps he'd always known that it would have been useless, and yet, planning, trying, and doing something had been a better alternative than agonizing powerlessly.

He still had the crushed seeds, though. Maybe they could be useful.

More and more small groups of Maris came and placed themselves in the different nooks in the wall surrounding the cavern. Sian could almost hear his heart and realized that if Maris hunted based on fear, he was likely not invisible at that moment. Fear was stupid, though. Useful as a warning, but not much more, and pointless.

So many creatures were coming. Of course they could overpower that obnoxious king, and it was a very logical thing for them to do.

Some of the Maris stared in his direction, likely thinking that his tribe had brought their fresh snack. Lovely to think that he was in a place where hundreds of large, deadly creatures considered him food. Then again, he'd already overstayed his time in Marisia for months, and took the time to appreciate this as another shot at survival.

The Maris settled as if awaiting something. There was something oppressive, odd about that silence. Sian also knew that Komiak would give the sign and the Maris would attack the king. How many would join them and how many would try to take the opportunity to gain the favor of the king was the remaining question.

An ear-piercing screech interrupted his thoughts. The king had spoken—or something. The stone didn't translate him, though. Sian was about to ask Komiak what was happening, but couldn't because all the Maris screeched in return. Some form of salutation, probably. On a nook in the middle of the chamber, a Maris screeched, then they stood in silence. The creature was likely communicating with the others. Komiak then screeched.

The stone said, "I'm sorry. Survival comes first." It then changed its tone, as Komiak screeched. "The traitor is here, among us, and we brought him as a prize to our king."

So that was it, then? They'd decided to turn against him?

Sian turned to Komiak. "Don't do this. He'll kill you one by one. He'll kill you all."

Komiak ignored him and continued, "In return for bringing him, we ask that he be allowed to challenge you as our champion."

Noises came from all the nooks, and Sian thought that they were some kind of laughter. Sian said, "I hope they make *you* challenge him and die."

"At least my brothers will still survive," the stone said, translating Komiak's thoughts. In Sian's mind he could see a large group of Maris going to Komiak's cavern and killing everyone. So that was his fear; that if he betrayed the king, they'd kill his people. But it could be avoided if everyone worked together.

It continued, "We've been betrayed. Fight him and keep in mind what you learned. Your chance is small, but it's a chance."

The king screeched.

"He accepts it," the stone said. "Reluctantly, but he does. Good luck."

Komiak grabbed Sian with his claws and they flew towards the center. King Sarat was even huger from up close. Sian knew from training that size was not always an advantage when fighting. Smaller combatants could be faster. That said, size mattered a lot in terms of power and resistance. Calculating his odds was pointless. All that he could hope for was an honorable death.

He saw himself reflected in those golden eyes, straight and proud, despite his gaunt and shabby appearance. In his mind he could see Siphoria, Malena, his friends, his brother, Karina, the Whyland throne, the day he closed all the portals and saved his land from the creatures he faced right now. It had all been worth it. And maybe, like Lylah said, he was destined for a short life, but not anyone's life; a hero's life. At least it had never been boring.

2

# CHALLENGES

Karina stood waiting, her heart accelerating, her face freezing. Months of trying and hoping beyond hope were finally coming to fruition. Hopefully.

The door opened and Karl welcomed them inside. He was a man in his forties, with greying blond hair and green eyes. The girls entered and hung their coats by the door.

Karina pointed to Zoe. "This is my friend, the one who helps me teleport." It was a lie, but it was her excuse for bringing her.

Karl smiled and extended a hand. "Ah. Nice to meet you."

Zoe shook his hand and smiled. Karina didn't see a place to put her boots, and the floor was hard, unfinished cement, probably too cold for someone to wear just socks.

Before she asked, Karl said, "You can keep your boots. Cold today, isn't it?"

Karina laughed. "I guess global warming doesn't translate into warmer winters, just wacky weather."

Karl's eyes were somber. "One more reason to go away while we can."

That was an odd thought. Perhaps humanity was indeed doomed, but she still considered it would take some two to five hundred years.

Karina had never wanted to teleport away just to escape some climate catastrophe. Okay, sometimes, when it was cold like that, she wished she could teleport to the Caribbean or something, but that was different. Still, she said, "True."

Karl turned around and showed another door. "Come."

Zoe stared at her and grimaced, probably also disagreeing with the man. Karina shrugged. The door led to descending metal stairs. This place had the feeling of an old, abandoned factory or deposit and Karina could feel her friend's tension. But then, of course a teleporting tower would be well-hidden. Or at least it should be.

The clank, clank, clank of Karl's shoes on the metal steps didn't feel as loud as Karina's own heart. Hers and Zoe's rubbery boots were silent. This could be foolish, irresponsible, dangerous. And yet, there was no way to stop it now, and no way she could have stopped looking for someone with a teleporting tower or any teleporting information, no way she could have stopped hoping.

There was that nagging feeling that Sian was in danger. True or false, she couldn't shut it off, and it overwhelmed all reason. And still, meeting Sian again was also scary in its own way. Would he have found someone else? Would he still want to conquer Whyland? Did he even remember her? She thought he did, but the heart had a funny way of influencing logic and thoughts. For all she knew she could be delusional, and perhaps all Sian had done was just because of her power. But then she always convinced herself that she had to find out the truth, and with that thought, she found her justification for what she was about to do—whatever it was.

Sian stared at the Marisia King, who stared back. If this had been a staring contest, he'd have very good odds. Unfortunately, it wasn't a staring contest. To make matters worse, being the first, he had no idea about the creature's fighting style. But no battle was won—or lost—until it was fought. Sian wasn't about to give up.

As he got in a combative stance, years of training kicked in, observing every muscle of his opponent, aware of every micro movement, as if time slowed down. No sound reached his ears other than King Sarat's breath, staring at him with a mix of curiosity and disdain. All of Sian's attention was focused on the creature. His entire life condensed in that moment.

The king lifted his claw and moved it to hit Sian, who waited for it to get close enough, jumped, and climbed the king's leg towards the top of his body. He ran towards the king's head, hoping to reach its eyes. The creature jerked, then rolled on the ground, and Sian jumped away before being crushed by that body. But lying down sideways, the Maris was an easy target, since his head couldn't move much. Sian jumped on top of its beak, again aiming for the eyes, but then unbearable pain shot through his entire body, and he fell.

Sian couldn't avoid the pain but he could pretend he didn't feel it in the hopes the creature would give up. He jumped on its neck, a place the king couldn't reach either with his beak, wing, or claws, and as Sian pressed his body against the creature, the pain stopped. Either the king had given up or being that close prevented him from making Sian feel pain.

So that was how this king won: by cheating, doing his weird magic to weaken his adversaries. Anyone with less tolerance to pain would have been convulsing on the ground. The creature jerked and moved to try to drop him, but he held on. If Sian had a sword or any cutting weapon, he might have won by now. But there was very little he could do with his bare hands. At that, the creature took flight and rolled so fast that Sian was thrown on the ground. The fall was short, and since Sian was used to jumping from heights, he rolled and cushioned his fall. All this because he'd lost focus for a second—no more.

Pebbles. If he could find pebbles he could aim for his eyes. But there was nothing. No, there was something; the stalagmites on the corner. He ran towards one, watching the king with the corner of his eye. As the creature lunged on him, he jumped away. Its beak cracked a pillar of rock. Sian jumped on it feet first—what a terrible time not to wear boots—and finished breaking it. Now he had a lance, a very raw, heavy, clumsy, blunt lance, but a lance nonetheless.

And then he felt it; again pain throughout his body, as if he were burning. The king eyed him, perhaps realizing that whatever he was doing had some effect. Sian let his pain show, contorting face and body and letting out the scream of pain that had been buried within —perhaps all the screams he'd buried. He focused on his pain and his rage, took his improvised lance, and threw it at the king's face. It buried itself deep in his eye. Sian had to bottle down his revulsion, as he ran towards the king, and jumped on the stalagmite, burying it even deeper.

King Sarat dropped dead. Silence overtook the cave.

Sian stared, only half believing it, only now taking in what he'd done, taking in the enormity of the obstacle he'd faced. It was almost as if another person had taken over him, commanded his reflexes, fought for him.

He knew who that person was: the son his father had always wanted. The magnificent, strong warrior; the one he'd honed, trained, and tortured Sian to become. Years and years of training, of pain and suffering, had just saved his life. His father had saved his life.

As much as Sian had always rejected what his father had taught him, had always believed that cunning beat strength, this time it was all he had. And he'd won because he'd been prepared. In fact, when thinking back about his father, he'd never yelled at him, never beat him in rage. The only pain and suffering he caused was training, believing it was for his son's own good. Perhaps a more compassionate father would have found a better way to train his son, or even wouldn't train him to face a cruel world.

General Keen gave his son what he could give. As twisted as it had been, it had been his way to love. His father's love had saved Sian. A tear formed in his eyes with the realization.

A screech pulled Sian out of his reverie. He hadn't prepared for this part because he'd never believed it would have come to this.

Maris in several nooks screeched. They were communicating. Perhaps they were planning something.

"Bring me the stone!" Sian yelled.

Komiak flew, but not to bring him the stone. Instead of going towards Sian's direction, he aimed at the cave's exit. Coward.

More screeches, and hard looks at him. Well, their looks were always hard. This was the moment Sian had to establish his authority.

He didn't care if they couldn't understand him. Perhaps they'd catch a little, perhaps they'd catch images or something. He yelled, "I'm your king! And you'll obey me!"

*Me, me, me*, his words echoed on the cavern's walls. The Maris stood in silence. After a few seconds, they flew in his direction. He knew what they were doing. They weren't coming to greet him for his victory but to finally enact the plan Sian himself had devised. Disobedience. Mutiny. They hadn't dared to do that against King Sarat. No, they couldn't defy the king who'd oppressed them. But now that their new king was smaller than they were, they had no problems getting together to gang up on him. Cowards. Perhaps all his suffering and training would turn out to have been in vain. Cowards. Cowards.

"Cowards!" Sian yelled and stood. The ceiling was high enough that the creatures flew in circles around him. So they wouldn't even dare face him on the ground, but fly and lunge at him from above. Cowards. Sian couldn't even call them dishonorable; it had been his idea in the first place.

Karina stared at the tower in what looked like brushed steel walls with some wires and copper-colored circles. Maybe it was a different type of teleporting tower.

Karl turned to Karina. "So, you think I need magic, huh? I assume you believe you have that *magic*." There was an edge about that last word, almost as if he didn't believe it meant what it meant.

"Maybe, but I can't be sure."

He stared at her. "You didn't come here just to see if my tower was real, did you? You want to go somewhere."

Karina paused, then said, "Well, that's the point of a tower, isn't it? Going somewhere."

"Somewhere specific, I meant," Karl said.

Zoe replied before Karina did, "Well, of course. No mystery there. She wants to return to a place she's been before."

Karina wasn't sure if it was good to be that straightforward, but the man didn't seem bothered.

He nodded. "Of course, of course. I understand. Now, see, I also have somewhere I want to go. If you can open the portal for me, you are welcome to use this tower to go wherever you want. How's that for a deal?"

Karina nodded. "It's fair. That said, I can't guarantee I'll be able to open the portal for wherever you are going."

Karl shook his head. "Nonsense." He picked up a metal plaque from the corner and brought it to Karina. "Can you see what's in this?"

It was just a silver plaque, but, as she stared, an image formed on it. It was the top of a tower, with windows facing a darkening sky and city lights below.

Karina was curious about that plaque. "What's this?"

"Lumina. The city of light."

Indeed it looked like a beautiful place, but Karina's question was different. "I mean this plaque."

"A rare object," Karl replied. "Together with rare archives with instructions. In theory all you have to do is look at this plaque while standing in the middle of this tower. I've tried, but it didn't work. Again, perhaps you know the secret I'm missing."

The secret was magic, but the man didn't seem to grasp the concept. To be fair, neither did Karina, at least not completely. If she had never seen it in action, she wouldn't believe it either, and even having used it, she didn't quite understand how it worked.

She took a deep breath. "Maybe. So you want me to stare at this picture?"

Karl shrugged. "I want you to do whatever you can to open a portal there."

Her heart beat faster. She didn't want to teleport to a place where she didn't know anyone and wasn't sure she'd be able to return. But just looking at the picture couldn't do anything, could it? There was more than that involved in teleporting. Maybe that was what Karl was missing. "Did you try looking at the picture and imagining yourself there?"

He frowned. "Of course. That said, the instructions are different. The idea is not to teleport there, but to open a way for them to come here."

A chill ran down Karina's spine, as she imagined strangers from another dimension entering her city. "Isn't it dangerous?"

The man rolled his eyes. "It's Lumina; the city of light, they are good people. And it's not a complete dimension like this, just a city."

Perhaps like the Light Gardens. Karina missed that place too, together with the chance of being a guardian, whatever that meant. Even then, opening a portal for strangers like that... "Why would they want to come here?"

Karl sighed. "They left the instructions."

Karina hesitated, taken by a nauseous feeling. She decided to pretend she was trying, then lie that she couldn't do it. Maybe later she could still find a way to go to Whyland. But then, yikes, what if her only way back was through this tower? And what if she teleported back when the building was locked? So many things she hadn't considered. She was just going to pretend to open the portal, say she couldn't do it, then try to stay away from Karl.

"All right." Her voice sounded cheerful. "I'll stare at it." She smiled. "Let's hope it works."

Karina looked in the direction of the plaque and the image. The city was beautiful, seen from windows among white walls, many lights below and a setting sun on the horizon. She didn't even keep looking to get more details, but relaxed her vision as if she were looking beyond it, so that her eyes didn't focus on the image.

She felt goosebumps. Since she'd returned from Whyland she'd get those when in the presence of strong magic. Often simple magic that goes unrecognized as such, as when someone sings a song with enough emotion. But she couldn't be doing any magic. It didn't make sense. She looked up.

"Don't stare at me. Stare at the panel," Karl said.

"I'm not sure it's—" she was going to say working, but Karl pulled a pistol.

Zoe ran in her direction. Heart speeding up, Karina stood in front of her friend and tried to sound brave. "You can't kill us. People know I'm here."

Karl shrugged. "I hide my identity well. C'mon. Stare at the plaque."

"I can't do magic if I'm nervous!" Karina pleaded.

"Just stare at the plaque, girl, and nobody will get hurt."

As the first Maris lunged towards Sian, he ducked, but then there was another close by, and its claw hit his shoulder, cutting his shirt and the skin beneath it. More Maris came, and they encircled him, while others, flying, attacked him. Sian ran towards King Sarat's body. He tried to take back his improvised lance, but it had been buried too deep. As a creature flew towards Sian, he jumped down, placing himself close to the fallen king's body, so that any attack could come from only one direction.

All he could do was duck, but at some point there were so many claws and beaks trying to reach him that there was nowhere to run. Death was facing him, calling him away from this world. The woman from the dream came back to his mind. Energy, positive, negative. Sian was kneeling, with arms around his face, but he decided to plant his feet on the ground and give it a try. So much magic he had never understood, magic that he'd been told he had even if he'd never felt it or recognized it. And if he had any magic that could save him, this was the time to connect with it. This or never.

He felt something on the ground, something in the air, something around him. Meanwhile, he moved so as not to allow the creatures to hurt him so much with their beaks, but his arms had deep cuts, metallic smell of blood overwhelming his senses. He'd never yield. He'd never yield. If all the strength he had wasn't enough, he'd call on whatever great power, greater energy he had access to.

Sian screamed as he saw a blue light surrounding him, expanding away from him. Electricity. It was electricity that expanded from him and hit the creatures who'd been attacking him. In the confusion of that blue light and some feeling he'd never had, he heard tormented screeches and a few creatures falling dead in front of him. Sian had found his magic. He'd never heard of it, as much as he'd studied; apparently he could make electricity. But he still hadn't won. If he didn't control these creatures soon, they'd attack him again. Ignoring the blood on his arms and forehead, he jumped over one of the bodies in front of him. He didn't care whether they understood him or not. Surely they'd get the meaning.

"I defeated king Sarat, so now I'm your king, and I demand respect. If you want to obey me, I'll let you survive. If you want to challenge me, you can do it one by one, as honorable beings."

A few Maris who had been attacking him stood staring, while a couple turned around to fly away. Sian felt the energy on his arms, and directed it towards the ones who were trying to flee, and then to more Maris who were going on the direction of the exit. They all dropped dead.

"Nobody moves!" he yelled. "You are going to stay and honor me as your king, as your tradition says you should. You were brave enough to challenge me, brave enough to attack me, don't you dare run."

*Show them, show them who has the power. Make them fear you, respect you. Only through fear you'll have respect.*

Somehow the creatures had understood him because they either remained on their nooks or around him. *Show them.*

"Now, defy me, and this is what will happen to you."

Sian used his weird electricity magic power and directed it towards the creatures surrounding him. They were killed instantly.

On the walls, on the nooks, the Maris shifted, uneasy. *Show them.* Nobody would ever defy Sian again. He felt high on power, invincible, as he could have killed them all. Killed them all, and it would have felt good. Instead, he directed his energy towards one nook and killed a random Maris.

"I can do this to every single one of you, but I won't. Go home. Go to your tribes and tell them—tell them who is the new king. Tell them to either fear me or come here and challenge me the right way." The creatures stood still. "Go!" he yelled.

Indeed the creatures understood him because they flew away. Sian felt the power flowing through him, causing such a pleasant feeling. He almost killed some flying creatures just for fun. Just because he could. Wasn't it the point of power? Doing whatever he wanted just because he could?

He stared at the bodies in front of him, proud of himself, when he heard a woman's voice.

"This is not you, Sian."

He froze and stared again at the carnage. While he'd been forced to kill some creatures in self-defense, he'd killed others just to impose his authority, just to feel powerful. Was that who he'd become when imbued with power? Was he just like his father? Sian trembled. Killing the attacking Maris would have been enough. No, he could have just injured them, and it would have been enough. They weren't brave creatures. There was no point in what he'd done. More, he knew that controlling subjects through fear was stupid, it only made them bid their time to turn against you. What had he done? He knelt, horrified, shocked at himself.

"This is not you, Sian," the voice repeated.

Tears were running down his eyes at the realization of the

monster he'd become. In a land of monsters, he'd become the worst of them. No. Wait. There was something else in Marisia, something else other than its creatures; Darloom. Horrified, Sian recognized that horrible creature's influence in the last minutes. From the moment Sian had found an upper hand, a feeling of invincibility, of being drunk on power, had taken over his mind, and he didn't fight it. So stupid.

"Don't you think you can avoid me," Darloom's shrill voice said. "You have nowhere to run, and I think I've proved we can be best pals."

Sian stared at his hands, horrified that he'd used that evil creature's energy, horrified. "You can't control me."

"Maybe not. That only proves that you are solely responsible for what you've just done."

No. Sian had allowed Darloom because he had been injured, afraid, desperate, and weak. Fear. Fear of being killed, fear of being betrayed, that was what had allowed those horrible thoughts to enter his mind. He was no longer feeling any of that. Sian remembered Whyland and this horrible creature's influence on the castle. It depended on a physical place, perhaps a place where there was some kind of portal. This cavern was his place in Marisia. Sian crossed the bottom of the chamber and climbed the wall towards the exit.

Darloom wasn't going to leave him alone. He said, "Leaving so soon? Do you want to go outside and be torn into pieces? Don't you realize that's what your beloved creatures are planning right now?"

"I'll deal with them. Don't worry."

Sian reached the exit on top, and looked down with a bitter taste in his mouth, seeing all the needless killings.

"Not needless, young king. You had to teach them to respect you," Darloom's voice said.

"Fear is not respect, dude."

Sian wasn't sure if his magic would work again, but he had to try. He pointed it towards the stalactites on the ceiling. His energy hit them—and nothing happened. No kidding, of course electricity wouldn't break stone. He had to find a way to collapse that cave, bury it.

"Really, my friend?" Darloom asked. "Are you ready to lose your power? To lose your protection? I can have you killed right now."

Sian just ignored that voice and made his way towards the second exit and stepped outside, in the sun. A creature flew in circles around him. Sian wondered whether he'd be able to use that weird electricity outside the cave, and feared that the creatures would attack him. The Maris landed by his side. It was Komiak, with the stone.

"I'm sorry," the stone said.

"I assume you had no choice," Sian replied.

"We always have a choice."

Sian shook his head. "That place is weird. It feeds into your fears. Maybe it had nothing to do with you. I'm also sorry."

"I heard what happened. You just defended yourself. It wouldn't have been necessary if maybe I had stepped up to defend you. You earned the title of king."

King. Hilarious. Sian had wanted it for so long, and now he'd finally earned it in a completely honest way. But he obviously didn't want to be the Marisia King, so the only victory that mattered was keeping his life. He was still worried about Darloom and what it could do.

Sian stared at the creature. "All right. Now, not as a king, but as your friend, I need a favor, the most important favor of all."

"What is it?"

"We need to demolish this cavern and block its entrance. This is the source of evil in your world."

"A cave?" the stone managed to sound surprised.

"Yes. There's a creature controlling it. It has done a lot of damage in my kingdom already, and has been influencing King Sarat. It has just influenced me, and made me do something horrible."

"We'll destroy it."

Komiak screeched, and after a few minutes more and more Maris came. Sian stood outside, observing the work they were doing. He was alert to any sign of danger, but the creatures were afraid enough that they avoided him. So he had gained authority with fear. His father would have been indeed proud. His father. In Siphoria's castle, under Darloom's influence for who knows how many years? Had it been his fault? And with his amplified fear, had it been such a mystery that he'd raised his son for a cruel world? Maybe he could claim that his father had chosen not to resist Darloom, but is it a choice when you don't know it?

Sian had felt and acted exactly like his father would—and would have continued like that if he hadn't received a warning. Perhaps he'd just had some better protection. He couldn't help but be overwhelmed with deep forgiveness and understanding, and even some regret at his bitterness against his father. He'd just been raising him to survive. And indeed, Sian was a survivor.

When the Maris finished their work, Sian asked Komiak to take him to the tower by the river. It was a human building, from an ancient time when people had inhabited this land. It could maybe also be a teleporting tower, and perhaps he'd figure out how to teleport away. He'd tried the river hundreds of times—no success. Perhaps someone would still come for him. He had to hope. He couldn't have survived just to die—abandoned and forgotten.

But he hadn't been forgotten. He knew he hadn't. Now, no longer bound by any promise, he felt that he had a chance of being rescued. He arranged a room in that tower from where he saw the desolate landscape below him. Pain shot through his upper body as he noticed a deep wound on his left shoulder. He'd better clean it—and hope river water would be enough to prevent infection.

3

# LUMINOUS

At gunpoint, Karina looked at the plaque in her hands. Zoe was behind her. Dragging her friend into this had been an awful idea. Just staring at an image was unlikely to open a portal, and she feared what the man would do to them if nothing was opened. Those goosebumps again. Perhaps it was only fear.

Karina had to stop being afraid and anxious and try to come up with a solution. Somehow, being threatened in her own world, with a gun that she knew was real, scared her more than any experience she'd had in Whyland. She wondered if she should try to teleport with Zoe. That, if that teleporting tower worked, of course.

When Karina was about to reach out for her friend's hand, convinced to try to teleport away, she heard a sound behind her. A sound somewhere between water boiling and wind. She knew that sound, and turned to see three young people wearing white hooded robes with golden rims and embroidery. It meant she had opened something, even if it didn't seem possible. She glanced at Karl, who still held his weapon but started to relax, his face in awe and surprise. Karina pulled Zoe's hand and ran to the door, taken by pure instinct that something not-so-pleasant was about to happen. It didn't make much sense. These people didn't look evil or anything, and if they were indeed from this city of light, there shouldn't be anything to fear. Despite that, alarm bells were ringing inside her.

A girl stretched her arm towards Karl. The palm of her hand had a light. Karina wanted to scream for him to lower his weapon, but before she said anything, a ray came out of the hooded newcomer's hand. Karl fell back, dropping his gun. Karina didn't know if he was dead or alive, and wanted to run, but didn't want to turn her back to that people.

The girl now pointed her hand towards Zoe and Karina, who wasn't going to wait to see what she was going to do. There was no time to think. Push. Explode. Whatever she did. It worked. The three newcomers fell back. Karina pulled Zoe's hand and ran up the stairs. One of the hooded people yelled "stop" or something similar.

Why had her magic worked in her own dimension? Perhaps residual effect of that teleporting magic, but it didn't really matter. All they had to do was run.

When they were at the top of the stairs she heard steps from below and closed the door leading down. Thankfully it had a lock, and she hoped it would hold. The girls ran to the door. Zoe was about to run outside without her coat, but Karina took both girls' coats and threw Zoe's to her.

"You don't want to freeze outside."

There was banging on the door leading to the stairs. The girls ran outside while still putting their coats on and kept running for two blocks.

When they got to a busy street with more lights and heavy traffic, Karina slowed to a walk.

"Wait. I don't think they can follow us outside." She couldn't run anymore, not after having run up those stairs in record time.

Zoe matched Karina's fast-walking pace. "What was that, Karina?"

"No idea. I'm so sorry."

They had to get away from that place as fast as possible. Still, the cold outside, the fact that those people didn't have coats, and being in a busy street, even though there were no pedestrians, calmed her.

"And what did you do?" Zoe asked. "When you pushed those people?"

"Something I didn't know I could do here." Magic in her own world was weird even for Karina. So far there had been a clear division between Whyland and her own home, between a place where magic existed and her dimension. She knew there was magic everywhere, but had never realized that magic that affects the physical world could also exist here, and more, that she could also have it here.

They were not very far from the metro, from normality.

Maybe not. A light appeared in front of her and became the girl, one of the three hooded people. Karina turned around to run but the two young men were behind her. How could they stand that cold?

"Wait," one of the boys said. "Wait."

"They're guardians!" the hooded girl protested. She was raising her hand and stared at Karina. "You can't fight us all."

Maybe. But she knew what they could do with their hands raised, and despite her disbelief whether she could do anything outside, in her own dimension, she had to try. Karina focused on her mini explosion and indeed the girl fell back. Her light shot sideways, breaking the accumulated melted and refrozen snow on the sidewalk. Shards of ice flew everywhere. No idea how no car stopped. Karina turned to the two hooded guys, about to do the same, but one of them had what looked like a protective field.

Karina grabbed her friend's hand and ran towards the street, away from those people, dodging cars until they reached the other side. "Maybe they'll die of hypothermia if we keep them out long enough."

Zoe was shaking. "They didn't look cold."

Indeed. No red nose or shivering, despite their thin-looking cloaks. Maybe it was revolutionary material, or maybe they were something different from regular humans. And of course, one of the boys appeared in front of them. He had long blond hair and brown eyes. "Apologies for my sister. I mean no harm."

Trying to run from them wasn't working, so it was time to change strategy. "What do you want?"

"Portals, that's all," the blond boy replied. "If you can open portals, you can help us."

Karina crossed her arms. "And how would we have helped if your sister had killed us?"

He shook his head. "Again I apologize, but she wouldn't have killed you."

"Is Karl, the man who had the gun, alive?"

The boy shrugged. "He had a weapon pointed at us. Were we supposed to wait?"

Talking. Talking was good. Maybe she could come up with a plan while they talked, but her mind was blank, unable to find an easy way out when they were outnumbered by people with superior magic. The boy was glancing at Zoe quite a lot. Karina didn't blame him; she was pretty. Hopefully that would count to their advantage.

Zoe must have noticed it, as she asked, "And if we help you, how do we know you won't hurt us?" She didn't sound angry or threatening, but mild and sweet.

"We're Luminous, from the city of light. We spread light, you see?"

Karina rolled her eyes. "I saw you spreading light to Karl."

"We were scared. We didn't know who you were or what you wanted. Let's all calm down, go back to that tower, and open some portals."

Karina was angry and about to say something snarky, but Zoe replied first.

"We're so sorry for that. We'll be happy to help you." She glanced at Karina, her eyes beseeching, then turned to the guy. "Of course we'll open whatever portal you want!"

Ugh, opening portals for people who kill first, ask questions later sounded terrible, but Zoe had a point that confronting them wouldn't help. It was better to pretend to comply. Hopefully they'd just teleport away and leave them alone.

"I'm Satwak," the blond boy said. He pointed to the girl. "That is Faizana." He pointed to the other young man. "And that is Geralm."

"Neat." Karina shrugged. "Let's open some portals, then."

"I'm Zoe," her friend said. "This is Karina."

Satwak nodded. "Again, I'm sorry this didn't start in the best terms."

Faizana and Geralm now joined Satwak, and they didn't seem as friendly. Karina wanted to run away. Instead, they walked back to the building where the tower was.

Zoe turned to Satwak. "It's freezing today. Aren't you guys cold?"

He stared down at himself. "No." He turned to his companions. "Do you feel anything?"

"No," Geralm replied.

"So interdimensional teleporting makes you invulnerable to cold?" Zoe was really into making conversation. It was nice that she managed to sound calm despite what they had just been through.

"Maybe that, maybe our magic. We can't be sure. We don't have ice like this in our city."

Weather; universal conversation starter indeed.

"What do you have in your city?" Zoe asked.

"The weather is usually mild; never too cold, never too hot."

"Sounds lovely," Zoe replied.

Satwak smiled. "It is. But there are other lovely things in the universe."

Lovely was the fact that they were being dragged back to the tower against their will. Then again, Karina couldn't face the three of them at once, and she didn't want to risk hers or her friend's life. Perhaps, like herself, they were just quite desperate to go somewhere.

They reached the building and found the metal door locked. The girl, Faizana, shot the lock with her hand light thingy and it opened. The way downstairs now felt gloomy, and Karina couldn't help dreading whatever was coming even if she kept telling herself that these were just scared people who wanted to teleport somewhere.

Zoe somehow managed to make conversation with Satwak as if

nothing weird was happening. Hopefully it would help diffuse the tension, and hopefully Karina and her friend would be free and left unharmed after doing whatever they wanted them to do.

They reached the tower. Karl was lying down, eyes open.

"Is he dead?" Karina asked.

Satwak nodded. "We thought we were going to be attacked, that someone was trying to invade our city. It was a mistake."

A mistake that could have cost Karina and Zoe's life, had Karina not used her weird magic.

Satwak looked at Karina. "No, no. As I said, she wasn't going to kill you."

Was he reading her thoughts? "That's great to know." She couldn't hide her sarcasm.

"I know you don't believe it, but we meant no harm."

Their meaning wouldn't help Karl. But perhaps she shouldn't be upset about him. Pointing a gun towards a portal from where you expect people from another dimension to come should win the prize for dumb idea of the year. He shouldn't have threatened Karina and Zoe either.

Zoe touched Karina's arm. "They meant no harm."

Her eyes were pleading. Maybe she had a point. *Let's be nice to the people who can kill us without warning.* Hopefully her friend wasn't pretending, though. Karina pointed to Satwak and whispered. "You know he can read our thoughts, right?"

"Not really," Satwak said from a distance. "Just glimpses, emotions."

He shouldn't have heard Karina, but at least he confirmed what she'd just said. Zoe tensed. So she was afraid despite her relaxed demeanor and previous chit-chat.

Satwak pointed to Karina's bag. "Can I see what's in there?"

His tone was polite, but it wasn't a question. Karina smiled. "Sure."

Her mind went back to Chemistry, as she visualized the periodic table and repeated: Lithium, Sodium, Potassium, Rubidium, Cesium,

Francium. Satwak definitely could read more than just glimpses, because he stared at her and grimaced. She wondered if chemistry was studied the same way everywhere. The boy took her book and his eyes widened.

Geralmis looked at the book as well. "Is that... the portal hub?"

Satwak chucked. "Looks like it. What a gift."

Fine. If they knew what it was, there was no point in chanting the first group of the periodic table.

"It's no longer a portal hub," Karina said. "It's been sealed." She shrugged, wondering if perhaps she'd made a mistake providing them information. "Not sure what you can do with a book, though."

"Open portals," Satwak said—as if it were the most obvious thing in the world.

Karina decided to be honest. "I tried. It doesn't work."

Geralmis now stared at her, eyes narrowed. "You tried. You mean you can—"

"Probably not," Satwak said. "See? She couldn't do it."

"How come she has this book, then?"

Satwak stared at his friends. "Objects sometimes travel to other dimensions. We can't know."

The girl, Faizana, was now close to them. "We'd better leave or guardians will find this portal. Let's bring them with us and see who's the opener."

"I think it was the man," Satwak said. He stared at Faizana. "Which you killed."

Karina again focused on the periodic table as if nothing else existed.

"Why were they here, then?" The girl pointed to Karina and Zoe. "We need to bring them with us and question them."

Satwak glanced at Zoe and Karina, then said, "I'll check them."

He put his hand on the top of Karina's head. "Why were you here?"

Despite Karina's effort, Sian's image flashed in her mind. She shut it off quickly, but not before Satwak noticed it. His eyes widened in what looked like a mix of surprise and joy, kind of like a kid who gets the Christmas gift they'd been wishing. Then he got serious again, and his posture straightened as if he'd become alert. Karina focused on the periodic table again, to see if it could deviate his attention, trying to shut down curiosity about his reaction.

Satwak turned to the others. "It's her. The other girl has nothing to do with it."

"Let's bring her with us, then." Geralm pointed to Zoe. "Her too, or she might talk."

Satwak approached Zoe and put his hand over her head. "No. She'll forget what happened here."

Karina wanted to do something, but she wasn't sure what.

"Where are you taking Karina?" Zoe asked.

Satwak hesitated, then said, "Our city, but she won't be harmed. I promise you."

Zoe's eyes had tears. "No."

"I'm sorry." His voice was almost a whisper.

Karina's heart beat faster. Should she try to use her magic and prevent whatever he was going to do? Would she be able to confront them? But before any smart idea could form in Karina's mind, Zoe closed her eyes and collapsed. Great.

Karina ran towards her friend. Still alive. She turned to Satwak. "What did you do?"

"Don't worry. She'll wake up soon. We have to go."

Right, Zoe had just been knocked out. Karina had seen it enough to believe it. The issue was that any escape plan was doomed, as she wouldn't be able to carry her friend. Faizana grabbed Karina's hand. Soon she felt as if she were falling or floating, and closed her eyes due to the intense brightness. When she opened her eyes, she was on the top of the tower she'd seen on the plaque. This was unlike any teleporting tower she'd been, because it wasn't at the bottom of a tall circular room, incorrectly called tower, but rather on the top of a tall building from where she could see a city below. The sun shone on triangular roofs and distant woods.

There were five more hooded people, hands in front of them, around the tower.

"Close it now." Satwak said, staring at Karina.

"What?" Was he even talking to her?

"Close the portal."

"I don't know how to do it."

"Yes, you do."

Karina closed her eyes and imagined that door closing, visualizing a cord being cut, and wasn't sure if it was right. She pictured doors shutting, a wall being erected, a light between worlds turning dark... She had no idea if this would close the portal and she was afraid of what they might do to her.

Karina opened her eyes. "Did any of this work?"

"It did."

A man with very long black hair approached them. "Who's this you brought?"

"A gift," Satwak said.

This sounded horrible, and that man gave her the creeps.

"A portal opener," Faizana added.

"She's friendly to our cause and wants to help us," Satwak said.

The man with the long dark hair raised an eyebrow. "Huh. Doesn't look like it."

"She's just afraid."

Karina started to think that Satwak was protecting her and wasn't sure if she should feel glad or worried about whatever he wanted. Hopefully this wouldn't take long and she'd be able to be back home soon. She'd told her mother she was going to sleep at Zoe's, but that would buy her a night only. And there was school and everything. Yuck. First she had to make sure she remained alive.

The man with the dark hair approached. "We need to test her. She could be a spy."

Satwak, who carried Karina's bag, took the book with the images of Whyland and tossed him. "This. Maybe she could open a portal there."

Just opening a portal, not teleporting, was something new and strange. Again, something she wasn't sure she could do. The man opened the book and his eyes brightened. Karina hated that.

He gave the book to Karina. "Stare at an image in it."

Karina shuffled the pages until she came to a picture of a misty forest, which she imagined was very far from any populated area.

"No, no, no," the man said. "Somewhere busier, like a city." He took the book from her and opened at the image of a city. Siphoria.

Her heart sank. What were her options, though? If she opened the portal, she could put her friends at risk. If she didn't open it, she could put her life at risk. She decided to unfocus her vision and just pretend to look at it.

"You're not looking at it," the man said.

"I thought that was the right way to open a portal."

Indeed, she'd been doing something similar to this back in her world, in that strange tower.

"She's too nervous," Satwak said. "Give me some time with her."

"Be brief, then," the man snorted.

"Come." Satwak's voice was again kind, and he led her out of that room, into a different corridor, then to a room with a chair.

Karina didn't sit and neither did Satwak. He just lowered his hood. He had golden wavy hair, brown eyes, and was younger than she'd thought at first, looking somewhere between sixteen and twenty-four.

"I'll be brief," he said. His voice was harsh. "That man you just met is my uncle Firis. You either help him willingly or he'll make you do it. It might hurt. And I don't mean just pain, but harm, and I'll spare you the details unless you insist. So if I were you, I'd do my best to help him—and pretend you like it."

"You promised my friend I wouldn't be harmed."

"That's why I'm asking you to cooperate. You have to help me."

"Why do you want to go to Whyland, though?"

Satwak shrugged. "Does it matter? We don't even care about that place, if that's what worries you; we just want to reach the portals."

This didn't sound good, but Karina couldn't see any way out of this. Plus, the portals were closed. Maybe it wasn't a terrible idea.

"There's something else," he said. "Some of us can indeed see people's thoughts. Firis is very good at it. So I'd be careful."

Karina narrowed her eyes. "You can read them too."

"A little."

He was lying.

Satwak smiled. "Fine, then. More than a little. But nothing like Firis. So if you value your life and your physical integrity, pretend you want to help us. Oh, my uncle has ways to use your magic without your consent. You don't want him to do that either. So you might want to comply."

Karina had a thousand questions, including: why were they doing this? What would they do to her once she opened the portals for them? Who were those people? She swallowed.

Satwak took a deep breath. "Portal openers are rare here. As long as you're useful, and as long as you don't cross my uncle, you'll have no reason to fear."

The question in her mind was: and *what happens when I stop being useful?* But the answer was obvious: *never stop.*

Sian sat down and stared at his shoulder. Maybe it would be better to remove his shirt, but he didn't want to do it. Ragged as it was, the shirt still covered his upper body. Maybe he shouldn't care about it, now that he was alone, but he couldn't help it.

There was goo coming from the wound and his shoulder and upper chest were swollen and painful. The Maris didn't use any herb to cure their infections. Their bodies were different. He'd seen them getting hurt and healing. He had to find something... Salt. The only answer was salt. That could maybe stop the infection. There was none there, though. Sian got up and stared out the window. All rivers went to the same place. Maybe if he followed the river he could come to an ocean where he could clean his shoulder—if the ocean was clean. The river didn't have any visible end, though, and he'd traveled in that direction, to the King's cave, and had not seen any sign of ocean. Sian could die trying to reach a distant source of salt water. He'd die alone and abandoned, away from the only place where there was any hope for him to be found.

KARINA FOLLOWED Satwak back to that room with all the guards. Satwak covered his head with his hood again. Everything was a blur around Karina. She tried to focus her mind on *helping these really nice people.* There was movement of more hooded guards coming in. Karina took the book and looked at it. It was a picture of the Silver River, Siphoria, and the abandoned tower. This must have been an old picture, as it didn't include the military tower. But no, she shouldn't be remembering any of that. Or maybe she should? To make sure a portal was opened? Everything that had happened since she'd left her home that afternoon flashed in front of her, starting with her eagerness and anticipation as she braved the extreme cold. Speaking of cold, she still had her icky boots and coat, and was starting to get hot. At least focusing on her physical sensation allowed her mind to focus on something.

"You have to reopen that portal," Satwak said. "We'll need to go through it." He then whispered, "And don't even think about tele-porting away."

Weird that the last thought hadn't even occurred to her. Maybe because fear was taking over her mind. Maybe because she wasn't even sure how to teleport, and then maybe because these people would follow her.

Comply. Perhaps Satwak was right, it would be worse if she were killed or forced away from her free will. Ignoring how much she hated what she was doing and trying to pretend she knew how to open and close portals, she thought about the tower in that building where Karl died, and about Siphoria.

"Go!" Firis, the dark-haired man, spoke.

Karina raised her eyes and saw some of those guards, soldiers, or something disappearing in front of her. So they were teleporting. There could be an invasion in Whyland, and she was allowing it. She focused on how hot she felt, trying to shut off any other feelings or thoughts.

Someone took her arm. Satwak. "I'll take her to interrogation."

Firis stared at her. "No. Put her with the others."

Karina felt Satwak shudder. "She's more useful conscious."

The dark-haired man had a grimace. "Too dangerous."

"But Lumina needs teleporters. I have an idea." Satwak's hand was on her head and then everything went dark.

4

# BREACH

Cayla watched as Darian buttoned up a beige shirt, covering up his collarbone. She was still sometimes awestruck at how everything about him was perfect, from his soft hands to his amazing smile.

He stopped. "You don't like it?"

"What?" Cayla was startled.

"You're staring."

She looked away. "Sorry."

Before she looked back, he was in front of her, planting a kiss on her cheek. "No need to say sorry."

Cayla turned to him. "You mean I'm allowed to stare?"

"As much as you want." He kissed her lips.

It was a long kiss she didn't want to break away from. He pulled her close to him and she knew they'd start it all over again. Two, three, five. No point counting. Their love was infinite. And just when she was ready to get lost in his arms again, her stomach growled.

Darian stopped. "I'm horrible. I said we'd have dinner."

"We lost track of time." Just then, a memory hit her. "Oh, no."

"What?"

"Alessa. We were supposed to go out tonight." She hoped he wouldn't be upset. "I thought you would still be up north."

"There's still time, you could still go."

Cayla wasn't sure she wanted to walk away from him. "But us..."

Darian pinched her chin. "There's tomorrow. And the day after. And after. And after. You've spent your life locked in this castle."

He had a point. "True. You can come if you want."

He kissed her forehead. "Go. It's good to make time for friends."

This would actually be the first time she did that in a long time. "Are you sure?"

"You'll be disguised, right?"

"I got a brown wig." Her hair was so distinctive that covering it up was enough not to be recognized—or at least she hoped.

He smiled and ran his hands through her hair. "You'll have to show it to me one day. Well, that, and the fact that you'll be out with a very well trained bodyguard... I'm confident you'll be safe."

Cayla had been rather thinking he could be jealous, but she should have remembered that this was Darian, and he had shatter-proof confidence. "Sure you don't want to come?"

Darian smiled and shook his head. Cayla kissed him and ran back to her room, hoping her friend wouldn't mind that she was late.

DARIAN WATCHED Cayla run away towards her friend. Since she'd told him more about her childhood and how sheltered her life had been, he'd encouraged her to get closer to people she liked. Alessa was nice. The thought of Cayla in a place with music, drinking, and all eyes on her almost made his skin break with hives, but hopefully he'd sounded unconcerned. This was important for Cayla. He'd better swallow his immature jealousy.

Darian put on his boots and decided to make his way to the kitchen to grab something simple to eat. As he walked out, he stepped on something. One of Cayla's knives. His heart warmed remembering her giggles, as he put the object on a table and then walked outside.

In a hallway, he came across Lylah. "Where's Cayla?"

"With Alessa. Were you looking for her?"

The woman smiled. "No. I was just surprised. You're usually together. Were you going to the kitchen?"

Darian still felt a little awkward around Lylah, and would have answered whatever meant that they wouldn't need to spend unnecessary time together, but since he didn't know where she was going, he said the truth, "Yes."

"We're two, then."

It would be odd to say he changed his mind, so he had to walk with her hoping she wasn't planning on asking him any intrusive questions about her daughter or lecturing him. He wasn't sure how much she knew about his relationship with Cayla other than the fact they were betrothed and wondered if he'd feel more or less awkward if she knew everything. Maybe he'd better not think about it.

They got to the kitchen and sat at a table together. Speaking with Lylah in an official capacity was one thing, sitting together in the kitchen as if they were buddies was another, especially right after...

"Did you ever have any news about your brother?" she asked.

She'd interrupted his thoughts to turn to a subject that only made him feel even more anxious.

"Should I? I thought you knew all about him and his need to live a hero's life." He sounded more bitter than he'd meant.

"I just wasn't sure."

"Isn't there a way to find out where he is?"

Her eyes were sad, or perhaps had pity in them. "Maybe there is, but I don't know it. I'm sorry."

Darian didn't like being pitied and felt annoyed. Still, he took a deep breath and decided to ask a question that had been bothering him for a while. "Lylah?" He paused. "When the Maris invaded, and you were in Arlenia, you said it was because you had predicted your death, right?"

"Yes. I also had a vision about Bianca's boy defeating them. I thought I could ruin it if I came."

"Can all of you predict your death?"

She tilted her head. "What do you mean *you*?"

"From the Light Gardens."

Lylah shook her head. "I'm not from there, even if I have visited that city and had close friends there."

Darian sat back. "Oh."

"My family's from a different ethereal city, one that no longer stands."

"What was its name?"

There was wistfulness in her eyes. "Gleam Fortress. It's been gone for generations." She then changed her tone. "But I don't think you're interested in history, are you?"

"Well, I am. I'd like to understand where I'm from, but—"

"Your mother. You want to know why your mother didn't prevent her death, don't you?"

Darian swallowed. He'd been going in circles, but yes, that was what he meant to ask. He nodded.

Lylah stared. "Well, not everyone has visions, and not everyone can see the future. Can you?"

"How would I know?"

"Have you ever had dreams or visions that became real?"

He tried to think.

Lylah didn't wait for his reply. "You would remember if you had visions. It was probably the same with your mother. She couldn't see the future."

Darian looked down. "Yes, but..." It was hard for him to remember that, remember how he saw his mother killed by common thieves, how he hadn't been able to help. "It just doesn't make sense. They were just regular thieves. She was from the Light Gardens. I mean... Even me, I knew how to fight—defensively at least." He recalled how he was able to defeat Liam easily, using a technique he'd learned when he lived in the Light Gardens. "We should have been able to deal with three men."

Lylah stared at him and took a deep breath. "Your mother was strong, but not invincible. And her strength was not in fighting. The time comes for all of us. It was hers."

"But you didn't go when it was your time."

"It probably wasn't my time, then. Maybe that was why I had the vision."

Darian was still unconvinced and anger was bubbling in him. "Why did it have to be my mother's time?"

"I don't know. I also miss her. She was my friend, too."

There was another question bothering him, and perhaps Lylah knew the answer. "Well, tell me then, tell me why she never mentioned my brother, why I came here and had to treat him as a stranger. Why?"

Lylah stared at him and paused as if measuring her words or thinking, then said, "Sian was born here, in this castle, but your mother and father left when he was very young. I lost contact with Bianca then. General Keen came back a year later with Sian, claiming his wife had died. I didn't know *you* existed. And never had time to know. I was locked in the white tower soon after he returned."

Darian looked down. "Do you think Darloom was influencing them?"

"It's a comforting thought."

Strange reasoning. "Why *comforting*?"

Lylah shrugged. "You shift the blame."

"So you don't think it was."

"I don't know, Darian, I really don't."

Darian sighed. "Do you know if my father gave my mother a love potion?"

"Those potions are quite useful. Again, you can shift the blame for foolish choices."

"So you think it wasn't."

"I don't know. People change. Your father, at first, seemed to be a decent man. So did Cayla's father. Was it Darloom that influenced them? Was it power? Or had they always been horrible people and the potion prevented us from seeing it? I can't know."

Darian looked down. Sad, angry, disappointed, he didn't even know how he felt. "I thought you knew more."

"At one point in my life I might have thought I knew all the answers too. As the years passed, I realized that I don't."

"Love potions do exist, though. Karina was given one."

"I heard that. And why do you suppose your brother's friend came in possession of it?"

"No idea."

"It's not that hard to guess who ordered it, Darian."

"You mean my brother. Are you implying he used it?"

"No. I think he changed his mind."

"And what does it have to do with anything?"

"Do you think he'd love her any less if he'd given her a potion?"

"It'd be a pretty disturbing kind of love if you have to force someone…"

"You just enhance what's already there. Keep that in mind."

"That's still horrible. And they say you'll go crazy if you give it to someone. Maybe that's what happened to my father."

"Maybe. Then, maybe it was Darloom. Maybe it was a combination of factors."

Darian exhaled. "I just wanted to understand why my mother hid my brother from me, that's all."

"Perhaps it was to protect him."

That didn't make any sense. "When he was living in the castle, where everyone knew he existed?"

"She could be hiding him from the Light Gardens."

"They're good people."

Lylah took a deep breath. "There are tons of reasons why a child could be endangered. You don't know."

"I guess I'll die not knowing."

"Maybe. They might know the answer in the Light Gardens."

"Which I'll never reach, since the passage has been blocked."

"It won't stay blocked forever, Darian." She frowned. "Did you hear that?"

He hadn't heard anything. "No."

Lylah got up and pulled his hand. "Come. This might be your lucky—or unlucky—day."

The servant still hadn't brought their food.

"What's happening?" Darian asked.

"I'm not sure, but I need to take you to an emergency portal."

He kept walking with her. "If something's happening, I need to mobilize our defenses, I need to get Cayla. What's going on?" Even though he hadn't heard anything, the worry on the woman's face was enough to alarm him.

"You're going to the Light Gardens, and they'll explain everything to you there."

"But the portals..."

"I can open an emergency passage. It's a last resort, but at this point it might be worth it."

"At what point? I'm not going anywhere if you don't explain—"

Lylah stopped and gave him a hard stare. "Do I have to knock you out and drag you?"

He wasn't afraid of stares. "I'm not walking away with Cayla in the city, without taking care of the safety—"

Everything went black.

Cayla was dazzled by the lights and the multitudes in the city. It was different being in it as if she were nobody special, and perhaps different being there without Darian—and with her hair well-hidden.

"We should go straight to the Junction. My sister's playing tonight," Alessa said.

Diane had been hurt and scared the last time Cayla had seen her.

It would be nice to meet her in more normal circumstances and hear her playing.

"Do they have food there?" Her stomach was still growling. "I didn't have time to eat."

"They do, and it's decent. How come you didn't have time? Evening meetings?"

"I was with Darian." That wasn't a good explanation. "Don't ask."

"I wasn't going to. He didn't want to come?"

"He was tired."

She didn't want to say that Darian wanted Cayla to spend time with friends because confessing she hadn't had friends in a long while was quite embarrassing.

Alessa stopped. "Wait."

"What?"

"I told you I'd show you Siphoria, remember? I think we can eat in a better place."

Cayla hesitated. "Are you sure? I don't want to miss your sister."

"Positive. I just remembered they're last."

Alessa led Cayla to a tiny restaurant, if that could even be called such. There was a counter at the end, some seats facing a wall, and three tables outside. The weather was good, and they sat at a table on the sidewalk.

Cayla watched the people walking on the street, a late-night rail transport passing in front of them. Everything and everyone so ordinary. She'd come to Siphoria before, usually wearing some kind of hood, but she'd never had time to just relax, sit, and watch the city live its life while ignoring her.

The woman from the restaurant brought them some sort of vegetable pie.

Alessa pointed to it. "Zafar. This is typical of Siphoria."

"I think they have it in the castle."

Her friend shook her head. "Some silly imitation. This is the real deal. You might be wondering why this place is not full, if it's so good, but it's because a lot of people buy it to take it home. They're also almost closing."

Indeed, the woman was cleaning the interior floor. Cayla felt bad. "I'm so sorry I was late."

"You weren't *that* late."

"I shouldn't have forgotten it."

Alessa shrugged, parted the pie, or zafar, and served it. It better taste good, since the service wasn't that amazing. Cayla poured water in two glasses, then took a bite of the pie. Yes, it was quite good, in a different way from the food at the castle, simpler, with less seasoning. The taste was more subtle. If anything, it was different.

Cayla smiled. "It's great."

Alessa nodded. "I told you."

As Cayla forked another bite, a sound startled her. No, it wasn't a sound, just a feeling, something. "Did you hear anything?"

Alessa looked around. "Did you?"

There weren't any guards around the restaurant and Cayla felt unsafe at that time at night, on a street where there were only a few pedestrians here and there. Maybe she was paranoid or just unused to being in the city. Maybe it was something else. She was about to suggest leaving when Alessa glanced behind Cayla.

"There's a weird group coming. Don't look. They might have nothing to do with us."

Alessa's posture was relaxed but her eyes were alert. Resisting the urge to turn, Cayla drank from her cup, ears perked for anything suspicious. The steps in the distance changed from walking to running, but then again, how likely would they be interested in Cayla and Alessa? The steps approached. Cayla tried to pull a knife from under her dress but cursed mentally when she realized she was completely unarmed.

Then, there was just a flicker of alarm in Alessa's eyes before the girl jumped over the table, pushing Cayla down, who got up and saw her friend moving fast, facing five people wearing hooded white cloaks.

Cayla reached for the water jug and broke it. Her right hand got cut, but now she could use the glass shards as weapons. Two people approached her. With a fast arm movement, she cut one of them, who stepped back. The other stepped back as well but reached out his hand.

Cayla's necklace, the one Darian had given her, the one she used to communicate with him, one of her most prized possessions in this world, was pulled from her neck. Cayla jumped and kicked the person to whom the necklace was going and he fell on the floor. So did the necklace, though. When she moved to catch it, she felt as if a strong wind wouldn't let her get near it, and another person caught it. It was a girl, satisfaction in her face.

No. No way those criminals would get her necklace. Cayla braved that odd feeling like a barrier and stepped towards the girl, but she threw the necklace to one of her friends. They seemed about to leave. So it had been about the necklace all this time? They would turn around and Cayla would take a while to catch them, and considering they could toss it between themselves, her chances of catching the necklace were very small.

Cayla did the only thing she thought she could do; she threw a glass shard towards what had been her most prized object. The orange stone shattered in hundreds of pieces, and the guy holding it fell back. Then Cayla felt again as if a strong current of wind pushed her back, fell and saw the girl with her hand up. Their attackers turned around and ran away.

Cayla got up and was about to run after them when she saw Alessa on the ground by the tables. There was blood around her. As Cayla approached, she noticed blood coming from the girl's belly, where there seemed to be a deep cut. Beside her, one of the hooded people lay down unconscious or dead. The woman from the restaurant came out and knelt with a cloth, helping to put pressure on Alessa's wounds.

Guilt consumed Cayla. "It was so fast. I didn't see it. I couldn't..."

"Hush," the woman said. "You did what you could. Hold it and I'll be right back."

She went inside as Cayla tried to stop her friend from bleeding to death. But the cut was so large! Alessa was silent and Cayla was glad that she wasn't making an effort to speak. A bell sounded in the distance. No, not distance, the restaurant. There was so much blood on Cayla's hands. The woman returned and helped her try to stop the bleeding.

Some city guards came, then soon came the medics. Cayla couldn't understand what had happened. If it had been really her necklace they were after, then it was unfortunate that Alessa should have been hurt. Cayla wasn't sure she could bear the responsibility for her friend's death. Perhaps that would not happen. Alessa was put on a stretcher waiting for a small urban lift to take her, when Lylah appeared.

She ran towards Cayla and hugged her, getting blood on her white dress. "How are you?"

"I'm fine." She pointed to Alessa. "My friend—"

"She'll be treated. You have to come with me."

"I can't leave her."

Lylah stared at her. "Cayla, we need to sort out who these people are and what they want. If they're after you, the best thing you can do for your friend is stay away from her."

Stay away from her. Stay away from everyone. Maybe that was the only useful thing Cayla could do. "Fine. I guess I'll have to stay in the castle then."

Lylah shook her head. "Sort of. Wait just a moment."

Cayla's mother spoke to the city guards giving them instructions, then to the woman from the restaurant. She examined the body of their attacker briefly, then told them, "I'll be right back."

She approached Cayla again. "Let's go."

Cayla felt numb. Had it been her fault? And the necklace. She had no idea what to tell Darian or how he would react. She missed that necklace because until then it had been like a piece of him near her, a reminder of their closeness, their love, their connection. Now it had been shattered.

Cayla followed her mother to a smaller street. Weird. She didn't seem to be heading to the castle. Lylah stopped. "Here. We can talk." She then noticed the missing necklace and looked the most alarmed Cayla had ever seen. "Did they steal it?"

"They tried. I broke it."

Her mother frowned in confusion. "*Broke* it?"

"I threw a shard of glass and it shattered."

Lylah still seemed puzzled. "Are you sure?"

Great. Amidst everything that was happening she had to face doubt. "I saw it."

Her mother still looked at Cayla with a suspicious expression, but exhaled in relief. "Good. Listen, Cayla, there was a breach. I'd rather you stayed away from here for a while. Just in case."

"What about Darian?"

"He's away too." Lylah shook her head. "If I had known you could be in danger..."

Lamenting the past didn't help. "Who were they?"

"I'm not certain. Follow me."

Lylah entered a small building with an empty room. Before Cayla had time to wonder what it was or ask, her mother held her hand and they teleported to the castle. This was not the blue teleporting tower, but a hexagonal room with mirrors and a well in the middle, but it was very different from the other room like this she'd seen in the Darloom castle. This room was lighter and had golden details. "What's this?"

"We're deep underground, below the Queen's Castle."

Their castle. It was odd when she used the name of the castle because it was as if she were referring to herself in third person. "How come these passages haven't been used?"

"When you open a door to get out, you might allow things to come in."

"So we shouldn't open it."

Lylah raised an eyebrow. "Not if we think they've already found a way in. I'll close whatever passage they're using, but I need to see you safe first." She pointed to one of the mirrors. "I think you can cross it. It'll lead to the Light Gardens. Darian's there."

Light Gardens. The place Darian had hoped and wished to visit for the last six months, the place he'd been thinking was lost to him forever. She couldn't hide her anger. "There was a passage to the Light Gardens and he wasn't told?"

Lylah shook her head. "Emergency passage, Cayla. Go. I have things to do here."

She still thought it wasn't fair but crossed the mirror and found herself in an empty teleporting tower with white marble walls.

5

# VISIONS AND GARDENS

Sian lay down shivering. Perhaps the infection would go away by itself. Perhaps he should find a way to contact other Maris. His guess was that their saliva had antiseptic properties. But the issue was that they could decide to challenge him, and he was in no state to fight anyone. Now that he'd witnessed their cowardice first hand, he thought it would be quite likely for them to attack a dying human. Dying. That word was horrible. Really? So he could defeat a gigantic beast but would be defeated by microscopic beings? Ridiculous.

"Well, it's a whole army, Sian."

He stared towards the voice. Karina was crossing the wall and entering the room. Funny he didn't remember she could cross walls. Wait. She could. At least mirrors. She lay down beside him and rested her hand on her arm.

"There's an epic battle inside you. The attackers are many, your defenses aren't ready, but there's always a way to turn the tide. No need to set everything on fire. Are you going to give up? Like that?" She shook her head. "Tsk, tsk, tsk. So unlike you."

Her tone was cold and mocking. Her eyes were still brown, her eyes, but different. She wore the blue dress he'd picked for her a long time before and looked stunning, but an uncomfortable kind of stunning, like a beautiful statue or work of art.

Sian stared. "You're not her."

She rolled her eyes. "So perceptive. How long did it take you? A minute? Is your brain getting fried?"

"Fried brain? Really? While I'm feverish and having visions. Who would have guessed? And who are you?"

That weird not-Karina person laughed. "Me? I thought that was obvious." She changed her form and became Sian, not as he looked now, but normal, well fed, decently dressed Sian. "Don't you know me anymore?"

"It's been a long time, pal. Go back to Karina's form. You can dress as well as you want, you're still ugly."

Weird vision Sian laughed. "How dare you?" He changed his form again. This time he looked thinner, shabby, and had a long beard. "What about this?"

"Hideous. What do you want?"

The vision transformed back to normal-looking Sian. "I want you to survive."

Sian shrugged. "What for?"

The vision transformed again into Karina, but wearing the leather pants and jacket she wore the first time they kissed. Sian felt a cold shiver in his stomach, a tinge of panic with the thought that something in his life was out of his control. Her eyes were cold and all wrong, but still... goodness she was beautiful.

She smiled. "For me."

Sian sighed. "I'll never meet her again." The vision wasn't Karina and there was no point treating it like it was. "And stop pretending you're her."

Karina vision rolled her eyes again. "I'm you. It's not like you never... I'm just doing it better, see?"

"Fine. Vision whatever, since you are here and all, do you have any tips for me to survive?"

"Find Komiak."

As if Sian hadn't considered that. "I can't make it to that mountain, and if I call them, they might kill me."

"Might is the key word here. If you compare maybe to sure, and if you're talking about death, maybe is a win."

"There's a chance the infection will go away by itself."

"You know it won't."

"So you think I should call Maris to kill me?"

Karina-vision shook her head. "You forget your powers."

"The electricity thing? That was Darloom."

She grimaced. "Fried brain. Sian, think. Darloom can only affect thoughts, perception. He could only cause pain, because it relates to thoughts. He couldn't even physically hurt anyone with that magic." She had a disapproving, disgusted face. "Very different from what you did."

"Don't give me that look. I mean, maybe do, maybe I deserve this death."

"Forget the look, Sian, think. What you did there, that was not Darloom."

That made some sense. Sort of. And yet... "What was it, then?"

"You."

Sian tried to take in the information, then laughed. "Nice try, but I have no magic."

"You know you do, fried brain."

"Right. I'll assume I have electrifying magic that I have no idea how to use. Do you think I can use it in the state I'm in?"

"Maybe you can't." She winked. "But the Maris don't know it."

Could she, he, whatever it was, be right? "You have a point there."

She smirked. "One of us has to have the brains, pal."

"Your impersonation of her is still awful."

"Ooooh. As if you did so much better."

"Unrealistic, maybe. Nicer, for sure."

He felt her hand on his, and was second-guessing his impression that it was a vision. Her clothes were now the pyjamas she'd worn the last night they were together. That was a low blow. His mind took him back to that moment. He could almost feel his hands over the soft fabric, under it, touching her warm skin, soft hair. They were like two lost pieces about to snap into place. So much want and so much need for restraint—and patience—under the bitter illusion that they'd have so many more nights and days together.

His mind took him back to the present time. For once vision Karina's eyes were sweet and loving like they were supposed to be. She ran her fingers on his face, shabby beard and all. "It could be all real, Sian. It can still be real. But you have to survive."

Sian didn't care that it was just some part of himself pretending to be Karina. He wrapped his arms around her waist and pulled her towards him. But there was nothing to pull; her body disappeared and then the vision was gone. Of course. He shouldn't even be surprised.

Survive. Weird vision was right. Wasn't he a survivor?

He needed to go to the top floor and ring the bell, but wasn't sure if he could even get up, let alone go up some flights of stairs. Weird vision had a point that the Maris would probably hesitate to attack him. He had to get up, he had to go up. Why couldn't that stupid vision do that, since it had been so intent on mocking him?

Couldn't he use his weird unknown magic to ring that bell? No. He had to get up. One last shot. He had to gather his last strength, go up, and hope everything went right.

Sian made a huge effort to open the door. The stairs to the top looked interminable even if he knew there were only three more floors. A movement caught his eye. A Maris was flying towards him. Sian wondered if he should lock himself in the room again when he realized who it was; Komiak, with the stone in one of his claws.

"You look sick," the stone said.

"Infection. Do you know how to treat it?"

The huge bird approached Sian. "You should take off that dirty cloth you use over your body."

Sian shook his head. "I'm not taking that off."

"Fine, then. Come back to our cave. You kept your end of the deal, got rid of King Sarat, and you're welcome back."

"I have to stay here. It's my hope of finding a way out."

Komiak tilted his head. "You don't like being king?"

Sian didn't want to say that he wanted to find his friends and his people, lest he offend him. Well, maybe he had no choice. "I want to return to my family." There. Family didn't sound so odd. "Before that, I need to avoid dying—if possible."

Komiak opened his huge beak. Had he changed his mind and was about to chop Sian's head off? Well, no. He put his beak around Sian's shoulder. Sian felt something wet. When Komiak took off his beak, there was a dark yellow slime around his upper body.

"This is our medicine," the huge bird said. "I'm not sure it will work with that disgusting thing... But it's your choice."

Weird. This wasn't like regular saliva. "Thank you."

"I'll come back tomorrow. Please consider removing those rags and coming back home. We can be your family. At least for now."

Komiak didn't wait for a reply and flew up to the opening. Sian barely had time to enter the room again and close the door before falling asleep.

Leena served Darian a bowl of soup. He'd been hungry but now he was so anxious he didn't know if he could eat. And he was pissed that he'd been brought unconscious.

"Darian," the woman asked. "Do you know where your brother is?"

He shook his head. "No idea. Why? What's happening?"

Leena had a worried expression. "Lylah mentioned a breach. We're going to investigate it."

He stared at her. "So?"

"So what?"

"Are you going to investigate or watch me eat?"

"I want to make sure you're all right."

"What do you think? Something's happening in Whyland and I'm not there. Cayla's there and I'm not there. Are you sure you can't take me back?"

Leena just stared.

Darian exhaled. "Fine. You won't. I guess it doesn't matter because if I protest you'll just make me faint. Screw free will."

"For the record, I don't agree with Lylah's methods. But Cayla's coming. Even if I could take you back, wouldn't you want to wait for her?"

Darian sighed. "Can you just tell me what's happening?"

"I will. Once I know."

He looked down then took a spoon of that soup. His chest was tight. So many things bothering him. Hadn't Lylah nominated him Grand General? For what, if he would be sent away at the first sign of trouble? And not knowing was gnawing on him. The worst part was not having news from Cayla and having to wonder if she was safe.

Darian shut his eyes, trying to think, trying to calm down, trying to find a solution, anything.

A hand touched his shoulder. "Patience, little one." Leena was standing beside him.

He did his best to hide a grimace. "Little one" was rather infuriating. Especially in a time like this.

His necklace shone, like always. Perhaps he could contact Cayla. He pulled the stone close to his mouth and was about to press it, when Leena put her hand over his. "Don't. By no means should you alert anyone to Light Gardens magic. Not now."

"Will anyone tell me if she's safe?"

Leena sat at the chair beside him. "Darian, it's neither a war nor an invasion, just a breach. It means someone or something is coming or might come from another dimension, but we don't even know what it is."

"If it's nothing, why was I brought here?"

"To keep you safe. Lylah thinks it might be some enemy of the Light Gardens."

"She *thinks*. Great. And what do I have to do—"

Right then, Darian saw something that made him chill. His right hand trembled as he held the necklace stone, now black. For a second, he wanted to believe that his eyes were tricking him, that it was a shade, a trick of the light or something. No. It was black. It could only mean... He didn't know. For so long he'd looked at his necklace as a reminder of Cayla, trusting that the light meant that the two people loved each other. Cayla's love couldn't have vanished like that. They'd been fine just a couple hours before. Could she... The painful memory of his mother dying and his necklace turning black hit him. Not again, not again, not Cayla.

His voice was cracking as he showed Leena the stone. "Do you know what this means?"

Her eyes darkened. "Lylah is coming. Cayla's her daughter after all. She'll know. It might be nothing."

That last part sounded quite insincere. Here Darian stood powerless, his heart pounding. No, he wasn't going to stand here. He got up. "I have to tell her. I know where Cayla went. She's not in the castle!"

"Darian. Lylah can find her. Wait. There's no reason to assume—"

Darian shook his black stone. "Explain this."

Leena sat and took a long, deep breath. "I can't use that portal, only Lylah can. She told me she was going to get Cayla. I'm worried too, but right now, all we can do is wait. Sometimes life's like that."

Darian sat down and put his head in his hands, hoping that his stone turning black didn't mean anything serious, hoping Cayla was all right, hoping so many things. And how he regretted leaving her. If only he'd come with her. If only... But when has regret ever helped anything?

~

CAYLA STOOD in the tower for a moment, surprised that she should be left alone in a place she didn't know. Venturing towards a door, she almost crashed with a girl coming in her direction. She had darker skin, brown eyes and very curly black hair.

"Are you Cayla?"

"Yes. Is Darian here?"

The girl nodded. "I'll bring you to him."

Cayla was stressed and upset, but she had to remember politeness. "And what's your name?"

"I'm Anika. I'm finishing my initiation this month."

"Nice." Perhaps Cayla should have smiled, congratulated her or asked something, but she was too worried about Alessa to care or make conversation.

Outside was a meadow. The sun was setting. Apart from some lights in the distance, there was just a small wooden house nearby and they walked towards it.

Anika opened the door to Cayla but left. Sitting at a table were Leena and Darian. He looked miserable, raised his eyes and saw her. His features were turning into a smile when he looked down at her clothes and frowned. Oh, no. The blood. He got up and stood in front of her, his face contorted in horror. "Are you hurt?" He turned to Leena, desperation clear in his voice. "She needs help."

Cayla took his hand. "I'm fine. Darian. I'm fine. The blood is not mine."

Darian exhaled then took her in a tight embrace. "I've never been so scared in my life. I thought you..."

"I'm fine." Actually, now that she thought about it, her hand hurt. The cut must have been deep.

He stepped back and stared at her. "What happened? Whose blood is it?"

Cayla was about to tell him all but she hated seeing his face in so much pain. She pulled up her hand and showed it. "I just have a cut."

"You need to stitch it." He looked down at her clothes, her hand, and her clothes, maybe trying to find a correlation.

"It's Alessa. She got a bigger cut." That was true. Cayla still debated how much she should tell him. She should tell him the truth, she should, but then she remembered the time she'd been locked in the castle by her father and even the brief time when Darian had been overprotective of her. "The table where we were sitting broke and some things fell on us. This is from the jug."

He raised an eyebrow, likely still suspicious.

"It's my fault. I got up quickly…"

Leena was standing near them and took Cayla's hand. "We'll mend it, but we should get going." She put a white paste on the wound. The bleeding and the pain stopped. "This will do for now."

Darian stared at her in silence. After a while, he asked, "What about the necklace?"

The question she'd dreaded so much. The necklace. The necklace. The one she missed so much it was like missing a part of her. Her insides felt hollow and her heart was about to climb out of her chest. "I'm so sorry. So, so sorry. I… I don't know what happened. I…"

Darian hugged her. "At least you're here. This is what matters. Don't worry about the necklace."

Cayla was relieved. She knew how important that necklace was, what it meant, and at the same time, she'd had no choice. Still, she didn't want to talk about all that right then. His face leaned against hers. She could hear his breath, feel his heart. The words left her mouth as if by their own will: "I love you."

He whispered in her ear, "You'd better keep telling me that now that I have no ratting stone."

She wished he'd said something different. "I don't have a stone either."

"Your fault. You deserve some guessing. No. It's obvious, isn't it?"

"I guess."

He kissed her cheek. "Very funny."

Cayla didn't share his sense of humor, but she didn't say anything. At least he wasn't upset about the necklace. Leena was staring at them. Cayla stepped away from Darian and looked at the woman. "We have to go, right?"

Leena nodded.

Darian made a stop gesture with his hand and turned to the woman. "Hang on. You said I was in danger because I'm from the Light Gardens?"

"It's a possibility, yes," Leena confirmed.

"So is my brother." His voice came low, almost as in a whisper. His face was realization and pleading.

"Indeed." Leena sighed. "Do you happen to know where he is?"

He looked thoughtful. "Maybe."

## 6

## NEW LIVES

Screeches. So many screeches. Sian opened his eyes to the darkness in his improvised bedroom. There was a faint light coming from a half-moon in the sky, but it was intermittent with shadows of Maris. Maybe they'd come to kill him. Maybe not. There was something sticky on his shoulder. Wait. He remembered his encounter with Komiak—and his vision. In theory he should have gotten better. The reality was that he couldn't even get up.

If the Maris decided to break his door and kill him, it would be his end. But then, if the Maris didn't, it would still be his end. Hero's life. What an amazing hero, killing people—or big birds—needlessly.

Well, he *was* tired of eating unseasoned worms and rodents. That was a positive in dying. He'd never given much thought to the afterlife. With so many conflicting descriptions, all he surmised was that no one had a clue. Still, he assumed the menu would be better there. If there was a menu. If there was a there. No more unseasoned worms. The thought gave Sian a smile. When had his needs gotten so simple?

There was a muffled yell from beyond the door, hard to distinguish with all the noise those Maris were making. Maybe they were not yells, just screeches.

Then he heard it: "Sian, Sian!"

There were also sounds of banging on doors. Yay noisy vision.

Sian mumbled, "Come in. Can't you cross doors? Walls?"

The steps sounded closer to his door. This time the knocking was there. "Sian, is that you?"

The voice was familiar. His brother's? The one who never knew he existed? Not familiar. Unfamiliar. So many people to impersonate, why did the vision decide to be him?

"Come in." Sian's voice was hoarse, but it still sounded loud enough to be heard from the outside.

"Open the door, please!"

"I can't get up." The mumble was low this time. Regardless, the vision should know.

More knocks. "Sian, please, open up." Darian's voice.

Sian sat up, then leaned on the wall to stand, but collapsed. Did fever do that? How could he know it when all his training was a blur in his mind? Did he even have a mind?

He stared at the ceiling. "Just come in," he managed to say.

There were voices inside the tower, in front of his door, and screeches outside. A loud noise, like something breaking, then two people walked in.

Someone resembling his brother knelt beside him and held his hand. "Sian, we're here. We're here."

The vision felt solid and real enough for Sian to wonder if Darian had died and come to take him. Why couldn't Sian get up then? By now, he should have a strong, shiny new body—or spirit—or something. Perhaps he should close his eyes and let himself go.

IT HAD TAKEN a lot less beseeching and imploring than Darian had imagined. It was a guess, but by elimination it made sense. Thankfully nobody doubted him. Leena had taken them to another tower, and Cayla stood holding the portal open.

Relief turned to worry when he finally found Sian. Thin and sick, he lay down as if he were dying.

"We'll need to carry him," he told Leena.

Her hands were up, casting the protective barrier to prevent Maris from coming in. The huge birds were outside, probably attracted by their visit, likely ready to strike. He wondered how his brother had survived for so long.

She sighed. "We'll need to bring more people."

"He's dying!"

"If I help carry him, the barrier will break."

Darian crouched, lifted his brother's body, then put it over his shoulder. It wasn't that much weight or perhaps he didn't feel it as he rushed down the stairs. He hesitated when he came across a huge gap. Would he be able to make the jump while carrying his brother?

"Wait," Leena said.

She lowered her arms. Blue light connected the two broken edges of the stairs. "It's a bridge. Hurry."

Darian walked across it. Once he was done, he heard Leena jumping behind him. He also heard Maris entering the tower, but then saw Leena's barrier on top of them. The creatures were inside but not close enough to reach them. Anika was downstairs also casting a protective barrier.

And Cayla... they'd better be fast. He wasn't sure if holding a portal open like that required effort, but he didn't want to take any chances. His brother also required urgent assistance. If only Darian had known that there was a way to find Sian, if only he'd known that they could open emergency portals, his brother wouldn't be almost dying on his shoulders. Perhaps it had all been Darian's fault for not asking, not insisting, not trying enough. No more of that.

~

KARINA OPENED her eyes and sat up, squinting against the strong light coming from her side. The entire wall was glass from where she could see a clear sky, as if from a great height. There were three other people in the room. Involuntarily she flinched at the idea of being helpless among strangers, but then maybe it was just a hospital. Quite a fancy hospital. Her double bed had white soft sheets and many layers of thin golden covers. The three people in the room were some awesomely good looking nurses or doctors. Perhaps she was having visions or this was a dream.

A young man with long blond hair sat on the edge of the bed. "How are you?" Apprehension, relief, and expectation were clear on his voice and expression.

He didn't sound like a hospital worker, but like a friend, a very close friend or even something more. He had small dark brown eyes, some small braids on one side of his hair, and overall was the kind of good-looking guy that didn't usually spare Karina more than two glances. Friend, definitely.

In front of the bed, there was a girl about Karina's age, with wavy dark hair and brown eyes. She observed but didn't seem as worried as the blond guy. Near her, a man in his forties or so with very long black hair. He was good looking the way actors in their forties or fifties can be good looking and had worry and concern written on his face, just not as much as the blond guy sitting on the edge of Karina's bed.

They were all well dressed, with some strange embroidery on their shirts. The older man had an overcoat. Combined with the fancy decoration in the room and the golden details here and there, Karina assumed this was a luxurious condo. Maybe something happened to her while in a very fancy party.

A few questions popped up in her head and almost came out of her mouth, like "Do I know you?", "Where am I?", or "Who are you?", but thankfully she used her brain before her mouth and found something that wouldn't sound offensive. "I... I don't remember what happened."

The older man approached her. "You went through a lot." He put his hand over her head like in a comforting caress. The gesture was intimate, as if he were a close family member. "Things will come back to you slowly."

The blond boy held her hand. Karina flinched. This was too weird. He noticed but held on tighter. "Do you remember me?"

Karina went over her mental files. Would she forget a good-looking guy? Well, considering she didn't spare many glances for guys who didn't pay attention to her, that was possible. But he sounded like a friend, someone who cared for her. Who was he? Who were those people? Perhaps she shouldn't worry so much about being rude.

"I'm sorry. I... I don't remember..." Karina looked around. "Any of you. Or this place. I don't know if should remember it."

The blond boy caressed her hand. It still felt strange, out of place, too intimate, and it wasn't like the older dark-haired man. He said, "Karina, don't worry. It will take some time. At least you're alive."

Karina flinched again. One, they'd said her name, and that she remembered. In fact, now that she was thinking, she remembered a lot of things; her family, her apartment, her best friends, Zoe and Tori. She remembered school subjects, even some memories from her childhood flashed in her mind. The only thing she didn't remember was how she'd gotten there. Also, alive?

"Was I in an accident? Did I hit my head?" Some temporary amnesia was possible, but she'd need to read more about how it worked. She wasn't sure if it was possible to forget just a period of time, and felt uneasy when she didn't know something, uneasy when she didn't have enough information to understand what was happening around her.

The blond boy turned to the man and the girl. "Could you give us some time?"

The man stared and nodded. "That's a good idea. Now that I know she's well, I can go back to my duties. Call me if you need me."

"I will, uncle."

He left the room. The girl got up after him looked back. "See you." She then also left and closed the door behind her.

The blond boy let go of her hand. "Don't strain, don't stress, don't worry. You don't remember any of this, do you?"

Karina shook her head.

"I'm Satwak, but you can call me Sat. You just saw my uncle Firis and my sister Faizana. Do you remember Lumina?"

Karina had no idea what he was talking about.

"It's our city. Where you live."

"How long have I been living here?"

"I'd say about two years."

Karina's heart sped up. That much? That much time was a void in her mind? And did it make sense to forget recent memories like a part of her life had been wiped away?

Sat sighed. "Karina, it wasn't an accident. You were attacked. With strong magic. That's why some of it might be a blur. It's almost as if... as if someone wanted you to forget us. To forget me. But you're here."

Wow, wow, wow. Hang on. "Magic?"

"Take it easy, Kah. I can show and explain everything to you again. I'm not upset you lost your memory, don't worry about it."

*Kah?* What the... Karina had a queasy feeling in her stomach. Memory loss. So he'd said it. Maybe she should just ask the questions burning her mind. "Can you just like, do a quick recap on how I got here? How I lost my memory? How I met you?"

"We met almost two years ago. You came to live here. We were trying to travel and the guardians ambushed us. They attacked you, but we saved you. You've been sleeping for a few days, but now you're awake. Don't be afraid to speak your mind, at least to me."

"A few days. Feels like a couple years."

"Probably."

"And what's this place?"

"It's Lumina, the City of Light."

The name meant nothing to her. She was awful in geography, but still, it was more likely she wouldn't know a city's location, not that she'd never heard of a place she should. "Does it have another name? Are we still in Canada?"

"This is an ethereal city. We aren't anywhere specific. Well, we should be tied to dimension and a geographic location, but we aren't."

This was all too weird. She wasn't even sure if she believed it. "So, is it like... floating in the air?"

"Floating in the void."

Was he joking? She decided to play along. "Is it flat? Or is it spheric like a little planet?"

"Not a planet, no."

Right. So here were some questions she'd always wanted to ask flat earthers. "What happens at the edges? Is it like a precipice into nothingness? A wall?"

He laughed. "You think I'm joking. I'm not. But yes. It's a barrier. You try to move forward and it takes you sideways. We don't go much to the edges, though."

"I'd like to see that." No kidding. What a scientific breakthrough.

"I'll take you there. I just thought you'd like to see the palace first, the city. Since you forgot it all, it will be as if it were your first time."

"Can we go now? I think I've slept enough."

Karina looked at herself. She wore what looked like a night-gown. It felt like cotton and had golden embroidery on the edges. She'd need to change and she had no idea if she had clothes there, or even what kind of clothes she wore. It all felt like a bizarre nightmare.

"Don't worry," Sat said, as if guessing her thoughts. "Your attendant will help you get dressed and then we can go. I think you're better now, and some fresh air might be good for you." He pointed to a table on the back of the room with two jugs and some glasses. "Do you want to drink something? Juice, water?"

"Some water." That was a great idea indeed. She was thirsty. And a little hungry too.

Sat poured water in a glass and brought it to her. It still felt odd, familiar, intimate. Could he be an attendant? Well, no, his uncle looked important. Karina took a long, refreshing sip.

She wanted to ask what he was in relation to her, but wasn't sure how to phrase it. "How did we become friends?"

"I saved you. A long time ago."

Something didn't add up. "And then I decided to move here?"

He looked down. "You were prevented from returning."

Home. That was a hard blow on her when she thought about her parents, her friends. Not school. That, strangely, she was glad of being away from.

"I see." Something was still strange, but the guy seemed nice. Perhaps they had been close. "And since I couldn't return you allowed me to live here? Cause you're my friend?" She took a sip.

"I'm your husband."

Karina spat her water.

7

GAP

Such a mix of emotions in Darian. Should he feel relieved that they were saving Sian? Should he feel angry that he'd been abandoned for so long when in fact there was a way to save him? Should he just be glad for this second chance to reconcile with his brother? Maybe it was everything and then more.

They'd brought Sian to a building away from the city. It was a hospital, but the rooms had earthy tones, plants, and large windows overlooking trees and flowers outside. Leena and Darian watched as two health practitioners put him on an examination table.

Darian felt strange at seeing his brother so helpless, thin, with a long beard and shabby clothes. Everything that had always denoted Sian's pride was gone. There was something strange on his right shoulder, like some widespread infection.

The male doctor took a knife and was about to cut Sian's shirt—but was stopped. Sian sat up, pushed the knife away and had his right hand around the doctor's throat.

"Calm down, it's us," Darian rushed to his brother's side.

"Easy, easy there," Leena said in her soft soothing voice.

Sian let go of the man.

Leena turned to them. "It's better if you all get out. I can take care of him."

The doctors got out, apparently glad to be getting away from Sian. She looked at Darian. "You too."

He was going to protest, ask why, but then realized there wasn't much he could do. "I'll be outside then."

"I'll lock the door. Make sure nobody tries to come in."

She said it as if there was going to be some super secretive activity there. This time Darian couldn't contain his question. "What's happening? Is he in danger?"

"Not a lot of danger, but I think privacy will be better for him. Do stay outside, as I might need some things."

"I will."

Darian walked outside and heard the door being locked. Cayla was sitting on a bench under a tree and came running to him. "So?"

"I don't know, Leena is examining him."

She ran her hands through his hair. "He should be good in no time."

He took her right hand. They had stitched it, and now she only had a bandage over her cut. "Is it better?"

"Good as new." She smiled.

"Thank you for opening the portal for us."

"Anything for you."

For him. Of course. Not for Sian. According to Leena, they opened the portal without consulting the Guardians, or even letting them know, and they shouldn't be opening portals like that. He was glad they'd done so, as his brother could have been much worse had they waited. But something else was bothering him.

"Cayla, I have a question."

She moved her hand away from his hair. "Yes?"

"Why did you lie?"

She squinted.

"About what happened in Siphoria," he added. "You know you didn't fall over a table or whatever you said."

She sighed. "I didn't want you to worry—"

"What happened?"

Cayla was thoughtful. "Some strange people, they were wearing white cloaks and hoods, they attacked us. It was fast, and as much as Alessa and I fought back, they had some strong... magic. One of them took the necklace. I didn't want them to have it. I threw a glass shard on it and it broke."

"Broke?"

"It did. I saw it. I'm sorry, I didn't want to break it, but they were many, they were cheating with magic, and I was afraid they'd take the necklace away. What would you have done in my place?"

"I wouldn't have thought of breaking it, but I guess it was a good idea. But you should have told me." He was worried about what happened to her, but he didn't want to make a fuss out of it, lest she think she had to lie to him again.

"I was just...overwhelmed."

Darian caressed her face. "I would understand. I always do. You need to tell Leena."

"I will. Lylah also knows what happened." It was odd how sometimes Cayla referred to her mother by her name. "I think it has something to do with the breach. Whoever was there wasn't supposed to be."

That made sense. "They were after the Light Gardens. That's why they came to you. They were attracted by the magic of the necklace, the magic of this city. If you hadn't broken it, they could perhaps open a portal here." He facepalmed. "I'm so dumb. I put you in danger."

"No. How could you have known Lumina would come? Plus, you used it to save me before, remember?" She looked down. "Not anymore."

Darian kissed her forehead. "Maybe we can find something else. It feels strange no longer being connected to you."

"We'll always be connected."

He laughed. "Always?" Darian kissed her lips softly. "I know... still, I liked carrying a reminder of you."

She had a sad smile.

"What's wrong?" he asked.

"Alessa worries me." Cayla looked down. "She had a huge cut. I hope…"

"Hush. She was being treated, wasn't she?" Darian embraced Cayla.

"*That* was my fault."

"It was the breach, Cayla, not you. Siphoria should have been safe if it wasn't for that. Don't blame yourself."

"Maybe. I hope Lylah brings news of Alessa soon."

"She will. I'm sure she will."

Darian hugged Cayla tight, hoping his love would ease some of her fears.

Karina felt numb, perhaps so overwhelmed with all this information that her senses shut down. Two girls helped her put on a dress. They were silent, and as much as Karina was burning with questions, she didn't even know where to start. Plus, since when was she so incompetent that she needed help getting dressed? Still, she played along. But the biggest question was another one: married? Satwak was certainly cute so it wasn't a huge mystery why she'd be interested in him. Still… she was so young.

These people, this place, this talk of magic, it didn't match anything she knew. Deep down there was some recognition, like when you hear a name you've heard before but can't recall. Like the name, she had no clue what any of it meant. Without two years of her life, it was as if she was being transplanted into a body that wasn't hers. It wasn't hers because she hadn't had the life experience that this married Karina had. Without the experience, she couldn't be that person. Maybe everything would come back to her mind, and then it wouldn't be weird. Maybe. For now there was a two-year gap in her life, not only two years, but very eventful ones of which she had no memory.

Even her underwear was weird, like some thinner material with a cotton feel but a shiny look, like nylon or something. Her bra didn't have wires and she hated that. At least they wore bras in this weird city. But then, perhaps this was just a prank. But who in their right mind would prank someone having a memory loss? It didn't make sense. How could she add things up, when she didn't know what to add up?

Her dress was white, with the stupid golden embroidery on the rims. Other than that the dress was simple, though, no details or anything, just some back ribbons that needed to be tied and required help. The dress was tight on top with a skirt up to her knees. Her boots were also white. Who chooses white for shoes? Maybe the attendants cleaned them.

She walked out of the room and Satwak, or Sat, was waiting for her, then he guided her to a hallway. At least he understood that she didn't remember anything and acted almost as if he were presenting the city to her, and explained a lot of things.

The palace was where they housed the government of the city and the royal family. His uncle, Firis, was the overseer, as they called their leader. Shouldn't that be mayor? And since when was an overseer family royal? Karina shut down those silly questions, when there were so many, enormous questions hanging unsaid.

They descended spiral staircases beside a glass wall overlooking a valley and houses. Karina did peek to see if she found the end of the world barrier, but she only saw horizon. In the middle of the staircase was a gap. Not a gap, as a metallic box moved up past them.

"What was that?"

"The elevator. It's for when we don't want to use the stairs."

"I know what an elevator is, but shouldn't there be cables?" Something, anything? That thing had shot up like a rocket.

"Our technology is different from yours, Karina."

"Did you explain it all for me and I forgot?"

He nodded. "A lot of it. I know you like technology. You've explained to us how your elevators use pulleys and electricity, and I've explained to you ours use magic... I don't mind repeating anything, though."

There had been something off in that interaction, but she couldn't quite put her finger where.

Sat chuckled. "You're upset I explained to you what an elevator is. I forgot you also had them. It's been a long time, and we haven't had those conversations in a while. Forgive me if I make mistakes."

Karina exhaled. That had been exactly it. He'd explained what an elevator was. They kept descending the stairs. But now the odd thing was that he was replying to her thoughts. Was he replying to her thoughts? Silence. Was he? He looked normal. Maybe she was imagining things.

"Like I told you, the top floor is our teleporting tower. We haven't used it in years, since the Guardians blocked it. Below it is the throne room, then our accommodations, and below are some government offices."

"Who are these Guardians?"

"There are other ethereal cities like this one. We used to be thirteen cities. Lumina was the most important of them. See, we have more advanced magic. But some people from those cities rebelled against us and locked us out. A city was destroyed in this confrontation."

"So you're saying they're the bad guys?" Again, Karina had a strange gut feeling telling her not to trust people who claimed someone else was a villain. Perhaps it was just common sense.

"I'm saying they isolated us. I'm pretty sure they believe what they do is wonderful."

"Is it, though?"

"They destroyed a city. They attacked you."

"Why would anyone attack me?"

"Because you were trying to get out."

"What does it matter to them? I mean," she was going to say she was worthless, but that was a strong word, "I can't harm them."

Sat shook his head. "They don't care about that."

"Are you going to tell me more about them?"

"Yes. In fact, my uncle can discuss it with you. He's very passionate about it."

"About Guardians?"

"About freeing Lumina."

Right. She'd really have to get more information about it, so that she could draw her conclusions and try to understand what was happening.

"How did I end up here?"

"A portal was opened by accident and you fell through."

She was trying to connect points a and b. "Right. But how would that make me be in touch with, uh, the royal family?"

"We hadn't had a foreigner in generations."

That would make her interesting, intriguing, and explained quite a lot. "So you called me here to compare elevator styles?"

Sat chuckled. "Sort of. Let's get to know Lumina, then we can try to retrace some of your past."

They got out of the palace. It led to a square surrounded by humongous metal statues. They had human forms, but weren't all in the same position. Some knelt, some stood, some were ready to strike, almost as if they'd been giants who had been frozen. Karina wondered if one day they had moved.

Sat pointed to the statues. "Legend says these are the real royal guards, guarding the royal family. But that's just legend, of course."

"They do look real."

"Maybe. Let's get to know more."

The square was at a hill and from there Karina had a better view of the city. It didn't look that strange. Houses had triangular roofs in many different colors. Woods surrounded the castle. They descended some stairs and came to another square, this one huge, with what looked like stores all around it. Each house had a big open door and people came in and out. Many inhabitants wore some kind of cloaks over their clothes. Many wore white, some wore light colors like light blue or yellow. When they had embroidery, it was silver.

Sat pointed to the square. "This is central Lumina. As you noticed, it's where you can buy things."

Karina nodded.

Sat added, "Only the royal family wears gold embroidery. That's why they dress differently."

"Do the colors mean anything?"

"The royal family and its protectors wear white, other people can wear whatever they want, but they prefer lighter colors."

"A whole lot of trouble to wash."

With everything that was happening, Karina shouldn't be thinking whether it was hard or not to wash lighter clothes. In fact, maybe they had some neat version of bleach and that was why they made that choice.

Sat pointed beyond the square. "That's where people live."

Karina had seen houses extending far away, then trees and fields. This was a small city. Karina guessed some three thousand people in total.

Sat nodded. "Our population is two thousand."

This wasn't the first time he was replying to her thoughts. But then, sometimes he seemed oblivious. Perhaps he was great at interpreting body language and caught her making a mental calculation face.

"Are we going to see the edge?"

Sat chuckled. "There isn't much to see, but since you insist..."

Oh yeah, she insisted. She needed to know how much of a prank it was, or if by chance she'd ended up with some brainwashed people.

Sat walked back to the castle. It didn't make much sense.

"Is it in that direction?"

"No, but it's not that close. We'd better take a capsule."

"I assume you'll explain what it is."

He stopped and sighed. "I'm so sorry. Sometimes I explain things you know as if you didn't, sometimes I just assume you understand what I say. I didn't mean—"

"That's fine."

"You'll see what it is. The edge is a bit far, and we'd take too long walking."

"But could we get there walking?" Karina was wondering about distances.

Sat shrugged. "You can get anywhere walking as long as it's in your dimension and there are no bodies of water in the way."

Dimension. Still that talk. But then, with all this weird technology, maybe she should be a bit less skeptical. Well, maybe, but the issue was convincing her rational mind.

They returned to the castle and entered that odd elevator. It didn't have buttons, just a lever, and it had no door. Karina stood back in the wall. Of course the movement of an elevator wouldn't cause anyone to move horizontally and fall, but still, being in that place, looking at the gap without any barrier made her scared.

Sat looked at her and pulled close a metal gate. "Better?"

She nodded.

He laughed. "I'm sorry, I'm just lazy."

They got off on the fifth floor and walked to what looked like a terrace or balcony. There were huge golden metal balls on it. Sat approached one of them. It had two seats and a window in the front.

Karina looked at him. "Now you're going to tell me this flies."

He had a small smile. "Maybe you're remembering things."

"Just being logical. I mean, it's not like you'd roll down the fifth floor with those things. Let me guess, it's moved by *magic*."

"Yes. Like almost everything in Lumina."

"You'll need to explain to me what magic is." It was obviously some kind of mechanics that were unknown in her world. This difference in technology was one point that almost convinced her about the theory of ethereal city. But then, who knows, this could be the future, maybe she'd been frozen in time, traveled in time. So many possibilities.

At least the capsule had doors. Karina wasn't a great fan of heights without a barrier between her and a fall, even if a fall wasn't likely.

They flew over the city. There were some large fields with plantations and some animals. Farms. Then outside, dense treetops in what looked like a forest. Sat landed on a clearing. It wasn't just a natural clearing, but a landing pad, with a small house beside it and markings on the floor.

"We'll have to walk to the edge."

"Of course, otherwise I suppose the capsule falls off." She still was skeptical and couldn't help the sarcasm.

"I told you it was a barrier. We would have hit it."

They walked on a man-made path with smooth stones. The trees were like trees in any temperate climate, even if she wasn't sure she knew the trees themselves.

A few minutes of silence convinced her to ask a question that had been burning in her mind.

"Satwalk." He had a face. "I mean, Sat. Can you read thoughts?"

He stopped then took a deep breath as if thinking. "A little. Sometimes, yes."

"I see." She felt a little invaded.

"I try not to, Karina. Don't worry about it."

It was just... she was among strangers in a strange land, alone, and couldn't even have the sanctuary of her own mind.

Sat took her hands. "You're not alone. I'm here with you."

All right. Weren't they a couple? She didn't even want to think what that entailed. Too much. "How long have we been together?"

"About a year and a half. We married a year ago."

Karina tried to recall the last information she had about her own age and her own life. "I was just a little less than fifteen. Married at sixteen?"

He let go of her hands and started to walk again. "Lumina is different. Marriages are also magical contracts. We protect each other. See, everyone in this city wields magic."

"Except me."

He nodded.

"So it was for my protection?"

"In a way."

"How old are you?"

He tilted his head, as if avoiding the question. "We age differently."

"How differently?"

"I'm fifty-three."

Something turned in Karina's stomach. She wondered if she'd be revulsed if he'd said one hundred or a thousand, or if it would just be the same. Then she remembered he read thoughts. "I'm sorry. It's just—"

Satwak was laughing. She didn't understand what was so funny.

"What?"

He had a weird face. "I was joking. This is not the legendary city of Gleam Fortress, where people were said to age slowly. We're normal. I'm seventeen."

Karina wanted to burn him with her stare. "Is it fun? To mess with someone who lost her memory?"

He looked down, serious. "It isn't. I'm truly sorry."

Idiot. Hopefully he'd heard that. Karina tried to think. With this talk of protection coupled with the fact he didn't seem to be the least in love with her, plus their own young age, Karina wondered something else. "Was it real? Us?"

"Try not to think about it."

"How can I not think about it, when you're making me wonder if we... you know what." There. She'd said it, and brought to her mind one of the things that spooked her out the most; the idea that she'd done something she had no memory of.

"My uncle Firis can read thoughts. Better than me. He's a good man and an excellent leader, but he fears that the Guardians might have brainwashed you. If you're in love, he'll trust that you'll be loyal to me."

Karina swallowed. "So we have to pretend?"

"I understand everything is strange to you now. Take your time. We'll get used to each other. For now, it's better not to inquire on the past, lest it bothers you."

"But I want to know…"

He raised his hands in the air, in despair. "We didn't. Happy?"

More relieved than she had expected, Karina exhaled a huge ball of discomfort from her chest. But that opened a whole lot of other questions.

He sighed. "Don't make this complicated, please. I'll teach you how to replace thoughts, but it might take a while. Try not to think about it, but know that I'm your friend."

"So you say."

"True. But I'm the best you got."

The path stopped. Karina walked forward on it, but then when she looked back, she'd moved sideways. It wasn't like a barrier in front of her, it was as if space curved or something.

"So this is the edge."

"Yes," he confirmed.

Karina shrugged. "At least I know you're telling the truth about this ethereal city idea."

"See? You can be sure of one thing."

"Among so much uncertainty." She wouldn't have said this out loud, but it made no sense to keep her thoughts to herself just to wonder whether he'd picked up on them or not.

"I'll give you more proof when we come back. And there's something I need to ask you."

It didn't sound good. "Yes?"

"Your vows, you don't remember them."

"I don't remember anything."

"I know," Sat said. "But that makes them void."

"You mean I don't need to be married to you." She felt relieved. Who would have guessed she wouldn't want to be with the hottie in front of her? Perhaps an ethereal city made people weird and illogical. Wait, he might have heard all that. She added, "Not that I wouldn't like…"

"I understand. I'm a stranger to you and it would be super creepy to be married to me. Is that right?"

She nodded. He got the creepy part right.

He continued, "So we could each go in a different direction."

Karina couldn't read thoughts but she anticipated what he was going to say. "Except I have nowhere to go." She felt hollow inside.

"You could find a place in the city. You could go somewhere. But I'd like to make sure you're safe. I don't want my uncle having unnecessary doubts."

His uncle, always his uncle, and it gave her an unpleasant feeling. "So what do you suggest?"

"We renew our vows. Tonight. We can pick our own words. We can make it about mutual protection and alliance, so that we don't have to lie."

"You sure won't be in any danger with mighty Karina protecting you."

He shrugged. "You never know. Don't underestimate yourself. Anyway, it will help us. Do you say yes?"

This sounded like a weird sham, and still… "Do I have another great alternative?"

"I don't want to force you."

She couldn't figure out what his motivations were. "Why do you care about protecting me?"

"You'll find out in time, as you remember things, or as I get to know you better. Why ruin things?"

"I'm anxious not knowing where I stand."

His expression was serious. "At least know you'll have an ally. Our vows are magically binding."

"What happens if you don't obey them?"

"Magic will make you obey."

"So you could make sure your partner never cheats on you? Is that fair, though?"

"It's chosen by both parties. They can also break the agreement in another ceremony."

Karina chuckled. "Like a magical divorce?"

"Yes, but it can be just different terms. You can do that once a year."

This was a difficult situation, as Karina was almost a hostage of these people. At least Sat seemed nice, but even then, who knew? And she didn't care if he heard her thoughts. "We'll make vows just to protect each other?"

"Yes, loyalty, respect, protection. It's good for you, Karina."

It sounded like a good deal, even if more and more she got the feeling Sat didn't like her. But then there was the question as to why, which he was avoiding answering. Then again, she was the one most at risk. Alone in a place she didn't know, refusing an ally would have been dumb. "Let's do it."


KARINA WORE AN ENTIRELY GOLDEN DRESS. Her hair had been braided in what looked like a bird's nest. She wasn't going to argue with Lumina fashion. Well, she didn't even know fashion in her own world. The thought reminded her of Zoe, and it hurt. Anyway, if they could change this agreement or even break it, it wasn't as definitive as it had sounded. Maybe Sat was right that it would be a good idea to have someone sworn to protect her in this strange land with strange people. She just had to remember to watch her thoughts and feelings in front of Firis.

She walked in the throne room. Firis sat at a high chair. There was a circle of chairs around the middle, where she stood. Satwalk entered after her, also wearing gold. Surprisingly, he didn't look as ridiculous as she would have imagined. It was a dim gold.

Firis took their hands. Sat was going to say his words first. Of course, he loved her and she loved him, even if she didn't remember it right now.

Sat looked in her eyes as he said, "At this point and time I bound myself to my words. I'll protect, respect, and support Karina, and make sure no harm comes to her. I'll measure my words and actions to make sure she's safe, well, and provided for."

Karina then repeated the words, trying not to think about what it would mean for her to provide for him. She wasn't supposed to think about any of that, considering she didn't remember anything. Her mind was focused on partnership and loyalty.

There was no party, nothing. Quite a simple wedding. After that, Karina was sent to a dressing room where an attendant helped her change to a nightgown, and she went to hers and Sat's room. Their room.

"You did very well," he said.

Karina already felt uncomfortable wearing a nightgown, even if it was very modest, more like a long t-shirt. She looked at the room and the fact that there was only one double bed. Okay, a king bed, not a real king's bed, but a king mattress—which was likely not what they called it here. "Where should I sleep?"

Sat shrugged. "You can sleep on the floor."

What a gentleman. "Didn't you just swear to protect and respect me?"

"Sure, but the bed fits two, doesn't it? I won't touch you. Still, if you are that bothered, we can prepare a comfortable bed on the floor. That said, I don't want my uncle having any doubt about your loyalties. We're stronger if we appear united."

Fine. The bed was wide enough. It wasn't as if she'd never shared a bed with friends during sleepovers. This could be the same. Kind of. She still couldn't call Sat a friend. "Do you kick or pull covers?"

"You never complained."

That mysterious past she had no idea about.

He lay down far on his side of the bed and soon his breathing steadied.

The temporary privacy for her thoughts was a welcome relief despite the discomfort of the lack of physical privacy. Thankfully he'd told her nothing had happened between them otherwise she'd gag.

Yikes. Nothing against him, it just—it didn't feel right. But then, maybe he'd said that just to put her mind at ease. But he didn't seem interested in her, so it made sense. There had to be more to this alliance than met the eye. If it was about mutual protection, she could understand why she'd need it. But what did *he* have to gain? Being nice? For what? No, there was something else. There had to be. The question was what.

His uncle. He'd given enough hints for her to fear him, so perhaps it had something to do with him. But how could she figure anything when she lacked years of information? When she didn't have her past self to guide her? How could she think and at the same time conceal her thoughts and doubts enough not to raise any suspicion? Not easy to use her mind while at the same time pretending not to use it. She'd have to manage, though, if she wanted to find her answers and her way out. There had to be one.

8

## LIGHT GARDENS

**B**irds singing. Sian opened his eyes and sat up panting. There was a soft bed beneath him, and soft covers over him. So he was no longer in Marisia. A few hours—or, who knows, days, months—before, he'd think he was dead, but his mind was sharp now. He was alive and somewhere else. His heart warmed hoping he was back in Siphoria. The room had orange walls and a huge window facing trees.

A familiar-looking woman was sitting on an armchair. Familiar. But it had been so long, like an eternity ago, before he'd been confined to a land where he didn't belong. He took a better look at her face. Yes, he remembered; she'd cast a protective barrier over him and Karina a long time before.

The woman noticed he was looking. "How are you feeling?"

"Alive." Words weren't enough to express how much it meant. "Who are you?"

"My name's Leena."

That didn't answer much. "Are we in Siphoria?"

She took a deep breath.

Sian saved her the need to answer, and said, "No."

He chuckled. "No need for drama. Whatever this place is, it's a huge improvement. Where am I?"

"We're in the Light Gardens."

He looked at the trees he saw from the window. "I see a garden. Does it light up in the evening?"

"We're the Northern ethereal city in Whyland. I mean, we were, before the portals were blocked. This is also where your mother lived and where your brother was born and raised."

Sian took in the information. It wasn't surprising that he didn't know anything about it and had always imagined Darian to have been raised in a simple village. To be fair, he'd never asked his brother much about his upbringing. "How did I end up here?"

"We went to Marisia and brought you back. Your brother carried you."

Sian looked at his arms. "Wow. Ain't I skinny?"

He didn't want to complain, but there was something he wanted to understand. "If you could rescue me, how come it took... I don't even know how long. Months? A year?"

"Six months. We had no idea you weren't in Whyland. There was a breach in one of the ethereal cities, Lylah opened an emergency passage and brought Darian. Cayla also came. The breach meant you could be in danger. Thankfully your brother guessed you were in Marisia. That's when we found you."

Sian snorted. "*Could* be in danger? Among huge beasts?" He waved a hand. "Nah, preposterous."

Leena nodded. "You're absolutely right. We failed you and could have lost you. We almost did. It would have been tragic."

Images from his battle against the Maris king, the attack on him, and his feverish visions flashed before his mind. At least it was over. Not sure why this woman was describing losing him as tragic, but he'd take it.

"Coming late beats doing nothing. When can I go home?" He could almost feel himself back in the city, seeing Malena again, eating her food, seeing his friends, Joel, even Raja. Karina was a long-gone dream, but at least getting his life back was a good start.

"There's a breach in Lumina. While this is not sorted out, you'll need to stay here, where you're safe."

"Lumina?"

"One of the ethereal cities."

Sian couldn't connect the dots. "Why would a breach in a city I have no idea exists be a threat for me?"

Leena looked at him and hesitated.

"What?" he asked.

"Every time we open a portal we risk Lumina coming in."

"So we're locked in?"

She nodded.

"Until how long?" he asked.

"I don't know. Days, weeks, a month."

"A year maybe?"

"I doubt it. Guardians are working on it and should have it all sealed within a few days. A couple months at most."

Sian exhaled in relief. That meant he'd be home in a reasonable delay. He'd lost hope of ever seeing Siphoria again, and having it within reach was like a dream come true. He could wait—as long as they had something other than unseasoned worms to eat. He looked down at his cream cotton shirt—and noticed he'd never worn it before.

He flinched. "Who changed my clothes?"

Leena shook her head. "Don't worry. You're right to protect your secrets, but they're safe with me."

He put his hand across his chest, feeling his privacy violated, knowing that she had seen him. "I never allowed..." He was rambling. Allowed what? Saving his life?

"I had no choice. You had an infected wound and poison. I had to clean it, but I did it myself. Nobody else saw you, Sian."

He was still uncomfortable, but he couldn't argue with the woman's logic. In a way, she did care for his privacy. "Thank you."

She nodded. "Since when have you known it?"

That didn't make sense. "Known what?"

She pointed to his chest. "That you're supposed to hide it."

Sian swallowed. Where was she going with this? He looked away. "Can you not mention it?"

Leena got up and patted him on the arm. "I'll bring you dinner in a moment. I bet you're hungry."

He *was* starving.

She continued, "Your brother is eager to see you. Can he come in?"

"Can't I go out?"

"You're still weak."

Likely. Still, it sounded boring. "Can you bring me something? A book? Maybe a book about this city, unless it's some secret I'm not supposed to know."

She smiled. "The Light Gardens keep no secrets from their own. I'll find you something."

She left Sian to wonder why he would be one of *their own*. The door opened again and Darian walked in.

"How are you?" His tone was cautious as he approached slowly.

Sian waved his arms. "Great or terrible depending on what you measure me against."

Darian looked down then back at him. "I had no idea, I had…"

Sian hated drama. He waved a hand. "You say it as if it were your duty to save me. It wasn't."

His brother bit his lip. "True, but…"

"Thanks for carrying me." Now that he'd said it, he realized it sounded kind of humiliating. Almost dying had its way of ruining someone's dignity. Sian smiled, "I'll wager you've gained some muscle since you first came to Siphoria."

"I hope so."

Darian went silent.

Sian hated those moments when conversation died and asked, "So, your hometown? I guess you'll finally introduce me to it."

His brother sighed. "I had no idea I was raised here. They wiped my memory."

That was something Sian had never heard of, but he didn't think his brother was lying. "Did it come back?"

"Yes, once I visited here. But I didn't know about it."

A thought hit Sian. "Was that why... Why you didn't know me? Why you didn't know my name when we met?"

Darian hesitated, then said, "Possibly."

"Brother, you're a terrible liar."

"Not really. I can be good when I want to. Not sure I want to lie to you, though. I..." He looked down. "Don't recall." He looked up at Sian. "Maybe I'm wrong, maybe there was something and I forgot it when my mind was..."

"Yeah, yeah," Sian interrupted. "It's fine, and I don't care. It's not your fault."

"Sian... I'm sorry..."

His brother's sad face was getting to Sian's nerves. "No issue." He smirked. "So, do you think they'll wipe my mind once I leave?"

"I don't think so. Of course we can't tell people about it, but I don't think they'd keep it from you."

Sian rolled his eyes. "Cause I'm so nice and not a threat to anyone. That's kind of sad, you know?"

Darian shrugged. "If you insist, they can wipe your memory. Maybe they will. I don't know."

"I'm just wondering because I asked Leena to bring me books about this place. Now, it would be awful if I'd spent time learning something just to forget it."

"You say it as if you'd never forgotten anything you read or studied."

"It's different when my brain chooses to discard unnecessary information."

Darian laughed, then became serious again and stared at him. "What do you plan to do once we come back?"

"Plan? Almost dying has its way of ruining any possibility of scheming."

"True. But now..."

"I just woke up."

"And what do you think? I mean, we'll have to stay here for a while, but you'll return to Whyland..." Darian was thoughtful, then added, "You're no longer king. I think you know that."

Sian rolled his eyes. "Really? While I wasn't around to defend my position, someone usurped it? How shocking. Nah, who cares about Whyland. Little brother, you're looking at the Marisia King."

Darian made a face. It was somewhere between disbelief or pity. He was silent, though.

"Not impressed?" Sian asked.

"Surprised, I guess. It's already impressive you survived for so long."

Sian closed his eyes and took a deep breath. "That what I was doing; surviving. Killing the king was part of the deal."

"What about Darloom?"

"I blocked the place where it was. Not sure if it worked."

Darian nodded, thoughtful, then, after a moment of silence, said, "I'm happy to see you alive."

Sian considered asking why, considered saying something snappy, but then he just said, "I'm happy to see you, too."

"You're different."

"Months without decent food does that to you. Speaking of which, is my dinner coming or not?"

Karina had a war to wage in her own mind. She had to understand the world surrounding her, and yet, had to watch her thoughts when near other people, especially Firis. Her life was coming into a routine, which should be comforting, except it wasn't.

Faizana apparently had been her friend. It didn't feel or look like it, but it was true that not all friends were people Karina clicked with, and perhaps that was the case—or maybe it was something else. Sat swore his sister couldn't inquire into Karina's mind, but still, she wasn't sure. Faizana taught Karina about Luminous customs and traditions, mostly what to dress. She was a very unglamorous version of Zoe, except that Zoe had been kind, and Faizana seemed to think Karina was an uncultured primate.

They sometimes hung out with other girls. They played a game similar to chess, called magic and matter. The similarity to chess must have made Karina pick it up quickly. Still, Karina made sure she always lost. Faizana usually had a satisfied smirk when beating Karina, and it was best if it remained this way. The girl scared her for some reason. But no, it wasn't just that, but perhaps a need to hide her strengths, act as someone meek, just to make sure nobody looked at her too closely. Not that winning a game was any impressive strength, but still... Karina wasn't sure why she was doing it, just that there was a greater game at play and she was going to be careful while learning its rules.

The best time of the day was when she was with Sat. They usually went out to the woods under the excuse that he was courting her again—as if he'd ever courted her. She didn't think he had.

What they did was something else. Something difficult and challenging. Perhaps that was why she liked it.

Today they were near a pond.

"So, what did you have for lunch?" he asked.

Answering that question was like threading a different pathway in her brain. Instead of going for her memory, she went somewhere else.

A weird image came to her. "Raw worms." She could imagine the feeling in her mouth, something slimy and tasteless. It should be disgusting, but she felt empowered instead. Maybe she was just creating a feeling of being brave and eating something so gross could be part of it.

"Hum, interesting. For a moment I was quite surprised at the diet you guys have in your world." He smiled, then got serious. "Until you were surprised at imagining something you've never eaten before. Karina, that could get you killed."

This was so frustrating. He'd been asking her to perform increasingly difficult tasks. "Your uncle will kill me if I lie about what I ate?"

"Maybe. I told you. Very soon he'll test you. Depending on what you're hiding..."

"I don't understand. You insist your uncle is good. Why then—"

"He's cautious, Karina. You saw what the Guardians did. They almost killed you. They've kept you from your family. They kept us isolated." There was anger in his voice. Like everyone here, he did hate those Guardians. He continued, "If my uncle believes Guardians have brainwashed you, I mean... I don't know... If he thinks you're hiding things, he could want to protect us."

Karina wanted to ask why Sat cared whether she lived or died, but he was as unlikely to answer this now as he'd been dozens of times before. Maybe he still didn't trust her mind to carry secrets.

"There are no secrets, Karina," Sat said, in his annoying habit of replying to her thoughts. He added, "I do that so you're aware of how much you need to watch your mind."

Karina stared at him, thinking that she could just stop talking, since he would understand everything.

Sat sighed. "For sure. You can be silent, but that's not what I want you to train. In fact, I mean, no. It's actually how you prevent someone from seeing your thoughts. You send a different thought. But it's usually in images. It can work in words."

"Is there a way to block someone from entering our mind?" Karina asked out loud because she was getting creeped out by his replies to her thoughts.

"Of course there is. But it has two problems: one, it's hard. Can you guess the second problem?"

Karina wondered what the issue would be with not allowing someone in your mind. Oh, that made sense. "It would raise suspicion. Like when you don't allow someone to get in a room or open something."

"Exactly. The person will wonder what you're hiding."

"I see." Well, she'd better learn to conceal her thoughts before Firis decided to test her. "Let's continue, then."

Asking Sat anything was pointless, and maybe the way to find answers was by first learning to dissimulate her thoughts. If he had anything he was hiding from his uncle, other than this training, he'd never tell her while she wasn't very good at it.

He ignored her thoughts or perhaps didn't catch them, and asked, "What were we doing here?"

Karina visualized them walking hand in hand while he showed her the pond and evoked a warm feeling of companionship and even love.

Sat nodded. "Nice."

The tricky thing was that whenever she pulled up those thoughts and tried to create those feelings she saw him differently, almost as if the feelings were real, and she feared falling in love, since he'd never correspond.

Sat stepped closer to her, lifted her chin and looked in her eyes. Karina shuddered, especially considering he'd just heard her thoughts. He said, "There's no danger. You need to feel in love when near my uncle. It will protect you. But there's no way you'd fall in love for real. For me. It's not in you, Karina."

Right. As if he were horrendous. "What's in me, then?"

"You'll remember it slowly."

They went back to training. Their time alone together had a lot less clarification than Karina would have wanted since they had to use all the time to practice. But it was good, she wanted to learn how to dissimulate and conceal her thoughts. That was the only way she'd be able to navigate this crazy city and maybe find her way out. If there was one. There had to be one and she'd find it, but first, she wanted to make sure nobody knew she was looking.

Karina then returned to the palace, where she had lessons about the history of Lumina. One thing was clear: they were arrogant. That wasn't the end of the world, though. In her own dimension, many countries thought they were better than everyone else, and that didn't mean they were evil. Not completely evil, at least.

Lumina was the city with the most advanced magic, the most

advanced ideals, the most advanced society. They were also the only city where every citizen was capable of wielding magic. Their food production, technology, everything had some magic behind it, and, again, that made them better than everyone. She got it. As bad as she usually was with history, hearing fifty times how Lumina was the best was more than enough to remember it.

Karina didn't want to think critically about the lessons anyway because she wasn't sure what could be considered rebellious thoughts and who could pick it up. Again, in theory the teacher couldn't feel other people's thoughts, but Karina didn't want to take her chances and focused on memorizing the lessons.

Still, her mind wandered while they went through their list of overseers. Weird name, right? They should have been mayors, but, again, she wasn't about to contest the information given to her. Lumina had a royal family which had been leading it for generations. Again, she had to hear names and names and how they were wise, fair, and intelligent. The line was passed either to male or female rulers. Usually the eldest was chosen, unless one of them was born with a special talent. Which talent was a secret, of course, and Karina wondered if that could be used for younger siblings to usurp the throne. But then, there were no accounts of sibling-to-sibling disputes. But then again, the history had been written by the winners.

There were a few battles against other cities that tried to attack them or that revolted against their fair rule. Karina wished she could know what happened and why exactly they'd been isolated. More than anything, she wanted to know how she'd ended up there.

So much to learn. Her heart ached thinking about her family and friends back home. Did her parents think she was dead? Did they suffer? That was a pain she didn't think was fair. At least she had to find a way to warn them, tell them where she was, tell them she was alive. No point dwelling on pain. What she had to do was learn as much as possible and get as good as she could in concealing her thoughts, hoping she'd be good enough to fool Firis. Yet, before doing anything, she had to make sure she stayed alive.

9

IMAGES

Sian's ragged image mocked him from the mirror while he trimmed his overdue beard. He stopped, considering what it had meant to him, and then decided to leave some hair on his chin. He shaved the rest, then braided the long part and left it as a reminder.

His hair wasn't as bad now that he'd washed it properly, just dry ends. Some trimming would be good but he could wait until he got back to Siphoria. He didn't really like the clothes Leena had given him; they were cotton pants and a tunic lacking any sense of style. Fine, the pants were black and the tunic was light green, it was a nice contrast. The tunic also had some beautiful embroidery. It was just not Sian's style.

He shouldn't complain, though. This was much better than wearing the same rags for months. And it was temporary. Still, it was annoying to depend on other people's generosity as if he were a beggar. He didn't even buy his own clothes.

His thoughts turned to Karina, when she'd been in the same situation. Of course it was uncomfortable, and yet, at the time he'd never considered it. He'd imagined that she'd be happy having everything given to her. He'd been told that was what women wanted. Well, perhaps it was his father who'd told him that. He'd also told him that they only cared about power—and that he should never trust them.

Ridiculous that he somehow allowed himself to be influenced by the guy whose wife ran away. Ran away with one child only. Sian wasn't as good at cloaking the pain as he'd once been, as he felt the sting with that thought. Misguided advice and harsh parenting methods were better than nothing. His father had been better for him than his mo—no, he wasn't going to call her that.

If there was one woman who'd filled those shoes for at least some time, that was Malena. He'd met her when he was twelve, and still, she became like a mother to him. His father had sent him to her business for reasons only later he'd understand. At the time, Sian was taken to the kitchen, got cake and stories. Somehow his father was satisfied that Sian enjoyed going to Malena's and kept sending him. From a father's very warped sense of education, Sian found a mother and later a business partner. He also found a sister.

Those were the things he had to look back and remember. Still, it hurt that his father hadn't even gotten a chance to repent. One time Sian thought he was threading on his father's steps. Not all steps, but the ones he thought were good. Now he didn't know where he was going anymore. All the power in the world didn't compare to time with friends. At the same time, time with friends was sour when powerless.

He was powerless now, and had been powerless all the time he'd been in Marisia, feeling as if his identity had been torn away. Well, it didn't matter; it was temporary. The only two things he could do for now was learn as much as he could, hoping they wouldn't wipe his memory, and maybe get to know Darian a little better. If he wanted, of course. Sian wasn't going to force an oblivious brother to acknowledge him. The thought stung. No, it didn't have to sting, he could put it away.

～

THIS TIME SAT took Karina to another pond. She was glad he didn't take her to a river, or glad that there were no rivers in Lumina because it would be very strange to explain from where to where they ran when in a small circle, and her mind would have a knot. Lakes made sense, even if the whole cycle of water was weird because there were no oceans. But then, many of the rules didn't apply. She was just trying to rationalize, trying to make it fit the logic she'd known until then.

"What do you like most about Lumina?" Sat asked.

It wasn't a question like a real question, but an exercise. Karina thought about the pond and nature.

He looked at her. "Do you think it's a good answer?"

"Is it not?"

Sat shrugged. "I don't know, maybe you should include me."

It wasn't that he was vain or self-centered, but that he must have thought it would convince his uncle better. Karina wasn't sure she agreed. "Can't I like the nature? I understood the question as being about the city itself, not people in it."

"Fair enough. Do you miss your family?"

The pain and the yearning were strong, but she made sure all her anger was directed at the Guardians. "Is it okay?"

"It's great. You can miss your family and your home, it's natural. And if you understand that it's the Guardians' fault you can't go back, it means you're our ally."

Karina sighed and hid the feelings bubbling beneath the surface. "Of course I'm your ally. It's insulting that Firis should think otherwise."

"Careful there. You don't want me to repeat myself, do you? It's not you, it's the Guardians. Firis fears they could have affected your mind."

"Do you think they did?"

"Of course not."

He sounded so sure. "How do you know?"

Sat shrugged. "Hunch. Now, I know you want to understand a lot of things, but we need to get back to training. We're shorter on time than I'd expected. Firis is going to examine you tonight."

That didn't make sense. "But I've seen him before." He'd called her to his throne room, asked how things were going, and Karina always made sure to watch her thoughts.

Sat shook his head. "It's not the same. He's going to touch your head and look inside it. It's a lot more powerful."

"And he told you that?"

"I picked it up. Which also means you have to pretend you weren't warned."

"I can do that."

"Yes, I think you can."

Karina wasn't a mind reader but a shadow of fear in Sat's eyes didn't go unnoticed. He was terrified of his uncle despite his assurances that he was a good man. Why? Perhaps one day she'd find out. Hopefully not tonight, though. She'd better be flawless and not let any stray thought escape.

THEY DRESSED Karina in a complicated dress again. It was light blue and had longer pieces of fabric wrapping around her waist. The skirt was puffy. The attendants didn't tell her anything about a special dinner or party, but it was obvious because of the dress. Well, the attendants probably didn't know anything either. As always, they entered and left in silence.

Karina wasn't supposed to talk to them, but the proximity with people while maintaining a cold distance made her feel lonely. Not a good time to think about that. Technically, mind reading was a rare skill in Lumina, but Karina didn't want to take her chances. If she wanted to spy on someone, sending an inconspicuous attendant would be the perfect way to do it.

They did her hair with some pins with glowing stars in it. Karina looked beautiful. Truly beautiful, not just cute as she'd always considered herself. Perhaps not always. Who knew what happened in the years lost in her mind? Then again, it was that odd feeling, like stepping in a stranger's body. Beautiful stranger, and still a stranger. Karina wondered if that stranger had the confidence that should come with those looks.

She stepped outside her dressing room and saw Sat, who wore a dress suit too, in light blue, with a long coat. He was sitting on a chair and got up and gawked at her.

"You look beautiful."

Time to start the show—even within her own mind.

Karina laughed. "I do, right? You look good too. What's the special occasion?"

"You won't believe it. My uncle is having a dinner in your honor."

Karina decided to be playful. "Since when do I deserve any honor?"

He laced his arm against hers. "We're honored to have you recovered and well again."

"Well, let's celebrate!"

They walked towards the throne room.

Sat opened the door for Karina and the scene surprised her. She'd thought there would be more people at the celebration, but no, it was just Firis, sitting on a round table with food on it and set for three people. Quite an intimate celebration.

Karina sat down, and even though she wasn't sure if she was breaking protocol or not, decided to show her appreciation. "Thank you for having us here."

Firis had a warm smile and a nod. "It's my pleasure to see you recovered and my nephew so happy."

Karina focused on all the food on the table, making herself feel happy to be invited to such an occasion, glad for the favor Firis was giving them.

The old man gestured to the food. "Let's not let it get cold." He got up, stood beside Karina, and took her plate. "What would you like?'

Was he offering to serve her?

Karina smiled. "I trust your wiseness' judgement."

Firis filled her plate. As they ate, she focused on the tastes and textures of the food. They then had an aromatic tea and a sweet fruit pie for dessert. Karina didn't know the yellow berries, and she thought she'd ask Sat that later. She wondered if there were fruits from her world she was forgetting, or if she had eaten this before and had forgotten. The sugar wasn't cane sugar either, and she'd have to ask later about it. Funny that in these last days she hadn't given thought about local sugar. Well, she hadn't eaten any sugar these days, so it wasn't surprising she hadn't wondered about it. Maybe she should have wondered about the lack of sugar.

Firis stared at her. "How are you feeling?"

Sat reached out and held her hand. She said, "I'm well. It's still strange to have a part of my life missing from my mind." She looked at Sat and smiled. "But I think some things, feelings, are coming back."

Sat smiled back and caressed her hand.

Firis noticed it. "Love sweetens everything, doesn't it?"

Karina imagined a warm feeling in her heart. "It does."

"Did any memory come back?" Firis asked. "Some information about the attack, something?"

She shook her head. "I wish it had. I still don't know what happened."

Firis kind eyes rested on her. "You're not supposed to be told, you have to remember it, or we won't get pure facts when you do."

"I understand."

"Are you happy here?"

Karina looked at Sat, with his delicate face, dark brown eyes surrounded with blond lashes, giving her a loving look. She turned to Firis. "Of course. Your nephew. This place. Everything is wonderful."

Firis narrowed his eyes. "Everything? Are you sure?"

He wasn't asking as if doubting or testing her, but as if her words hadn't made sense. Well, of course. "I miss my family and I worry about them." Karina tried not to focus too much on her lost home, as she didn't want pain to spoil that moment.

Firis nodded. "You wish you could visit them. Of course. So do we. It's not fair that you should be locked here."

Karina shrugged. "It's life. I'll do the best I can."

Firis got up and walked around the table, standing by her side. Karina wondered if he was going to pour her some tea, but instead he put his hands on her head. "I'm just checking your mind. I need to see if you are recovered."

Karina's heart filled with gratitude at being so kindly treated by this great, wise man. Of course, his kindness was because she made his nephew happy, and still, it filled her with gratitude. In truth, Sat made her happy. She recalled their moments by the pond, when they walked hand in hand. She could feel his lips against hers, his arms touching her, how they ended up lying on the grass, his hands under her dress, her dress tossed aside, the comforting feeling of skin against skin...

Firis hands moved away from Karina's head while Sat's hand tensed holding hers.

"Lovebirds." Firis chucked. "I won't take any more of your time, as I'm sure you're eager to retire to your quarters."

Sat got up. "Thank you, uncle."

Karina also got up and followed him to their room. She wanted to collapse on the bed, exhausted from the mental strain of creating false memories, feelings, and images. Sat sat on the bed, rested his forehead on his hand and sighed. He looked stressed rather than relieved.

Uh-oh. That was bad. Had she failed her test? "Is there something wrong?"

Sat shook his head, still not looking at her. "You were more than perfect."

"But you're worried."

He looked up at her. "I'm just tired."

Karina wondered if it was straining for him as well. Now that she was outside Firis mind-reading range, she had to remind herself that Sat's googly eyes were as false as the images she created, even if they could feel so real. In truth, she did feel exhausted. "I'll call the attendants."

She was walking away, when Sat held her hand. "Don't."

Weird.

He added, "My uncle thinks, uh, we're tired and not going to need attendants. Turn around. I'll untie the dress. I think you can figure the rest on your own."

Yes, he did untie it, and Karina went to her dressing room and battled that thing until it was out of her body so that she could put on her nightgown. She didn't want to ask Sat to help her because he was cold, distant, and weird. Plus it would be horrible if he saw her half undressed.

She wondered if he was thinking that the feelings and images she'd conjured at dinner were real, if they were her desires, fantasies. All she'd done was pretend they were a real couple, maybe too real, but that was because she'd been eager to get Firis out of her head. Sat must have seen those thoughts. But what had he expected? Anyway, she'd better not think about it now. It was never safe.

All she wanted was to sleep. Sat spent a long time in his bathroom. When he came back, he brought a thick blanket. Karina wondered if he had a fever or something, but he made a bed on the floor. More space for her. Perhaps she should have imagined making out with Sat a long time ago if that was it took to get the bed for herself.

He fell asleep soon, and she had some respite to have her own thoughts. Was Sat disgusted? Why wasn't *she* disgusted? Had the desire been fake, or had it been real? Or had she faked so well it felt real? Regardless, that wasn't the point. What mattered was that she had been capable of concealing her thoughts from Firis, the so-called best telepath in Lumina. So-called, because she had a hunch that their overseer was only second best.

Karina's thoughts gave way to slumber and strange dreams. She walked in a dark forest trying to find someone. There was a thick fog and, even carrying a lantern, she could see no further than a meter ahead of her.

Heart racing, she sat up, recognizing her bed in the Lumina palace, then wondering where Sat was until she recalled he was on the floor. That was his problem, not hers. The dream... it had been important. Her chest ached. There was someone, something she missed. Probably home, her family, her friends. No, it wasn't any of that. It was someone else, someone important. She'd been looking for this person, but she couldn't remember who it was. So many things she couldn't remember. Still, she missed that person—and it hurt.

THE NIGHTMARES HAD STOPPED. Sian wasn't sure if he should be relieved or disappointed. Only now he realized how much Karina had been in his dreams. At first, he thought the medicine was making him sleep more deeply. Now that he was well and treated, nothing had changed. The dreams still hadn't returned. Could it be something in the Light Gardens that affected the way he slept? Maybe. Or had it been his desperation, loneliness, and pain while in Marisia that led him to these dreams?

No. The pain in Marisia had turned them into nightmares. Karina had been in his dreams way before, since after he'd just met her for a short while, knowing only that she was the girl traveling with the princess, and then later realizing she had mysterious magic. At the time, he wouldn't have imagined... Then the dreams came, like memories that wouldn't go away. Now they stopped. Something was different, and he didn't know what it was.

Sian got up and went to the kitchen. It was strange to share a house with Darian and Cayla, as if they were a family. Well, in a way, they were. The sun hadn't risen yet. Solitude was something he came to appreciate in time. He poured milk and grains on a pan, wondering if he should also make some for his brother. No. They'd wake up later and it would be cold. What he wanted to do today was find Leena. More than books, he was going to take this opportunity to learn—and convince them not to wipe his memory.

~

KARINA COULDN'T WAIT to be alone with Sat because the idea that he was upset at her for wanting him made her feel angry, rejected, humiliated, and who knows what else.

Of course, she had to drown all those feelings under a peaceful ocean of tranquility while she had breakfast with Faizana and her friends. Well, maybe not. Karina realized she could test whether people read minds, and imagined something very inappropriate concerning the girl. No reaction. Phew.

Sat had told her over and over that the only known telepaths in the castle were him and Firis. That meant her thoughts were safe around her. Or sort of. In the castle, one could never know.

Later, when she was alone with Sat in the woods, Karina didn't wait for him to start.

"What was the problem last night?"

His eyes widened. "Problem? You were perfect. I have to say, I was quite impressed."

That didn't make sense. "You were weird after."

He shook his head. "I was tired. Don't think you're the only one who had to strain your mind."

"Is that why you slept on the floor? Because you were too tired for a soft bed?"

"You talk as if you missed me." He wasn't sarcastic or teasing, just... she wasn't sure.

"I didn't. But if I did something wrong, I'd like to be told about it, not be given subtle signs in the hopes that I'll guess what it is."

He shook his head. "No signs. I just thought we'd convinced my uncle well enough. If anyone catches me sleeping on the floor, they'll figure we argued or something. I knew it made you uncomfortable, so I stopped once it was no longer necessary."

"Oh." That made sense. And it didn't. Karina wasn't crazy, there had been something odd about him. "You're not telling the whole truth."

"Are you also a telepath now?"

"No, but I can read body language, voice tone, like most human beings."

Sat shrugged. "People misinterpret body language. It was a tense night."

"True." Still, she had to say what she'd come to say. "Sat, what I imagined when Firis touched my head... I just wanted him to stop, I just wanted—"

"Aren't we glad my uncle's not a pervert?"

"You were also in my mind. What does that make you?"

Sat raised an eyebrow. "A concerned party. But you don't have to explain yourself. You did great. For a moment even I thought it was a real memory."

"I'm glad it seemed real. It's not like I've ever kissed—at least that I remember. But that was what I was supposed to do, wasn't it? Pretend our feelings were real."

"It was, and you were better than I expected."

"Thanks." Then a thought occurred to her. She didn't bother trying to hide it, and stared at him. "You're better than your uncle."

He raised an eyebrow. "Did you also imagine making out with him?"

Karina laughed. "Yuck. I mean you're a better telepath. You don't even need to touch people's heads."

Sat's playful mood was gone in an instant. "No. No, no, no. If I were a better telepath, I would pose a risk for my uncle, wouldn't I? That means I'd be in danger. So that's not a thought you want to have."

That pretty much confirmed Karina's suspicion.

Sat frowned. "It doesn't confirm anything!"

Replying to thoughts. That was definitely not a sign of a strong telepath.

Sat shook his hands. "Whatever. Maybe. Just don't entertain that idea."

"You just said I was good at concealing what I think. Can't you trust me?"

"I just did."

"Trust me more, I mean. There's a lot you're hiding."

Sat sat on a rock and picked a blade of grass. "You too are hiding a lot. I'd rather not strain you all at once. Some truths are more dangerous than others."

Karina sighed. "You're playing a dangerous game, aren't you? And using me." *Using me for my magic* came to her mind, but that didn't make any sense.

"Life in Lumina is always dangerous. I'm trying to protect you."

It didn't seem dangerous, but then, perhaps walking on a knife's edge with Firis wasn't the safest situation either. "You're protecting me for a reason."

Sat cocked his head. "Maybe."

Karina hated depending on Sat, hated not knowing what was happening. "I guess one day I'll find out."

"Definitely." Sat crossed his arms.

Karina wasn't imagining, he was colder and more distant. She had to finish what she'd been planning on saying. "Let me just get it out of my chest: I'm sorry if I disgusted you or made you feel invaded last night. I was just doing what you told me, and pretending we were a couple."

Sat looked down and shook his head. "No need for apologies. It was amazing."

She still wondered why he was strange.

He looked at her and added, "I'm not strange, but you're so good that we don't need to work at creating false intimacy. You can conjure it out of thin air. It's better that way, isn't it?"

"Yes." Was it, though? Did it feel better knowing that the person who was closest to her didn't want to get too close?

"I meant romantically," Sat said. "We'd never fall in love, that's all, and it can sound strange because if we imagine it well enough, somehow it can seem like a good idea. I hadn't considered that."

Why was he insisting on that? "I'm not saying it's a good idea, I just wanted to know why you have to keep such a distance."

He stared at her. "Why? Would you like to kiss me the way you imagined last night?"

"No." Her voice was dry. "And that's why you don't need to keep reminding me that we'll never have anything with each other. It's not like I'm going to grab you in the middle of the night or jump at you and kiss you, you know?"

"I know. Sorry if I gave that impression. I'm just being normal."

Karina looked down. "You're my only friend here." That was what really bothered her, and why it hurt to feel he was so cold. She hated admitting it, but perhaps being around a telepath was teaching her— or forcing her—to open up.

He was standing in front of her in a second, put his hand under her chin and raised it softly so that they looked at each other. "I'm still your friend."

His eyes were darker than usual. He opened his mouth as if to say something else but took a deep breath instead. For a second she did wonder what it would be like to kiss him, before she turned her thoughts to what she'd eaten at breakfast.

Too late. He must have picked that up as he stepped back, his voice cold. "We won't train anymore. Soon, soon, something big is going to happen. Meanwhile, try to study about the royal line."

She was going to tell him that the brief curiosity about a kiss was all it was, curiosity, but it was better not to make a big fuss out of it and he must have read her thoughts anyways. Changing the subject was a better idea.

"I've been studying. The royal line, they have a unique magical skill, right?"

"Yes," Sat replied, not looking at her.

"Is it telepathy?"

He turned to her. "Cause my uncle has it? No. I'm a telepath, and I'm not in the royal line."

"You're in the royal family."

He shook his head. "The skill marks the royal *line*."

"Genetics don't work like that."

"It's magic, it's different."

"What other skill does Firis have?"

"Firis? No. It doesn't mean that everyone in the royal line has the skill, just that it only appears in people in the royal line. Rarely. From time to time."

"And what is it?"

"All I know is that it's been conveniently erased from our records."

10

# PLANS

Leena had agreed to take Sian to the edge of the city. He wouldn't call it a city, but rather a strange area, since so much of it was forest. He sat on a boat with her.

"What happens to the river? I mean, if we're in this ethereal place…"

"We're connected to the land beneath," she replied.

"Even when we're blocked from it?"

"Yes."

The boat moved faster and faster, carving its way on slower moving water. It wasn't going with the flow of the river, and there were no sails to pick up wind. Pure magic, and he should have known it. But something else was in his mind. "What if the land were destroyed? Would this city die?"

Leena paused as if wondering why he was asking that question. Hopefully she didn't think he wanted to attack the Light Gardens. Well, who would want to attack a city that barely existed? It was just curiosity.

She finally spoke, "We could move, but it would be painful, like when you move a plant from one pot to another."

"So there is a connection."

Leena nodded. "There is."

She clearly enjoyed teaching about their city and even about magic to Sian, and he was going to take the opportunity to learn as much as he could. But then... learn for what? Last time he'd decided to learn as much as he could about magic had been for a very precise goal. Now he had no idea where his life was going.

The boat then turned, as if there were a revolving body of water beneath it.

"What's happening?"

The old woman smiled. "Try to guess."

The river went on, but they didn't.

"There's a barrier. Is this the edge of the Light Gardens?"

"It is."

Sian touched the running water. "If I were to throw something on the river, would it go on?"

"What do you think?"

Asking questions was Leena's way of teaching. He wasn't going to argue even if he thought that just giving the answer would have been a lot more efficient. Sian pictured an object from the Light Gardens, and then realized it shouldn't pass the barrier. "It wouldn't continue. How does the water continue running, then?"

"You've guessed a lot. I'm sure you know the answer."

Had he known he wouldn't have asked. But the woman enjoyed getting the answers out of him, and he wasn't going to complain. Sian considered. There was a barrier. Nothing could cross it, and yet, they were tied to the land.

"It's not the same water."

Leena smiled. "Yes, we're like a copy from the land below, but not the same."

Very freaky stuff. Karina would want a logical explanation for it, so he'd better learn what it was to tell her. A knot took the place of his heart. *Tell her.* When? Sian tried to bury the horrible feeling that came with the idea that perhaps he'd never see her again. And yet he'd known. They'd known their goodbye had been forever. But then he'd been dreaming about her during all his time in Marisia.

"Are you alright?" Leena interrupted his thoughts.

"I guess. I do want to go back to Whyland. I miss... so many things."

"You won't have to stay here long. A few days at most."

"Don't get me wrong," he said. "I'm enjoying the opportunity to learn."

"It's your city, it's past time you learned about where you are from."

Sian smiled. He didn't really agree, though. His city was Siphoria. He didn't want to say anything not to lose Leena's goodwill. There were a lot more things he wanted to learn about the Light Gardens before leaving, and the woman was kind and happy to see him so interested in their customs, magic, and tradition. It was knowledge. The more he knew, the better he could be, even if he didn't know what he was going to be better at.

KARINA HAD some rare moments for herself, between her lessons and dinner. Nobody had told her she couldn't explore the palace, and in theory she should learn everything she could about Lumina, so she set out to explore. Nothing in it ever rang a bell or even feel remotely familiar. Very hard to believe she'd lived in this palace for the last two years. Maybe she hadn't.

She'd come to the conclusion that Sat was a mind-reading prodigy, since he was way better than his uncle. In theory Firis was the greatest mind reader in Lumina, but he had to touch a person's head to get a decent reading. Sat didn't need it, but even he couldn't read minds from behind walls, so she stopped watching her thoughts as much when she was alone.

Karina took a back door that only servants used. Again, in theory, nobody had said anything about servants' areas being forbidden. She passed by the kitchen. There were some five people preparing food. The place was calm, organized, and yet something about it was creepy. Well, yes, the silence. Every servant she'd seen so far was quiet. Was this an order, some spell, or were they mute?

Karina decided to try, and turned to a girl rolling some pastry. "Hey, I'm lost here. Do you know how to get to the bedrooms?"

The girl didn't lift her eyes and pointed to the door. That didn't go as well. All right. There was a lot more to explore. Karina had seen an external elevated area near what she thought was the second floor. She went to the third floor instead and looked for a window. There was something to see indeed. About a hundred people practiced different forms of combat, most of them using what she would describe as magic. A few colorful balls of energy attracted Karina's eyes. Faizana was shooting and controlling them. The girl seemed very powerful. Near her, another girl made a defensive shield. Sat was at a corner listening to a short woman with purple hair who seemed to be a teacher.

Further down, some forty people trained manipulating metal spheres in the air. They sometimes flew high, and even had formations, like airplanes. On another corner, a small group controlled what Karina would call drones. They were not drones, though, at least not like the drones in her world. They were probably controlled by some kind of magic. So a lot of people in Lumina used telekinesis. And they were getting prepared for some kind of battle. Perhaps they were just ready in case someone attacked. Who knew? Her history lessons mentioned wars, claiming Lumina had liberated a few cities. Karina did wonder what *liberate* meant.

Her eyes scanned the grounds until she found Satwak again, this time dodging balls thrown in his direction. He was surprisingly good. Well, it shouldn't be surprising, as he'd probably be able to guess his opponent's next move.

His opponent's next move. That was what Firis was good at. Karina wondered... And yet, he seemed to be the legitimate overseer. Sat's mother had been his younger sister. Karina had paid careful attention to that part, wondering if there had been any foul play or maybe Firis had taken one of Sat's parents throne. Not the case. Why did she have to pay attention to the royal line, then? Why, why, why? Those were the thoughts that consumed her, and not only why watch the royal line. Why everything.

In a way, she should be glad Satwak was now cold and distant. He'd never been her friend. She was a prisoner, even if perhaps he also was. One thing that had puzzled her was why he insisted so much on them pretending, but making clear he felt nothing for her. She'd tried to brush away these thoughts, thinking maybe it was her own hurt ego wondering why he was avoiding her, but now she came to a different conclusion: she wondered about it because it didn't make any logical sense.

If he was so afraid of his uncle, and if his uncle had to think Karina and Sat were a couple, it would make a lot more sense to simply try to seduce her. Less risk. She had to admit he was good looking, so of course he had a shot if he made it seem that he liked her. Then, maybe he didn't want to pretend all the time. No, it didn't justify the risk. What was it, then? Did he have someone else? Maybe he just knew he didn't like her for real and didn't want to deceive her. That would be honorable, but didn't make sense. When people are cornered and afraid honor goes down the drain, and he was clearly afraid of Firis, who, for some reason, had to believe they were a couple.

Maybe it was something in her past. If Satwak tricked her into falling in love with him, perhaps he'd be in big trouble when her memory returned. Her past. She'd been searching in vain for an image, a sound, something from the last two years. Nothing. Nothing. Just emptiness.

Karina felt someone behind her and turned. Firis. Her husband's dear uncle.

His stare was intense. "Like what you see?"

She smiled. "They're phenomenal. So much magic, power. I can't stop falling in love with Lumina. Sorry, I know in theory I should know it already, but..."

"Your love is welcome." He looked at the window. "They are powerful. And that's why the Guardians had to isolate us; they stand no chances in a direct fight. Cowards. Afraid of power." He stared at her. "Are you afraid of power?"

"I wouldn't mind having a little more of it," she blurted.

His stare was piercing. "That can be arranged." He caressed her hair. "If you ever want someone to confide in, if you ever find my nephew is not being good to you, I'm here."

Karina looked down. "Thank you."

"Any time you need. Come to the throne room. To my personal room. My nephew doesn't need to know."

"Thank you, your wiseness." She felt deep gratitude at having the favor of such a great man.

"Call me Firis."

Karina nodded. "If you'll excuse me."

She ran away, up the stairs all the way to her bedroom, closed the door, then sat on the bed, shaking. What had that been about? Yuck. His touch still felt as if a disgusting spider had walked on her hair, and the worst is that she had to block all those feelings while he'd been doing that.

Had he been *flirting* with her? Had they ever... No, no. Maybe he was just testing her. That made sense. He had to touch her head, right? To know what she was feeling. And he had to check if she was loyal to his nephew. What better way to do it than to flirt with her? He probably thought he was hot. Well, he could be good look-ing, if he didn't look like he was forty or even fifty, and if he weren't creepy.

Karina prepared her bath. She wished she could bathe in alcohol or something. It couldn't be. She was imagining things. It had been just a test, which she really hoped he never repeated.

When she came out of the bathroom, Satwak was there, worry written on his face. "What happened?"

That was surprising. "Can you pick up thoughts from that far away?"

"No. My uncle. He was feeling satisfied about something to do with you. Feeling smug, superior, and, erm... You ran from him, confused. I couldn't get more than that."

Karina wondered whether she should tell him anything, but then realized that while she was wondering, her encounter with Firis had played in her mind. "Did you see it?"

"Not clearly. Can you remember it again?"

Karina brought up the memory.

Sat's face was somber. "You're wondering if you're imagining things or getting confused. You aren't. Firis has done this to me once."

"Flirt with you?"

He had a thin, amused smile, but then his face turned sad. "I wish. He stole my love."

"Oh." Karina's mind was buzzing. So Firis was capable of that. "But he's so old."

Sat shrugged. "Being overseer has its perks, I guess."

"What happened to her?"

"Died. Accident, in case you're wondering. And no, I'm not going to talk about it."

"Is that why you hate him?"

"Of course I don't hate him. I love my uncle. All he did was show me who she was, and that was good. If anything, I'm thankful."

"Awesome. Maybe you'll be thankful now." Karina knew it wasn't truly what he thought, but couldn't hold her tongue.

Sat shook his head. "He's going to pay more attention to you now, and that's the problem. Keep thinking of him as family, and keep pretending you don't notice his advances."

Karina couldn't bite her sarcasm. "Really? I was thinking of flirting back."

Sat rolled his eyes. "Whatever. Just don't let him know you find him repulsive. You ran away from him today, but you're lucky, he thought that was cute."

"I guess he *is* a pervert."

Sat sighed. "Maybe."

Karina was thoughtful. It didn't make any sense. "Why, though? Does he get a kick out of thinking he's better than you? Is it to test me? To annoy you?"

Sat shrugged. "He wants what he wants, that's all. He doesn't care enough about me either way to bother me on purpose or to spare my feelings. Try not to worry, though. Soon something will happen, and we won't spend much time near him."

"Right. Let me guess. You aren't going to tell me what."

Sat shook his head. "Sorry."

Great. As usual. Her thoughts turned to Firis again, and she tried to clutch on a small piece of hope. "You said I had to convince him. Maybe he didn't buy it, and that's why he's testing me."

"He bought it quite well, Karina. Perhaps too well."

Cayla was glad to finally see the portal tower, the seat of the Guardians. She knew that just by being able to open portals, in theory she could count as a guardian, but these were the real deal, they went to other dimensions and met with volunteers from other ethereal cities and dimensions.

The teleporting tower was guarded, as they were still on high alert because of the breach. Anika then took her to a different room, high in another tower, with twenty chairs around a well. This was their center, where they met. Not everybody had to come in person or teleport there as the room had small blue crystals on the floor, from which members could project their images. Cayla's own castle had some of those, and now she realized that they were meant for communication with the guardians.

There were twelve ethereal cities, but only eleven kept contact. The twelfth was Lumina, which had been sealed off. Somehow, they'd found an opening, and it was most likely their people who had attacked Cayla that night. They were interested in finding and destroying the guardians, so that nobody would prevent their expansion anymore. And that was what the Guardians were trying to find right now; how exactly this breach had happened. They were also on alert and avoiding opening portals until they were sure Lumina was sealed again. Cayla didn't know how they'd do it, but she was willing to help as much as she could.

Her own mother had never told her any of that. Now Anika showed it and explained it to her. The girl had been nice, but Cayla tried to keep some distance. Being Cayla's friend was dangerous. Still no news from Alessa, nothing. Her mother couldn't send a simple message, as usual.

As they left the tower, Sian and Leena came towards them, deep in conversation. It wasn't fair. Just because he'd almost died, now he got special treatment? Yes, he was Darian's brother, and no, she didn't think he should be executed, she was very glad she'd helped save his life, but he should at least face trial. If he had suffered, it was his fault only. Actions have consequences.

Perhaps it just bugged her that Leena seemed to pay more attention to Sian than to Darian, as if he were as important or even more important than him, when he wasn't. Sian was a war criminal with no history or interest for the Light Gardens, except perhaps for his own gain.

Sian saw her and waved, the signature smug smirk on his face. "Hey, sis!"

"Hi." Cayla had a half-smile.

It reminded her of Karina. Oh, Karina, it just broke Cayla's heart that he'd manipulated her so much. True, he'd been willing to die for her. Perhaps he did have feelings. Hard to believe, but maybe.

Hopefully Karina was happy back in her own world and had been over him for a long time now. She had to be, once she came to her senses. First, he wasn't that good-looking, second, detached and sarcastic as he was, it was doubtful that he could incite any deep romantic feelings regardless of his willingness to die for anyone. It wasn't even that noble. He wouldn't need to sacrifice anything or risk his life if he hadn't put Karina in danger in the first place. And maybe that was what pissed Cayla off so much. After all he'd done, here he was, like some welcome guest, even perhaps illustrious guest, when he should be nothing but an unwelcome burden until they could return to Whyland.

～

DARIAN SAT down by the lake. Rae, the young man beside him, had once been his childhood friend. One more of those forgotten memories. Their lives had moved in such different directions. Now they talked about magic, recalling his innocent years when Darian yearned for the day he'd find out what he was good at. Rae for his part wasn't exceptional with magic, but he could create protective shields and manipulate small, light objects.

Rae stared at him. "We could ask Master Siren to teach you, you know?"

Darian wasn't actually looking forward to lessons with his old master. It would be like regressing to his childhood again. "No. I wanted someone closer to my level, who still remembers how to get the basics."

"I guess. You forgot a lot, didn't you?"

"They *made* me forget." Darian had to make an effort not to sound bitter or angry, realizing then that he still carried these feelings.

"But now that your memory is back, don't you recall your training?"

"That's now how learning works, is it? If it were, nobody would need to keep studying or practicing anything."

"I see." Rae was silent, thoughtful for a moment. "And you think you're a spell speaker?"

"That's what I've been told."

"Hum. How do you do it? Do you imagine what you're going to convince someone to?"

Darian waved his arms. "That's the thing, I don't do it. I have no idea how to do anything." He added, "That's why I thought you could help me."

"Well, I'm not a spell speaker. What I do is I imagine what I'm going to create. It starts with an image. That said, you deal with words, right? It should be something sound based. But I'm guessing."

Darian scratched his head. He didn't know, he didn't want to ask any of the masters, he wasn't even sure if it would make any difference in his life. For the last three years he'd lived away from magic, and found his identity in the process. And yet, there was something stirring inside him, as if wanting to burst out.

"You know what?" Rae said. "Just stop trying to figure it out. Let's just sit and feel the wind and the sun. If something comes, great, if it doesn't, it doesn't."

That perhaps made sense. Darian closed his eyes, focused on the moment, on the nature around him, letting his thoughts flow. If there was magic to come, it would come out of its own will.

KARINA WAS AGAIN DRAWN to the yard where she'd seen people training. The encounter with Firis had been troubling but at least she knew that the area wasn't off-limits for her. Plus, perhaps it was her way to see people. This time she went to the second floor, found the door leading to the yard and walked to its edge. The worst that could happen would be somebody telling her to go away. Big deal. Then she would go back to her room or to the studies where she should be listening to more history of Lumina.

From up close, they looked even more spectacular and numerous, divided in groups here and there, many of them manipulating balls in the air, some making shields, some just wrestling. Karina was awed with so much power. As much as she disliked Lumina, she figured people born there were happy, learning so much magic. Of course a part of her wished she could go in that yard and train, move things with her mind, just... feel powerful. Karina closed her eyes and took in a deep breath. She was what she was, and all she had to do was find a way back to a world where she mattered.

"Want to try?" A woman's voice broke her out of her reverie. It was she short woman with purple hair.

"What?"

"Train. You should train as well."

The woman was cheerful but firm. There was something pleasant about her. Karina felt sorry she'd have to refuse her offer. "I don't have magic." The woman stared at her. Karina thought she hadn't been convincing, so she shrugged and added, "Sorry."

The woman cocked her head. "Fair enough. I'm here if you want to give it a try."

Karina smiled. "Sure."

Right. What would she even do? Maybe learn some self-defense. Anyway, she wasn't even sure if she was allowed to train. The idea of whether she was or wasn't allowed to do something irked her. Not even at home, as a teenager, she had to watch her step. At home her life wasn't on the line either.

The woman with the purple hair was now near a group of people wrestling. Karina didn't understand whether they were using any kind of magic. Maybe it was just regular wrestling, which was kind of stupid. If they could shoot projectiles and conjure shields, nobody was going to get close enough to anyone in order to wrestle.

Some guys wore no shirts. Nice view. Like everyone in Lumina, they looked almost too perfect. Perhaps it was just that they trained a lot.

Satwak was there. Well-toned like the others. There was something, though. Something odd about it. Perhaps it was that he should have some kind of scar. He should, if he'd been in fights. Maybe he hadn't. Still. Suddenly she closed her eyes and it was all wrong. As if in a dream, he wouldn't take off his shirt. Was it Sat, though? Karina felt a shiver. It was as if she'd caught the thread.

She walked in her mind with a vague idea where to go, holding to an end of a line, in a dark hallway. There was a memory there. As scary as the dark hallway was, she wanted to continue, even if it felt like walking through something thick and viscous instead of air. Hard to move, but the memory was there. Just there, and she held the thread.

"Hey," Sat's voice startled her.

The thread, the hall, and her memory were gone. Karina came up quickly with something to say. "Nobody told me I couldn't come here."

"Not a problem." He held her face with his two hands and kissed her forehead. "Marital love," he whispered.

*A public performance?* Karina thought.

Sat nodded, then laughed. "You aren't playing your part, though."

"I was staring at you bare-chested. What do you call that?"

He thought for a moment, then said, "All right. We'd better go up."

"You don't have to stop."

He shook his head, then whispered. "We have more important things to do. We're leaving as soon as we can."

More information that didn't make sense. "Leaving. Weren't we isolated?"

"I've found a way. To another ethereal city, at least."

Right. And nobody had told her anything. Something else worried her. "Won't your uncle be upset if we leave?" Not that she cared what he thought, just that she feared what he could do.

"No. He'll be quite happy."

KARINA LOOKED at her suitcase over the bed. Not really hers. Suitcases, clothes, accessories, they were all strange to her. All she knew were her nightgowns and some dresses. Very little that she could call hers in this strange body and life.

She hadn't seen Firis any more since their last encounter, which was a relief. Perhaps she had over-reacted and maybe even Sat had misread his uncle. If he truly did have some past trauma in that regard, couldn't he also mix things up, the way regular, non-telepathic people did with words and body language? It made sense. Karina avoided thinking about that in front of Satwak, though. He'd still been distant, and it was a great reminder that he wasn't her friend.

Sat came in. "Everything ready?"

"I guess. Are you going to tell me where we are going or should I figure it out once we get there?"

He took a deep breath. "We're opening a portal to an ethereal city; Forestglare. The idea is to lure some guardians there and pressure them to attend our demands."

"Oh, now you can open portals. Weren't we isolated or something?"

"We figured a way. It's new and it's going to be a game changer for us."

"Can't you go to my dimension? Or to the city where the Guardians are?"

Sat shook his head. "These passages are too well guarded. Forestglare is tiny and nobody would think we'd strike there."

Karina didn't like the idea of striking a possibly defenseless city for no reason.

Sat shrugged. "We have no choice."

Well, maybe it would be her opportunity to find a way back home, and an opportunity to stay away from Lumina—and Firis. "And how come you need my help?"

"To open the portal. We'll be five people doing it. The strength of us all will make it open."

"But I don't have magic."

"It doesn't matter."

"Fine, I guess."

They walked to the teleporting tower.

Faizana, a guy, and another girl sat in a circle. There were more warriors around them. At the opposite door, more warriors ready to enter. It wasn't as if Karina had any power to stop them.

Firis was there too, and walked towards them. "My nephew and his wife, the loveliest of them all."

Literally everyone in that room was better looking than Karina, but okay. She was happy Firis was being kind to her.

Sat gave her a plaque, with the image of a very tall room, like a hollow tower. "Just look at it and imagine opening a portal there."

Karina looked at the picture, imagining herself there, as if this tower and that could merge. She felt goosebumps and something else, as if for a moment she could float and see her own body and the circle of people there. Light surrounded her.

The warriors stepped forward and disappeared. Sat put his hand on her head. She shouldn't let him. She imagined pushing him away, and his hand didn't touch her. For a moment she felt she could destroy that place. A second hand touched her head. It was like a metal hand, heavy, and there was no way she could fight it. She didn't feel or see anything else.

# 11

# CROWN

Karina woke up in a large room with tree trunks and leaves surrounding the walls. The floor had moss but she sat on a sofa with a soft fabric.

Sat removed his hand from her head. "How are you?"

Karina blinked. "You. Your uncle. Both. You made me pass out."

"You were having a reaction to the magic. It could be dangerous."

He was lying but she didn't want to waste her time trying to dig out the truth. "We're in Forestglare."

"Yes. It all went very well."

For once it was as if she could see Satwak more clearly. In fact, her mind was making more sense of things. Karina looked around. "Are we alone?"

"You can never be sure. So many trees. They say the people here can talk to them." Sat twirled his hand and a blue light encircled them. "Now we're good. What is it?"

"Wouldn't it be easier to hear my thoughts?"

"You get annoyed. And I can't be sure the trees aren't telepaths."

Karina rolled her eyes.

He added, "In any case, you can't hear mine."

"Right." Then she decided to say what she was thinking. "You want to depose your uncle, don't you?"

"Of course not. Can't you see I'm here, taking this city, to help my uncle? That I'm devoted to him?"

"Cut it off. You want to depose your uncle and you need me. I mean, that's the only explanation for this fake marriage. What I don't understand is why."

"And you think I'm going to tell you?"

"No. But I can learn a little from your reactions."

"I'll watch my reactions, then."

"Careful. It's very easy to force me to cooperate when I have no other choice. Things can change."

Sat snorted. "Considering taking my uncle's offer?"

"Ugh. Can't you read my thoughts?"

Sat sighed. "You are getting into something, fine. But the less you know, the safer we are. Please always consider me as a devoted nephew, unless you would like to see me lose my head, or worse, be put in the stasis room."

"What room?"

"A place for dangerous people. Like a prison. What matters is that a tiny hint of suspicion is all it would take for my uncle to kill or imprison me, Karina, so I'd be very careful. Same thing with you. I mean, he might not want to kill you, since, you know, you're the loveliest and all."

Karina laughed. "Are you jealous?"

"Worried."

So was she. "I'm glad I'm far from him."

His face was serious. "The passage is open. He could drop by at any time."

"What is it you fear?"

"I don't know. It wasn't clear. I thought I'd take the opportunity to be away from his range, so I'd have my freedom with my thoughts, but I forgot an important detail; he's away from my range too."

"So he could be planning anything and you wouldn't know. But don't you guys connive together? Like attacking this place? Whose idea was it?"

"Mine. As a gift to him. I think he believed it. But he might think I'm no longer necessary."

"Find a way to be useful, then."

Sat sighed and looked down. "Yeah."

"I'm not sorry for you. You are deceiving, manipulating, and using me."

"I know…"

Karina stared at him. "So you confirm it?" For once it didn't feel good to be right.

"Maybe. You're the one saying it. I understand how you feel."

Not convincing. But what bothered Karina most was something about his eyes. "You're scared."

Sat shook his head. "The usual. I just don't have to pretend I'm not."

"Right. So here we are, playing a life-and-death game for which I don't know the rules. That's so helpful."

"Not knowing the rules could save your life."

"Not *my* life. That has been lost somewhere in my past."

Sat waved his hands, as if in despair. "It could save your physical and mental well-being. Don't you dare say it doesn't matter."

Karina stared. "Were you worried about my well being when you made me aware that our marriage was a sham? Firis could have caught us."

Sat laughed and looked away. "That would be easy to explain. I'd tell him I was going slowly with you." He pointed to a corner. "There's a dress there. I'll go out and you can change. The ceremony will be soon."

"I guess they don't send attendants in an invasion."

"Not in the beginning, but that won't be a problem for long."

Karina walked towards the dress. It was dark green. "Why do I have to change in this room?"

Sat laughed. "This is our house and bedroom."

"There are no beds."

He pointed to a corner, where some fabric hung. "Hammocks. They are extended at night."

Karina looked. "More than one. Neat."

"Forestglare people don't believe in sleeping together. They're smart."

"Is that why their population is small?"

Sat laughed "Sleep. It's different from... I suppose you know."

"That was a joke."

He cleared his throat. "I did laugh. Right. I'll be outside. Knock on the door when you're ready."

That place had warmth, life, and yet it was so simple. So different from the rich gold and white of Lumina. The dress was some kind of thin velvet. Karina was going to dress up as moss, perhaps to blend in with the environment.

She still hated not knowing so much, as if she were in a chess game without being able to see all pieces. Sat should trust her. Since Firis had revealed his creepo side by flirting with her, she knew who she thought was worse.

Even then, she shouldn't assume Satwak had noble intentions. It could be just a thirst for power, perhaps desire for revenge. And how did he even intend to overthrow his uncle? If that was indeed what he was going for, it was a dangerous game he'd gotten Karina into. In theory they were here to lure the Guardians. What was Sat's plan, then? Get them to help him? But if they had no way to defeat Lumina, it couldn't work, could it?

The dress was simple, one piece with a flowing skirt. One more dress she had no say in, like everything in her recent life. Well, if that body was strange to her, no surprise that the clothes over her body would be strange too. Karina closed her eyes. No, she had to have hope, and this place could give her that. If it was true that Lumina was isolated, and Lumina only, it meant that she could perhaps find a passage from here, a way out. Yes. She'd have to. Meanwhile, she had no other choice than to play whatever games they wanted her to.

She knocked on the door and Sat opened.

He came in and didn't look at her. "It's a crowning ceremony," he said. "Just sit, smile, and pretend you're happy, regardless of what you see."

That meant Karina wasn't going to like whatever was out there. "Who's being crowned?"

He had a face as if she'd asked a dumb question. "Us."

"How was I supposed to know?"

He shook his head. "You weren't. Sorry."

She took a second look at her dress, which seemed inappropriate for such an occasion. "*This* is for crowning?"

"We're in local fashion."

"I thought Lumina was supposed to *enlighten* the other cities. Shouldn't we bring our *civilized* ways?"

Sat snorted then rolled his eyes. "Yes, but we're peaceful, understanding, and don't impose anything."

"That's great."

"There's something else you need to know. They have a well. To communicate with other cities, and with the guardians."

"A well?"

He nodded. "Many people use water for communication. There are even portals made with water. But that's not what I'm getting at. We'll need to talk to them."

"What are we going to say? Hey, Guardians, come and get us?"

"Pretty much. But not with these words. I'll do the talking. But you need to say something."

"Like: yay, I'm so proud to bring light to this dark place?"

"If you sound sincere, it works. Don't try to say anything against Lumina or Firis. He'll be watching us. Mind your thoughts too. You need to be the perfect, obedient, loyal Lumina subject."

"I can do it—on one condition."

He raised an eyebrow. "Condition?"

"Tell me what you're planning."

He laughed. "In Lumina one must never share plans."

"Great. Then I'll just be sarcastic."

"Great. Firis will put you in the stasis room."

"Maybe I can stay silent. He's not going to punish me for that."

"Stay silent, then."

"Sat, I just need to know where you stand," she pleaded. "Do you hope to align with the guardians and depose your uncle?"

He stared at her as if she were crazy. "I never said I wanted to depose anyone."

She exhaled. "I guess we're getting nowhere."

"Nope."

SIAN RAN his hands through the books in the Light Gardens library. This was completely different knowledge than even what he'd found in the Darloom castle. Darloom. That had been so long ago.

Steps echoed in the room.

Leena was beside him. "Enjoying your read?"

"I'm just looking." More looking at the way things were organized. He wanted to mention something else, though. "I've been thinking... Darloom. I never defeated it."

Leena shrugged. "Defeat evil. That's a romantic and idealistic thought. How can you defeat something that can regrow at every time? You control it, and keep your eyes open for any sign of return, that's all."

"Do you think it's coming back?"

"Darloom? No. I think it will look for someplace else."

Sian exhaled. "I see. It's just... Lylah said I would defeat it. Perhaps she was wrong."

"Maybe. Maybe you're misunderstanding what she meant. Why does it bother you?"

Sian looked down. "Not bother. Just curiosity."

"You're wondering if you'll have to play hero again."

"I never played hero."

Leena nodded. "I suppose nobody does. It's other people who call them that."

Sian snorted. "I don't see anyone calling me a hero."

"No."

Her face tightened in worry as she looked at a bracelet whose red stone started to shine.

Sian was curious. "What's that?"

"Emergency meeting."

"Can I come?"

Leena looked uncertain.

Sian added, "I just wanted to learn everything."

She stared at him for a moment, then said, "Come. It's your right."


THERE WERE some three people already sitting and waiting. Sian, as not part of their assembly, got a chair in the back, behind the main circle. He wasn't sure exactly why he wanted to see it. Perhaps it was part of his idea of giving his stay a motivation, a goal; to learn as much as he could about this and other ethereal cities.

Whatever they were going to discuss would remain within the Light Gardens, since there were no transmissions from other cities. They were just waiting for everyone to come in, when Cayla came with Anika. She stared at him as if he were a hair in a soup. Stupid. As someone with no ties to the Light Gardens, she had fewer rights to be there than him. Not that he wanted to think about his ties with that city. Or that he even cared. Her disgusted look shouldn't bother him either, except... Her ties to Darian. A reminder of how unwelcome he was to his family. It didn't matter.

Some few more minutes passed until a couple people came in.

A man Sian didn't know got up. "Forestglare has fallen. It's been taken by Lumina."

Murmurs of surprise echoed through the room. They shouldn't be surprised. If there had been a breach and there had been no news for a while, it could only mean they were planning something.

Here was the result of their enemy's planning. Quite obvious, frankly.

"What do they want with Forestglare?" a woman asked.

The man shook his head. "Nothing. They want the Guardians to strike. It's possibly some kind of trap. But I'll let you all watch it and see for yourselves."

The image was going to be formed on the well. Sian was far and figured he wouldn't be able to see much. A sphere came up from the well, though, as if it was some steam. Soon he was looking at the image of a couple; a young man and a young woman with crowns that looked like tree roots. The first thing he noticed was how beautiful they were.

No, how beautiful *she* was. The perfect queen of Sian's dreams.

Literally.

The one who's been in his dreams. It couldn't, couldn't. It had to be a trick, something. She'd told him she didn't want to be queen, she'd told him all she wanted was him. How could this be possible?

The young man's words didn't reach his ears. All he could hear was the loudest buzz he'd ever heard. Was this some kind of torture? Sian looked around. Why was everyone sitting normally, looking at the images? How come nobody was contorting with pain? Nobody was horrified, deafened with that sound? He raised his hands to his ears. Pain. Just pain. Nothing. He could block it. He should bock it. But the buzz was stronger than anything and took hold of his body, or came out of his body.

All this energy; pain, anger, he didn't know what else, suddenly took form and was about to explode. He fell on the floor. Everything was blue around him. So much blue, then it all faded to black.

~

Cayla should be feeling anxious, but she was excited and giddy instead. For the first time she'd attend a Guardian meeting, see them in action, learn what they were about. Perhaps she should feel guilty because whatever they were going to see wasn't good news. Well, but it wasn't bad either. Not knowing was worse than knowing where they had struck. With information, one could plan action. Perhaps something would finally happen and end their waiting.

As Cayla followed Anika to the meeting room, she noticed that many seats were empty and that there were no transmissions from other cities. Sian was already there, looking bored. Well, why go, then? And what was Leena thinking? You'd have to be insane to allow Sian near any type of confidential information. Darian's brother or not, he'd proved to be untrustworthy before. Again, it was not that she wanted him tortured or anything, perhaps not even imprisoned, it was just that it was so out of place... Well, she wasn't making the decisions. And it wasn't her private information to worry about. She should rather worry about the silence from her mother's end and about Alessa. It just gave her a nauseous feeling. Maybe she should focus on learning what was happening. Maybe she could even be useful.

A man spoke. So Lumina was setting up a trap? It sounded naive. But then, if they'd been isolated for hundreds and hundreds of years, perhaps they'd lost the ability to make complex plans.

The image transmission was something she'd never seen before. She'd imagined that the well would be like a portal, like the one in the Darloom castle. Well, maybe it was like it, but it was being used differently. A mist came out of the water, and on the mist, the image that had been sent to the Light Gardens.

The couple on the image didn't look anything like what she'd imagined people from Lumina would look like. They were quite young and seemed nice. Wait. The girl, it couldn't be. Karina? What was she doing there? Cayla glanced back at Sian. His eyes were fixated on the image, but his expression hadn't changed.

The young man in the image said, "We're happy to bring back a Lumina tradition to Forestglare, incorporating it to our kingdom, as had been the case for generations. The people in this city are happy and we'll proceed with local coronation traditions, since, even though we're devoted to Lumina, we're also Forestglare's king and queen."

King and queen? That sounded strange. Cayla glanced again at Sian, wondering if he'd react. Still the same. No, something was odd, it was as if he'd been stuck in the same position.

The young man continued, "As much as we're glad to bring back enlightenment to Forestglare, we also want freedom for Lumina. We beseech again the Guardians to open our portals and let us go from place to place. We can negotiate the terms, and even give up on Forestglare or any other city."

So that was what they were trying to do; free Forestglare in exchange for having their portals open. Cayla wasn't that well versed in Lumina and Guardian politics, but she could already see that it was an insane request. With Lumina free, they could conquer all cities. Why this transmission then? Was this a first warning that they were going to conquer more cities? And what was Karina doing there? Since when she'd been in Lumina? Since when she could be queen there? Something was off.

Karina said, "We thank you for considering our request..."

A sound startled Cayla, and she didn't catch the rest of her friend's words. Sian was on the floor, shaking. Leena turned quickly and created a shield around him. Cayla looked around, wondering if they were being attacked. The shield dissolved. Sian was fallen on the floor. Hopefully not dead.

Leena said, "It's fine, fine. He's been sick for a while and fainted. It's nothing."

The people in the room got back to their seats and murmurs stopped.

Cayla exhaled in relief. She couldn't even start to imagine what Darian would feel if his brother died like that.

She approached Leena. "Will he be all right?"

"Yes, yes," the woman said as she gestured for someone to help carry him.

"What was that shield for?"

The woman's eyes were pleading. "You must have imagined that. You must. Nobody else saw anything."

Cayla nodded. "I guess." So apparently the shield was a secret. She'd ask Leena when she caught the woman alone.

The woman turned to everyone. "Please continue without me."

She seemed to be in a hurry to leave. There was something odd happening.

Cayla was torn between running to tell Darian what was happening and watching the rest of the meeting. She had a queasy, uncomfortable feeling about Karina. It was so completely unlike her... With that came a fear: seeing another friend hurt. As much as in theory, Karina in Forestglare, representing Lumina had nothing to do with Cayla... Didn't it? Cayla was the one who'd brought Karina from her dimension.

She tried to pay attention to what they were saying.

The man went on and on about waiting. He continued, "... until we know what we're dealing with. If we strike now, we'll be doing exactly what they want."

"What about Karina?" Cayla blurted.

They all stared at her. She knew she wasn't supposed to say anything.

The man said, "You can talk to one of our representatives later. Would you mind leaving?"

Cayla leaned back on the chair. "Yeah, I do mind. I'm not leaving."

The man shrugged. "Stay, then."

DARIAN WAS GETTING CLOSE. It was odd to look for something without knowing what it was. He sat quietly by the lake, feeling the breeze on his face, the sound of rustling leaves, the movement on the water, his breath interacting with the environment around him. Beneath all that was his magic, the magic that was still unknown to him. He didn't try to latch onto preconceived notions. Yes, he'd heard he was a spell speaker, but that wasn't *his* truth.

Whatever he was, he needed to find it by himself, not be told. Sitting in silence, he felt as if something was about to emerge. Even his friend Rae had left him. Strange to realize how he appreciated solitude. And there, almost there, like an old name he was about to remember, it was coming to him.

"Darian!"

He loved that voice but was startled at the shrillness in it. Cayla ran towards him, breathless, looking distraught.

Darian got up. "What's wrong?"

She looked around him. "*That's* what you've been doing? Sitting here?"

Cayla didn't usually annoy him, but she was getting close.

"Not just sitting," he explained.

She was breathless. "We need to do something. Your brother. He collapsed. Karina. I think they're doing something to her."

"What? Karina's here?"

Cayla rolled her eyes as if he should have understood her disconnected fragments. "No. She's in Forestglare. With Lumina. They sent a message. Your brother saw it, and he collapsed. He's in the hospital now. I guess you'd like to see him, right?"

"Yes. Soon. Is he still unconscious?"

"I don't know. I ran straight here. But that's not only it. Darian, the council wants to wait, gather information, then do a sneak attack or something. Karina is there. She's not with them, I'm sure. We need to do something."

"I'll go see Sian in a few hours. Then we can talk about Karina."

Her eyes widened. "A few hours? What kind of brother are you?"

"You say it as if you cared about Sian."

"I don't, but you should."

"Well, I do, and a couple hours won't make any difference. I'm doing something important now. I guess... you don't understand, but I feel it's urgent that I connect with my magic."

She stared at him in silence for a few seconds, then said, "Your magic. Great. Once you *find your magic*, do you think you'll help me get my friend back?"

"Didn't you say the council was onto it? I'm pretty sure the guardians have a better plan than we do, not to mention more experience. I know you're anxious, but sometimes you need to wait and trust."

Cayla squinted. "So you're not going to help me?"

"I didn't say that."

She looked down then nodded. "I see. And I guess your priority now is to remain sitting there."

He took her hand. "Cayla, that's how I can help. I can't do much when I have no idea who I am. Meanwhile, trust the council. Patience. Hurry never accomplishes anything."

"Find yourself then." She turned to leave, but she was angry.

Darian held her hand. "Wait. You do know I'm going to help you, right?"

"While trusting the council and spending your day here."

Darian didn't see what the problem was. "Well, yes."

"Great. I'll talk to you later."

"You're angry."

"Wow, you're so perceptive." She then changed her tone and looked down. "I wish you were more helpful, that's all."

Darian stared at her. "If I come back running with you now, I won't accomplish anything. Let me clear my mind, find my answers, then we'll talk. I promise."

He held her hands and she didn't pull them away. Cayla sighed. "Fine, then. I guess."

She kissed him on the cheek then turned around and ran.

Darian would take some two or three hours to get back where he was. No matter. Cayla was always a priority. It saddened him to see her upset, but she would understand. He sat and closed his eyes.

~

DROWNING. Drowning, drowning, drowning, not in water, but in a black, viscous liquid. Was that how Sian was going to die? He felt a jolt on his wrist, then sat up, panting. That hospital room again. Leena was there, staring at him with worry.

The memories came back all scrambled and out of order. Blue energy around him. Karina, the beautiful queen he'd always imagined, but sitting by someone else. An image formed with mist. Strange memories and fragments, and something exploding.

Perhaps the woman staring at him could be of some help. "What happened?"

"Do you remember anything?"

Really? She'd make him dig the memories? He took a deep breath. "A message from Lumina. In another city. Then... I don't know."

"Do you know what happens to magic that's repressed for too long?"

It was lovely and all that she wanted to start with her teaching and rhetorical questions, but couldn't she see the state he was on? Still, he replied, "No."

"What about feelings repressed for too long?"

As self-controlled as he was, this time he'd have to forgo politeness. "What are you getting at?"

"Explode. These things explode, Sian."

"And?"

"Your magic went out of control."

"My magic?"

She looked at him for a moment. "I thought you knew. Are you going to tell me you do not know what your magic is?"

He ran his hands through his hair. "I've been told... different things." Karina telling him that he was a spell speaker came to mind. "But to be honest, I never felt I had any magic."

"That complicates things."

"Not if you tell me instead of going in circles." He then added quickly, "I don't mean to be rude."

She shook her head and patted him on the head. "Don't worry. Now, tell me, have you ever felt something like electricity in your body? Or the ability to control electricity around you?"

Sian didn't like those memories. He looked away. "It happened once. In Marisia. But that was related to Darloom, wasn't it?'

Leena shrugged. "Maybe you were being influenced by him, but the electricity is your own."

"How come I never felt it before?"

She tilted her head. "These things can take time to manifest. Or maybe they'd been repressed. Now, I don't want to alarm you. Well, maybe I do because it's serious. I saw what happened and conjured a shield around you. If I hadn't been there, your energy would have killed every person in that room."

Sian heard the words but had trouble making sense out of it. Kill? Could it really be? He snapped his fingers. "Like that? The energy would have fried everyone? But how?"

"Like an explosion."

"So I'm a walking bomb."

"Sitting-in-bed bomb."

He smiled. The joke was terrible, but he appreciated her attempt at levity. "And what does it mean? Will I have to live in isolation?"

"No, but you need to learn to control it."

That made sense. "I guess you'll assign me some super electrifier who knows what they're doing?"

She had an odd look. "Nobody else has that specific type of magic, Sian. But we can help you find your balance."

He sighed, dreading what was coming next. "Meanwhile, I guess I should be put in complete isolation lest I explode again, right?"

"Oh, you'll be of no danger for the next few days, depleted as you must be. But yes, you should learn to control it, for the future."

Sian nodded, thinking that they'd use this to delay his return home. His mind kept coming back to Karina's image despite his efforts to forget it. He had to find some distraction, purpose. Being in bed did little to help him.

Leena continued. "I'm not sure you're aware, but nobody should know about your magic."

Sian frowned. "Why?"

"It's very—unique."

"Lots of people have unique magical powers."

"Yes, and some of those powers have special meanings and need to be kept secret."

Sian stared at her. "I'm assuming you're not going to tell me why."

"I can't. I can't, Sian."

"Great."

Leena left the room and Sian's questions. After a couple minutes she was back, with something in her hand. She approached his bed and showed a glass sphere.

"I was waiting for the right moment, but waiting might only make things worse."

That was Light Gardens magic, magic he hadn't read about in the Darloom castle. "What is it?"

"Take it. It has a message."

Sian took the ball and examined it, looking for markings of some sort. Instead, an image formed in it.

A beautiful dark-haired woman spoke, "My beloved son. I hope to give you these words in person..."

Too much for one single day. He wasn't about to listen to why his mother had abandoned him. He threw it against the wall. Sian heard a crash and didn't bother looking to see what happened.

12

SECRETS

ayla waited in the garden outside the hospital. So much waiting. She almost understood why Darian hadn't come with her. Maybe he knew he wasn't going to see Sian and didn't want to waste his precious time. Super precious, because sitting was soooo important. Nevermind. Maybe he was still digesting all the time that had been wiped away from his mind. Sometimes she still had to come to terms with the idea that his upbringing had been very different from hers and that he was from the Light Gardens.

Leena came out when the sun was already setting, holding something in her hands. Cayla ran to her. "How's Sian? What happened?"

The woman was startled. "Fine, fine. He was malnourished for so long, he's weaker than we thought, but he's being treated."

The woman was lying, not about the fact that Sian would be fine, but about what had happened to him, but Cayla let it slide. "You were missed in the council. They want to wait, but Karina is there, and I'm afraid..."

Leena seemed puzzled. "Karina? The girl that came with you last time?"

"Yes, she's in Forestglare."

"I saw the message. She's not there."

"She is! I can show you. And the council wants to wait and do nothing. She's my friend and I think she's in danger."

Leena stared at her in pity, which was quite infuriating. "I'm still watching Sian, but I'll come with you to look at the message. Is that all right?"

"I guess." Cayla noticed that the woman held three pieces of a sphere. "What is it?"

"Nothing anymore."

OTHER THAN A BRIEF visit by his brother, who didn't seem at all concerned, Sian was left alone. In a way perhaps it was good that nobody had paid attention to his breakdown. On the other hand, it felt... How did it even feel?

He left the hospital in the early evening, with a warning that Leena would come see him the next day. That had been all. As if almost killing a bunch of people or perhaps getting close to dying didn't matter. Maybe it didn't. And again, Darian didn't seem to know anything about it and Sian was happy not to discuss it, glad to be alone with his thoughts.

Karina's image in the transmission wouldn't leave his mind. Part of him still doubted what he'd seen, but it was likely his heart tricking him into stupid hope. So it wasn't that she had anything against being queen, her issue was with being queen beside Sian.

But anger and resentment were stupid. Who knew what had happened to her? She'd left Sian with the conviction that their parting was forever. He'd screwed up and he knew it. Time had passed. She'd moved on. And still... All this time, she'd been in his dreams. Perhaps it had been Sian's own foolishness to hold onto hope. Love was stupid. Had he really fallen so low?

And yet... Had he been in Siphoria, with his friends, with his power, he'd just shrug it off and move on. Here, alone, after half a year in starvation and suffering, he lacked even the ability to lock away this stupid pain. And it was stupid.

He knew he should never trust any girl, no matter how sweet she was, no matter her declaration of love. Maybe it had been true then. It wasn't now. But what about her morals? Had they been fake? Lumina had killed some people to invade Forestglare, and apparently she had no problem with that. When Sian had wanted to take Whyland, he wasn't going to kill a single person, and yet she ran away from him as if he were a criminal. Hypocrite.

He had to forget these things, he had to let these thoughts fade away. What did it matter? He'd soon return to Whyland, Siphoria, his life. Tons of pretty girls there. Why settle for one? Perhaps what hurt more was the realization that he'd been so dumb. Poor dignity. At least nobody had noticed.

He lay awake on his bed for a long time, perhaps afraid of what his dreams would bring him. Afraid of seeing her again, afraid of the lies his sleepy mind would make him believe.


"HEY," a girl's whisper woke him up.

He opened his eyes and sat up. So sleep had caught him. The room was dark and he couldn't see who it was other than the outline of her hair. True, he'd been thinking about finding other girls before falling asleep. That was fast. Too fast. Maybe it was a vision. He reached out to touch her hair but ended up yanking it instead.

The girl slapped his hand. "Ouch. Stop it."

The slap made him awake, which he hadn't been a few seconds before. "Sorry. Just making sure you are real."

"I'm real and it's the middle of the night."

Sian's heart beat faster. He wasn't sure who she was, what she wanted, and if she wanted what he was thinking she wanted, which, by coincidence was exactly what he'd thought he'd wanted before falling asleep. Oh, weird difference between theory and reality, between things you think you want and the true desires, those that get buried deep. Bury deep. That's what he had to do now. He smiled, wondering if she'd see it in that darkness. "To what do I owe the pleasure of such a lovely visit?"

"I know it might sound weird, me being here, but you're the only one who can help me."

Perhaps she didn't want what he thought, and he wasn't sure if he was relieved or disappointed. Also, why wake him up in the middle of the night? "What kind of help requires whispers in the dark in my bedroom?"

"There's only one reason I'd come talk to you."

Crap. One sure-fire way of getting rid of a girl was to make an inappropriate proposal. It didn't always work, though, because there were always those who said yes. But what could he say to scare a girl already in his bedroom? Plus, she could know Leena, and he didn't want wild rumors spread about him. No, maybe wild rumors would be good. He needed to be left alone. "On my terms, then. You need to do everything I ask you."

She snorted. "Are you insane? You don't know anything about it."

Prick. He got up and came to the lamp by the window. As the light flickered, he saw who the girl was, and was taken by revulsion just at the mere thought of what he believed she wanted. Sian was frozen in shock.

She got up quickly and turned off the light. "Nobody can catch us."

Uh, catch? This was more like a nightmare. It was hard, but he found his voice again. "I think you entered the wrong room. You do realize I'm not Darian, right?"

"Well, duh. But other than the fact that he's more interested in spending his days sitting by himself and he trusts the council like a fool, he can't do what you can do."

Still weird. For a nice moment he'd been convinced with the theory of the wrong bedroom and perhaps drunk Cayla. Now... But it was something else.

"Which is?" he asked.

"You saw her in the message, didn't you? Karina."

His entire body tensed and he felt like punching somebody. Was she here to tease him? Before his body language gave him away, he leaned back on the wall. "Yeah, so?"

"So? *So?* That's what you have to say? Did you believe for a single moment that she was there by her own will? That nothing wrong is happening to her? I thought you, uh, I don't know, liked her at least a little. Weren't you willing to *die* for her a few months ago?"

Sian took a deep breath. "That time it was my fault. I had to fix my mistake. This... I mean, she's free. We weren't married or anything. And we parted ways. I'm good with her decisions."

"And you think it's her decision to invade a helpless city? Do you have anything in that mind of yours? I thought you knew her, I thought you two spent time together. I thought you... I mean, you collapsed in the meeting room."

He felt as if the girl was poking a wound. "Just tell me what you want."

"We're going to rescue her."

"She didn't look like she needed rescuing."

"Sian, of course she does! Either they are mind controlling her, or maybe it was a love potion or something. It's not her, I know it. I thought you'd know it too."

The thought had occurred to Sian, but he'd done his best to ignore it, perhaps because it would mean clinging to hope, risking getting even more hurt than he already was. Still, Cayla could be wrong. And there were other issues with the plan. "Fine, let's assume she is controlled, whatever. How do you propose to get there, how do you think you can counter her love potion, and why do you need me?"

"I can teleport better than most people here. I think I know how to get to Forestglare."

"You... *think?*"

"Uh, I'm almost pretty sure. As to countering whatever they did to her, that's why I need you."

"Me?"

"Well, yes. You know what can break most spells, don't you?"

All he knew was that all this talk about Karina gave him a horrible feeling in his stomach. "Tell me."

"Sian, you can kiss her. I, uh, I think you like her, at least a little. I..." She looked down. "Saw your reaction in the meeting. And she... poor Karina, has terrible taste, unfortunately. Despite all you did, she still... liked you."

Opposite feelings were competing in his mind. On one hand, he was ready to follow Cayla to hell, if that was what would give him at least a tiny chance to get Karina. On the other hand, so many reasons to believe she no longer wanted him. "That was months ago. A lot could have changed."

"Well," she sighed. "I mean, true. She must have come to reason, right? You manipulated her and almost got her killed. It's only obvious. That still doesn't explain why she'd side with Lumina. It doesn't, Sian. And even if she no longer likes you, which I hope, you... I saw your reaction."

Sian was wondering if she always offended people when asking them favors. Nonsense. Why wonder? This was Cayla, of course she offended people. And she had no qualms wanting Sian to risk his dignity. Again, not surprising. "So you want me to go into enemy territory, then force a kiss on its queen, illegitimate or not?"

"Well, yes, to break whatever they're doing to her. They're doing something, Sian, and you know it as well as I do. If she's there, it's our fault. My fault for first bringing her to Whyland. Your fault for bringing her again. Now be a man, assume your mistakes, and make up for them."

Sian got up. "What are you talking about? I assume my mistakes. I went to Marisia to save her. I got separated from her to save Whyland. It cost me months living in a horrible place. I almost died. Don't you come and tell me to make up for my mistakes."

"Well, then, let's go. Let's get Karina back to normal. The worst she'll do is slap you."

"Karina's sweet. She doesn't *slap* people." Sian could imagine her looking at him with tears in her eyes, an apologetic look, but not anger.

"That's too bad," Cayla said, bringing him back to reality.

Whatever his brother saw in that girl was one of the greatest mysteries of the universe. Speaking of his brother... "Did you tell Darian?"

"Are you kidding me? Like I told you. I tried. He's all, 'let's trust the council'. And worse, he claims he didn't see Karina there. Leena says the same. It's not her. I mean, are they that amnesic? How can they forget her face? Her voice?"

How indeed? Her face had taken over Sian's thoughts and dreams ever since he'd first met her. And he hated that, especially when she was far away, beside another man. He tried to focus on the issue at hand. "Maybe there's something in that message." He tried to recall what he'd heard about projections and messages. "There's a way to disguise a person in a message so that they'll only be recognized by those who..." He stopped, suddenly aware of what he was about to confess.

"Love them?" Cayla asked, with no qualms as to how it made him feel.

His voice was tight. "Or know them well. Or something like it."

She had a smile. "See? Your kiss will work."

Yeah, yeah. It felt great to have his one-sided love thrown on his face by someone who would probably mock him and humiliate until the end of his days. "It doesn't mean much. You also saw her, didn't you? Are you going to tell me your love is romantic?"

"No, but I like her as a friend."

"Great, because I was going to tell you I'm not sure you're her type."

"Of course I'm not. I'm not a manipulative jerk."

Just a heartless prick. Of course that wasn't Karina's type. He decided to change the subject. "And when do you want to do it?"

"Tonight. They're going through Forestglare's coronation festivities. There should be a ball in a couple hours."

"You can't be sure. There could be a time difference."

She shook her head. "A time difference, yes. Time passing differently, no. And I'm basing my prediction on the time they sent the message."

Sian got up. "All right. I'll get dressed." His brother came to his mind, and he stopped. "I still think you should tell Darian."

"No. He'll try to stop us."

Sian felt uneasy. "Won't he be jealous?"

"Oh, yuck." She put her hands on her mouth. "Sorry. Sorry. I didn't mean that. It's just, you're Darian's brother."

Sian laughed. "The feeling is mutual, sis." Not only because she was almost his sister-in-law, but nevermind explaining the rest. "But I didn't mean like that, I meant... I don't know, you trusting me, not him."

"It's not like he wasn't the first person I ran to. He decided sitting was more important than me, Karina, even you. Anyways, he'll understand—once we bring Karina back."

Sian sighed, realizing his effort to bury his worry and pain was unsuccessful. "We might not bring her."

Cayla shrugged. "We'll explain what happened."

Sian nodded. "Just a moment, then."

He got dark pants and a light tunic, more than ever upset that he didn't have access to his own clothes. He went to the bathroom and changed, then cut off his braided beard. Reminder or not, he wasn't sure if she'd like it, and he didn't want to take any risks. Risk of her not remembering him, of course. He still had dark circles under his eyes, and his cheeks were unnaturally hollow. The tips of his hair were still dull. Sian hadn't been super privileged by nature, but he did the best with what he had, except that right now he was far from his best.

Karina had walked away from him when he had a castle, power, and was looking great. Now he was nobody, thinner than before, lacking all sense of style. He closed his eyes. True that she'd told him she loved him. And yet, how firm was her love? What had happened in these last few months?

A knock on the door startled him. Cayla's voice came from the room, "Sian, we can't take forever. If she's over you, she's over you, if she still loves you, you could come in rags."

He opened the door. "You assume too much."

"I'm just saying. Plus, if she fell in love with you, it's obvious she doesn't care about looks."

For a split second he wanted to ask her how she knew, what she knew, what Karina had told her, but that would be pathetic. Plus, Cayla was obviously trying to offend him. Give and take. "Yeah. Just like my brother."

Cayla chuckled. "I know, right? Plus he's either a compulsive liar or has serious vision problems."

Sian was stunned. Her reply had been natural, as if she hadn't noticed his jab. Maybe she hadn't. He thought about Darian. "Perhaps he says it because he knows it's not obvious." Cayla had a weird look. He had to explain. "See, other than one weird time when she asked me if my queen was pretty, I never told Karina she's beautiful. It would be like telling her she has two eyes or her hair is brown. Dull conversation."

"Very dull." Her voice was tight.

Now it was Sian who'd taken a jab at her without noticing, too busy involved in his own memories. Oh, well. Cayla deserved way worse than that. If it weren't for the fact that she cared for Karina and had helped save his life, he wouldn't even be talking to her. Hang on. If she hadn't saved his life he'd be dead, so this conversation obviously wouldn't be happening. Months of semi-starvation had indeed affected his brain. He'd better recover soon, as he'd need his wits.

But Cayla then smiled. "Yeah, your kiss will definitely work."

Sian was about to tense, but he caught himself in time, relaxed, and shrugged. "Because I didn't like to tell Karina what she looks like?" He smirked. "Interesting line of thought."

"Indeed. We were explaining how she's fallen in love with you despite your looks, which led you to your brother, who I assume you believe is in love with me, and then you voluntarily mentioned yourself. Crazy jump, right?"

Yeah, Cayla was going to rub his feelings for Karina on his face until his death. He'd better ignore her. "And it's not interesting?"

"No. Just logical."

Sian nodded. "From where are we teleporting?"

"The small tower. The one we came from."

"There might be some security there."

"Not as much as in the main tower."

They were about to do something quite dangerous, and he wasn't sure if the girl in front of him realized the extent of how dangerous it could be. "I need to get weapons."

"No kidding. Question is: where?"

Weird. "What do you mean *where*? The weapons room."

"Oh. I... You mean the guardians have a weapons room? How are we going to break into that?"

Sian walked to the chest by the wall, picked up a key, and smiled. "With this. I wouldn't call it breaking into, though."

"How come you have a key? How come you know about it?"

Sian shrugged. "I guess Leena trusts me."

Cayla snorted. "People are stupid."

"At least I got the key."

They walked outside, towards the main tower. Sian took the lead, walking among the trees bordering that part of the city.

After a while, Cayla asked, "Are you planning something, Sian?"

"Right now? Planning on doing illegal teleporting to an enemy-occupied place, to kiss someone just to make sure being queen beside a handsome king is something she chose for herself."

Cayla snorted. "You think she'd choose to be with the Luminous? Did you ever talk to her?"

"Hey, I'm just prepared for the worst." Hanging on to hope would only bring pain. "And you? Since when you're best buddies and know her so well?"

"She was ready to do the right thing when she came to Whyland."

Sian waved a hand. "Right, wrong, it's all relative. Maybe they convinced her this is the right thing."

"Exactly. Brainwashing. Which you can put an end to."

"And that's why you need me."

"For sure. And before you point out the irony of it, please remember that even enemies sometimes form strategic alliances."

"Oh, I'm your enemy now."

"Maybe not now, but a few months ago you did take armed action against my kingdom. Unlike your brother and the people in the Light Gardens, I'm not amnesiac."

"I'm not either, Cayla. I know who you are."

"Sure do."

Sian suddenly stopped. "What's your motivation?"

"She's my friend."

He stared at her. "Doesn't cut it."

"Why? Do you know what it's like to care about people? I..." She took a deep breath and closed her eyes. "I don't want to see any friend of mine getting hurt because of me."

"She looked anything but hurt."

"Yeah, and you think she forgot you, which she should, and now you're butthurt."

Sometimes he wished he could strangle her. "Goodness, Cayla, you're so hilarious. Nothing funnier than a guy who risks his life and spends months in hell for a girl then sees her beside another man."

"I'm sorry. It's just... it's true. You're feeling jealous, maybe wronged, and because of that you're convinced that Karina doesn't need to be rescued. It's a problem if you don't believe in it, because you might not try as hard as necessary."

He turned and pointed a finger to the annoying girl. "Hey, it's my neck and my pride on the line, but I'm not a coward. If there's even the tiniest bit of chance that I can save her from her horrible fate of having a comfortable life as a queen from Lumina, I'll do whatever it takes. That doesn't mean I have to go there under a stupid illusion."

"Suit yourself."

Leena had told him he wouldn't be a danger to anyone for a few days. He hoped she was right, because he felt very close to exploding again, and he didn't want to kill his brother's girlfriend, regardless of how she treated him.

No, Leena was definitely right, otherwise Cayla would have been fried a few times already in the last few minutes. Sian also feared what would happen if he had to kiss Karina and be rejected. Nevermind the difficulty of getting her to kiss him. Would he have to force a kiss? He didn't like the thought.

They approached the building where the weapons room was. There was nobody around it, and he gestured for Cayla to follow him. As he was about to enter, he heard a voice.

"Halt!" A young man Sian didn't know came in their direction. "Where are you going at this time?"

Sian showed his key, then pointed to the door. "What does it look like I'm doing?"

"It's... Do you have authorization to come at this time?"

Sian shrugged. "Leena told me I could come at any time. I mean, any time. How do you interpret any time other than *any* time?"

The young man narrowed his eyes. "Why do you need weapons now?"

"Sleepless. Wanted to train."

The young man nodded. "Right. And you are?"

"Sian."

"Oh. Right." He changed his tone. "Good seeing you. Let me know if you need help."

Sian shook his head. "I'm fine, thanks."

He walked in with Cayla. She said, "That was weird."

"Not really. Same thing as Darian. I guess our family... something important, whatever." He didn't want to be reminded of his mother.

"I know your mother's from here, but other than that... Do you know why you're important?"

"Me? I didn't even know this place until some time ago. Apparently they didn't know about me either. That just goes to show how super important I was."

He found a sword and strapped on his back.

Cayla made a face. "You aren't going to a ball with that thing."

Sian sighed, putting the sword back, and took some knives and a belt. The loose tunic covered it. Cayla was checking the knives.

Sian handed her a short one. "I think you can also get some. If you know how to use them."

"I can demonstrate on you. Wanna try?"

"Careful who you threaten."

Cayla made her lemon sucking face. "I was joking, Sian."

"I wasn't."

He passed by the wall with pistols, but ignored them, since they didn't work in the ethereal cities. Perhaps it was worth a try. No, where would he put them? He turned to Cayla. "Got everything?"

"Yeah, I mean, I'm hoping we won't need to use any of this."

"That's why you bring them. Cause then you'll curse saying, 'why did I have to carry this stuff?'. If you don't bring them, you'll be cursing otherwise."

"Right. Let's bring weapons as a not-need-weapons amulet."

"That's what I'm hoping."

Cayla shrugged. "Well, Luminous have very strong magic. If trouble finds us, a few knives, or even swords, won't help us."

Comforting thought. They left the room. The young man nodded, and they again walked towards the woods bordering that part of the city, going in the direction of the small tower.

"So," Sian finally decided to ask, "Do you have a plan, or is it improvise as you go?"

"No plan is perfect... But like I said, they should have a ball in a few hours."

"Why? I missed the end of the transmission, but did they send their schedule or something?"

Cayla chuckled. "Pretty much. That young king said they would proceed with the traditional Forestglare festivities."

"And you know what these festivities are."

She nodded. "Exactly. There should have been a banquet yesterday, and there will be a ball today."

"And you assume there won't be any security at this ball and we'll be able to sneak in."

"Pretty much."

That made no sense. "Did you hear what I just said?"

"Yes. There won't be any security."

"Care to elucidate why?"

"Well, Sian, it's obvious."

"In your mind, maybe."

"Think. Why do they send a transmission basically saying 'we're here, and these are our plans for the next five days'?"

Sian took it in. "It's a trap."

"Obviously."

"That just means we go in, but not out. Is that your plan?"

She stopped. "No, no, no. See, they're waiting for Guardians, which we aren't. Not really, at least not the ones who do security, who would be going there to either gather information or try to do something."

Sian saw a bunch of holes in her reasoning, but decided to listen in silence.

She continued, "How do they know? You may want to ask. Well, easy, people who often travel through dimensions will have some kind of residual energy."

Sian chuckled. "You think they'll have a sensor or something?"

"Maybe. Their magic is very advanced."

"So advanced that they won't see us."

"They might see us. I don't know. The thing is, they are expecting something big to happen, like an attack. Other than getting Karina, we won't do anything else."

"She's the freaking queen. She'll be the most well-protected person there."

"It's a ball"

Sian sighed. There was no real plan. How predictable.

Cayla looked at him. "Do you have a better idea?"

"Not yet."

He agreed with her that the fewer people, the easier it would be to sneak in. Other than that, if they were caught… "Does anyone know where we're going?"

"I left a note for Darian."

That made sense. "I guess he's your backup plan, then."

"No backup. We'll succeed."

They came to the small teleporting tower. Nobody was guarding it, which was somewhat surprising. But there was another problem. "You do realize that there are people in the main tower right now, monitoring all portals, right?"

Cayla smiled. "All *known* portals. Forestglarians have houses in hollow trees."

"So we'll bust into someone's house?"

She shook her head. "I got a map of the city. They also have a place called silent sanctuary. There shouldn't be anyone there."

"And you can create a portal where there isn't one."

"Like Karina, yeah. She's a bit stronger, though. That's why the Guardians won't find us either. They'll be looking at a portal-to-portal communication. They won't be monitoring this tower either."

It was lucky that Cayla could open portals. And despite her attitude, her initiative to save Karina was wonderful. Sian turned to her. "I'm glad you're her friend and you're doing this."

"I'm glad you're coming to help me."

Cayla extended her hand. Sian took it and closed his eyes, wondering what he'd find on the other side. The chance of getting Karina back sent thrills through him, while at the same time, he could be risking his life just to have his worst fears confirmed. Fears. He wasn't going to be paralyzed by them.

13

## A FORESTGLARE BALL

Karina couldn't ignore the fear in the faces of the Forestglare residents. From overhearing conversations, she gathered that the most rebellious citizens had been locked up, and the remaining ones either were too weak or scared to be a threat or had loved ones incarcerated. That fear couldn't come from nothing. Karina realized that some people were killed and felt revulsion in her stomach for being part of this. City of Light. Yeah, right. More like City of Death. Perhaps the Guardians had a point in keeping them isolated.

The dress she was going to wear was black, for once, which was a relief. If she returned home, she'd steer clear of any white for years. She sighed. If she returned. It was ridiculous to get dressed for festivities, as if the Forestglare citizens were thrilled to have a queen and king from Lumina. But if those were the rules, those were the rules. Karina would play the game. She put on the dress. Well, *you play the part, you dress the part.*

Karina felt a sudden chill. The sentence rang in her mind, trying to connect with a faint memory. The tip of something was in her mind's hand. If only she could pull it... But there was this barrier blocking her. She knew there was something there, there was something she had to find. The question was what. And how to get there.

~

CAYLA OPENED HER EYES. They were inside a huge hollow tree. That meant the first part of her plan had worked. Hopefully they were in the right ethereal city, there would indeed be a ball, and they would be able to rescue Karina. She let go of Sian's hand. Weird to ask for his help, after all he'd done. But he seemed to truly like her friend, plus he was Darian's brother.

He looked around. "Seems like you did it, sis."

Yes, she'd done it. Realizing they'd actually teleported and now would have to sneak in a Lumina ball gave her chills. She smiled, "Of course I did it. We still have a couple hours, from my calculations. The first thing we need to do is find out where they are having the ball."

"Not *we*."

Cayla just stared at him. "Care to explain?"

"Don't you get it? You can go back. Go back now and be safe."

"Right. And how do you intend to bring Karina back?" Cayla had the horrible feeling that he still didn't believe her friend would return with them.

"You did the hardest part; opened the portal. Karina's a teleporter too."

"We don't know. They could have done something with her magic, for example. We don't know, it Sian. Plus, if something happens, what are you going to do? Start living in Forestglare?"

"You say it as if you'd miss me. Plus, this is a huge improvement from the last place I got stuck trying to save Karina."

"You had it coming." Yep, she said it. She almost felt sorry when she saw him almost dying, but it didn't change the fact that he was simply facing the consequences of his actions. And just because they were working together didn't mean she was going to be a hypocrite.

Sian nodded. "Absolutely. Have you considered that maybe I have more stuff coming? It's my life. Not your life. If something happens to you, how am I going to look my brother in the eye?"

How dramatic. Cayla rolled her eyes. "The same way you spent your entire life: not looking."

"I had no choice in that, sis. Here we have a choice. You also studied military strategy, didn't you?"

"Of course."

Sian had a half-smirk. "Which is hilarious because your mother made Darian grand general, with his grand total of zero classes on the topic."

"Your point?"

Sian got serious again. "I was getting there. Strategically, it makes sense for you to return. You can bring reinforcements if something goes wrong."

"They can't fight Luminous."

"Not fight. Sneak in, I don't know."

"And how am I going to know that something went wrong? Plus, we need a quick retreat. Just for a second imagine you get Karina back and she has difficulty teleporting for some reason. The delay could cost your escape."

Sian paused as if trying to come up with a retort, but he couldn't. He thought for a moment, then turned to her. "Stay here, then. Wait for us."

"She's *my* friend."

"We need to be ready for a quick retreat. That's your part, getting us out. Plus, if we're going to sneak in, the fewer people, the less attention we'll attract."

Something clicked in her. His reasoning suddenly made total sense. She didn't even understand how she'd disagreed with his idea before. She said, "Fine."

"If I don't get back by sunrise, you should return without me."

No freaking way she'd do that. Still, she didn't owe him explanations—or truths. She nodded. "Sure."

He stared at her. "It's serious."

"I'm serious. I'm gonna be here. Long, boring, night."

Sian shrugged. "Doesn't Darian spend hours sitting in nature? Maybe it's your chance to learn what the fuss is about."

"Yeah, I'll be here with eyes closed and meditating. That will definitely help us with a quick retreat."

"Just wait. Wait here."

There was something about his voice. Hang on. "Hey, are you trying to do your spell speaking thing on me?"

"I'm trying to convince you. As far as I know, I have no ma..." For a brief second he looked troubled. He continued, "No... magic spell speaking thing."

She wondered if his hesitation was because he had some other magic. Hopefully yes, if that would help get Karina back to normal. He'd better get going. "Good luck."

He nodded in acknowledgement, then turned and disappeared in the mist. One guy in a Lumina-occupied territory. She didn't want to think about his odds.

FROM THE TOP of a tall tree, Sian observed its surroundings. It was a unique type of tree, with a very thick trunk, and branches only on its top, so it was very hard to climb. The months of practice in the Marisia cliffs and mountains paid off.

A clearing had been decorated for the ball, which was going to happen outdoors. Some people arrived. Wearing masks. They were half hoods with holes for the eyes, with drawings portraying animals. At first he thought only the Forestglare citizens would wear it, but he noticed someone who was giving orders to a group of people also wearing a mask.

Perhaps it was a local tradition and they wanted to keep it. Still, what was odd was how this arrangement would make Forestglare and Lumina citizens indistinguishable. He'd already thought about his chances of getting in, and considered that people from Lumina could think he was from Forestglare and vice-versa. Very easy for a stranger to walk in. With masks, it was a piece of cake. This was too easy.

Of course, many of the Lumina attendants were likely highly trained warriors ready to step into action if anything happened. So that was how they were setting up the trap. Maybe there was something else Sian was missing, but if not, they mostly counted on their numbers and perhaps their alleged magical superiority. A tight bet. A lot of things could go wrong.

A group of some ten people came in. They didn't wear uniforms, but Sian could tell by the way they walked that they were guards. A couple came behind them, without masks. A blond young man and... the air left his lungs.

She wore her hair loose, a black dress, and no mask. In her head, a tiara, matching a necklace. Karina had never looked so beautiful. Sian closed his eyes, feeling his stomach turning to ice. Radiant and healthy, what were the odds she needed any type of rescue? The young man beside her wore a crown and no mask. He'd seen him in the projection, and yet, it was unnerving to see how good he looked. King. Karina was queen. There was no question what they were to each other. Not only that, she and the young man exchanged glances in a way that conveyed ease, trust, intimacy even. Was there any more to see? Anything to try?

Perhaps it was time to turn around and go back, leaving her to her beautiful dress and conquered throne. Both things she'd refused when it was Sian who offered. When blond pretty-face offered her, she had no issue.

Sian took a deep breath. Anger clouded judgement, and he needed his mind if he was going to give this a try. Did he even want to give it a try? To hear it from her lips? He had to do it, just in case, in the tiny chance things were not what they looked like. Plus he'd given his word to Cayla. Not that Cayla mattered, but his word did.

Karina and that stupid king sat on a dais. Sian thought the guards would stand around or behind them but no, they spread around the clearing. Fine, maybe they wanted to be on the lookout for any suspicious activity, but shouldn't someone guard their royalty?

A couple came in, and they greeted Karina and blond pretty-face. They were from Forestglare. Sian had thought that the two populations would be indistinguishable, but it wasn't true. The local citizens had defeat and perhaps even despair in the way they carried themselves. As much as perhaps they tried to pretend to be cheerful, it was a thin layer over a broken interior. Sad.

Lumina people stood tall and proud, feeling superior. This was another factor Sian would need to consider when his turn to sneak in came. But what struck Sian about the couple was how close they got to Karina, when there were no guards near them.

Sian scanned the trees to check if there were guards ready to jump into action or shoot anyone who tried anything, but no.

What kind of idiot leaves their queen in such a vulnerable position when they were hosting a party attended by their enemies? As much as there were guards around them, it was just a matter of one fast movement, and Karina could be dead. Their head of security needed a serious lecture.

Maybe it was something else, though. Were she and the stupid king bait? Sian fought the urge to go down there that instant and do something. If he wanted to rescue her, he needed to watch and plan, and now he was very much convinced that she needed rescuing, despite whatever she thought. If she wanted to be conqueror queen, fine, but please do so with competent security.

*Look beyond.* As with any situation that doesn't make sense, there was probably more to be seen. Sian fought his revulsion and took a closer look at the silly king, who smiled and seemed relaxed as he greeted people.

Then, it was just a brief second, but it looked as if he was examining the guests, checking them for something. How, though, in a brief hello? He also looked around a couple times.

Blond pretty-face expected something all right. Why he had no security around him was the question. Maybe he was super powerful and thought he could deal with any possible threat. Still, that left Karina in a quite vulnerable position. She for her part looked… hard to say. Calm and serene were perhaps the words. The perfect queen —as Sian had known for a long time.

*Put it away.* Better not think about the past and focus on getting to her. From the way things looked, that part wouldn't be hard at all. The issue was how to kiss her, and how to escape after that. He'd figure it out later. Sian took a deep breath and started his descent, the cool wind agitating his tunic.

THE HOUSES in Forestglare were in the middle of the forest, not like a village surrounded by woods, but instead they were part of the forest. Since most of them were hollow trees, an unaware visitor could even miss them. This made it easier to walk in it without being seen, moving from tree to tree.

He wondered how the Luminous had conquered this place. As much as the citizens were peaceful, all these trees should have made it a challenging territory. Perhaps they'd threatened the Florestglarians into submission and cooperation. That wasn't too hard to do. Imprison and threaten somebody important and well-loved. That could be the case. He still felt uneasy, afraid of what a desperate citizen could try and what it could mean for Karina.

Far away from the clearing, he found what he wanted; a couple leaving a house. He had two sleeper pouches on his pockets. In a swift movement, he ran to the two people and pressed them on their noses and mouths. They fainted, and Sian pulled them inside. So far so good.

Since they were home, the odds that someone would find them were slim. Still, Sian had better hurry and get finished soon. He took the man's mask. It looked like an eagle or some kind of bird. A Maris? How interesting. He took the woman's mask too, just in case, checked if there was anyone outside, and then left and closed the door.

He hid his belt with weapons under a bush. It would be foolish to attempt to enter the ball with that. Hopefully he'd have time to come and get it back, otherwise, well, too bad. Climbing on another tree, he examined the area. There was only one entrance, and Lumina guards dressed as partygoers all around the clearing. But they blocked people from entering only, not from leaving, as he watched a couple walking towards the trees.

In the clearing, a band played. Sian didn't know those instruments. People danced in groups, in slow movements. Hang on. Everybody did everything slowly. Something was odd.

He stared at the entrance again. Right. They were handing wooden cups with a blue drink inside. It was probably the drink that made them slow. Interesting. Was that what Lumina was counting on? That their enemies would drink the blue thing and get too slow? A little risky as far as strategy went.

Still, how to avoid that drink? In other circumstances, it would be super easy. His father had trained him to force himself to vomit. Almost killed him in the process, but thankfully Sian had been a fast learner and didn't die from poisoning. So it could be super easy; drink it, go to a quiet place, and get rid of it.

The hiccup was on how he was supposed to try to get Karina back. He suspected that she wasn't into puke-flavored kisses. To just pretend to drink and spit it out wouldn't work either. The guards were watching the guests carefully. Sian took a better look at the middle of the clearing and how the guests were behaving. He noticed that even some Lumina people were also intoxicated with that drink —or perhaps pretending. Slow movements. Right.

THE GUARD HANDED him the cup with the sky water, as they called it. Sian lifted it slowly to his mouth, but poured it on his chin, as if he was having trouble with his coordination.

"Oops. Can I have one more?" he said slowly, with a drunk voice.

The guard poured it again. Sian took the cup and looked at it.

"Pretty." The cup then slipped from his hand and rolled away. "Sorry." Sian smiled apologetically. "Another cup?"

The guard gave him an annoyed look.

"Please?" Sian pleaded.

Another guard stepped close to the first one. "Just go in. And don't cause trouble."

Sian smiled. "No trouble. This is wonderful."

He staggered into the clearing.

There were already about a hundred people there. The band played cheerful music, but he couldn't help but notice their sad, resigned faces, even beneath the colorful hoods covering half their faces.

The people danced in groups, some alone, a little like people danced in Siphoria at the Junction. The only issue was that the people here had no sense of rhythm and their slow movements didn't match the beats of the music. The drink, maybe? What kind of drink makes people off beat? Anyway. Not everyone danced, and this was his chance to walk, or rather, stagger, and observe. He found a place where he could see Karina from afar. She was whispering in blond pretty-face's ear, then turned. Her eyes immediately found Sian's.

WHAT AN AWFUL POSITION, to have a celebration where the attendees had to be drugged so they would look cheerful, plus who knows what threats were used against the citizens so that they would come.

Satwak had told her the drink was a Forestglare tradition, but still, she saw the way it was being forced on them. It was all wrong. Hopefully no one would attempt to kill Sat or Karina. Drugged or not, all it would take was one wacko. Plus there could be some Guardians coming, and who knows what they would do or what they would try. That was what she thought this whole celebration was about: luring them in.

Karina leaned over to Sat. "I know you're good." She meant a good telepath, but she didn't want to say it out loud, not even whispering. She continued, "But it's a lot of people. You couldn't possibly, you know, get a sense of them all."

"Of course not, but when someone is not in the same syntony as the others, it's striking and noticeable. Even non-telepaths can detect suspicious behavior in a crowd; it's like raising a red flag."

"Guardians would be smarter, wouldn't they?"

Sat shrugged. "Being smart doesn't mean you can change the way you think."

Just then, something made her turn. On the far corner, leaning against a tree, was a tall guy, looking at her. She caught her breath, unsure if it was the intensity of his stare, his brown curls coming out from under the half-hood mask, or his lips.

Damn it, Sat was just beside her, probably hearing her every thought. He'd certainly understand that she'd find a guy hot, though. Right? And she and Sat were not romantically involved anyway.

Sat leaned over. "Hey, this looks like so much fun. I'm going dancing. You should go too." He got up and joined the crowd.

This was so strange. Karina had been expecting that he'd reply to her earlier thought, maybe tease her or something, not that he'd ignore her and plus walk away. But it wasn't as if he were jealous or upset, just truly interested in the party. Perhaps he'd seen something and wanted to check. She still felt uneasy sitting there alone, when she knew most of the people there considered her an enemy. But then, Sat was so calm, and he'd sworn an oath to protect her. Maybe she should trust his judgement.

She looked again towards the brown-haired guy, but he was no longer there. Had she imagined him? No. She looked at the crowd. There he was, in its middle, moving with them. Again he looked at her. Who was he? What was odd was how he stared at her directly, something nobody in Forestglare had yet done. And she was staring back.

Karina caught herself and looked way. She was almost out of air, though. Well, no wonder, who wouldn't be breathless when a super hot guy looked at her that way? All right, she couldn't see his entire face, just his eyes, lips, and jaw, but still, something about him...

She scanned the crowd for Sat and found him dancing among a group of people, as if he were just as intoxicated as them. A walking —or dancing—target, though, because, like Karina, he wore no mask. That was some trust in his mental abilities.

Her eyes met the brown-haired guy's in the crowd again. Karina felt awkward because she didn't know how to flirt. Zoe always told her to look at a guy, count three seconds, then look away, but Karina always feared she'd make a fool of herself. This guy, though, she had trouble looking away. She had to know who he was. Sat was dancing, and he'd told her to do the same. Maybe he had a point.

Karina got up, descended from the dais, and walked towards the middle of the clearing. From this position, it was hard to find the guy, because she no longer had the advantage of the high platform, and she wasn't tall. The people were having fun and ignored her. She just moved with the music, while trying to get closer to the position where he was.

Never in her life—at least in the life she remembered—she'd wanted so much to get close to anyone. She wondered if that strong wanting wouldn't send flares that Sat should be picking up from a distance. Well, he'd told her to dance. Maybe he was too busy paying attention to something else.

Not very comforting to know he could be ignoring her, when he'd said he would watch for any threats or intruders. Still, at least he was leaving her alone, and perhaps finding the brown-haired guy was worth risking her life. She felt lost in that crowd, though, and also wondered if he'd really looked at her or if she was imagining it. Plus, she couldn't find him. Again she wondered if he'd been a vision or something. Did she still have her sanity, with her memory loss and all?

Walking and looking around could look suspicious. There was a circle of people dancing and she joined them, so as to look more natural. Did she look natural, though? Their dance didn't make much sense.

She felt something over her head. Before she screamed, she realized it was one of those hood-masks. Somebody held her waist and turned her, swiftly throwing a shawl over her. Karina was face-to-face with the brown-haired guy.

14

UNMASKING

He leaned over and whispered in her ear. "Let's go outside slowly. I don't think they'll notice us."

Karina's heart beat faster. He was quite direct, as if it were obvious Karina wanted something with him. Well, it *was* probably obvious. Too late to play hard-to-get and she didn't even know how to play anyway. He took her hand. Her heart was going to explode. They walked towards the woods outside the clearing. She feared someone would stop them, but perhaps Sat or the guards would only notice something if she felt threatened. Maybe the fact that she wore a mask and had a shawl over her dress meant people didn't recognize her. Still, shouldn't someone be wondering where their queen was? Well, not her problem.

The music faded behind them. As she felt there was nobody around them, she voiced the question that had taken over her mind, "Who are you?"

He stopped as if surprised, looked around, then said, "Let's go a little farther."

So there was something important he was going to tell her. They walked a few more minutes, then he pointed to a thick fallen branch and said, "Let's sit."

He sat beside her and pulled out his mask. His face was quite striking, but what she liked the most was his eyes and the way he looked at her. He brushed his fingers against her mask. "So you don't know who I am?"

She almost apologized, explained she remembered nothing from the previous two years, then thought it was better to be cautious even if perhaps he was someone from her past. "Should I?"

"That's a good question."

His hand moved to the bottom of her hood-mask and he pulled it up. He caressed her forehead and brushed her hair away from her face. It felt natural, comforting. More than anything, she wanted to kiss him. Her eyes closed.

His forehead leaned against hers, then his nose touched her face. Was she really going to kiss a complete stranger whose name she didn't know? His lips were touching hers, and she parted them, inviting him in.

There was so much feeling in that kiss, and if felt so good, familiar. Images then passed through her mind. Her and the brown-haired guy, in another kiss, beside a well. A place with giant birds and pain. A girl with shiny black hair. Silver shoes. A woman with black hair. Flying machines. His name came to her mind; Sian. He was not a stranger. Realization hit her.

Karina gasped, pushed him away, and stared at him. "Me and you. We are..." She paused. Her memory was still blurry and she wasn't sure exactly how to explain what they were to each other.

"In love," He said. "Me at least. Do you remember me now?"

Sian felt like an ass having thought that she had forgotten him, that she had willingly chosen blond pretty-face. Karina had tears in her eyes, exactly like in all his dreams. Everything about her was like in his dreams. He wondered how she'd ended up as a Lumina representative, but he'd have time to ask that later.

She looked down as if thinking. "It's all mixed up. They brought me to Lumina. They made me forget, forget everything."

He kissed her cheekbone. "It's fine. Can you come with me now? I'll take you away from here."

She nodded.

He caressed her hair and kissed her forehead. "Let's go."

"Sian, I think there's a trap, they're planning something."

Sian kissed her hairline. "I know. But we'll leave soon." He kissed her face twice more, then got up and reached his hand towards her.

She looked so lovely he wanted to just sit there and keep kissing her, but they had to leave as soon as possible. Well, two seconds wouldn't make a difference. He pulled her closer and kissed her lips again, and perhaps it was a terrible idea because it took a lot of effort to stop it.

Karina smiled. "We need to go."

"Exactly what I was thinking." He promised himself no more kisses until she was safe in the Light Gardens. "Come."

One more wouldn't hurt. He kissed the corner of her face before turning in the direction of the sanctuary and their portal, walking at a fast pace.

They were walking hand-in-hand as if nothing had ever come between them. For now at least. Once they were back, he'd certainly have to talk to her. Marisia had given Sian plenty of time to go over his actions, and he wasn't proud of them. He'd need to find a way to explain, a way to apologize. Still, for now, she held his hand as if nothing mattered. Not surprising considering her memory was probably still damaged.

What bothered him most was how easy it all had been. Sian kept his ears perked for anything unusual. He picked up his belt with the knives, then put back his mask and Karina's, sorry to hide half her face.

FLASHES OF KARINA'S life were playing in her mind like movie trailers without dramatic music and narration. Images and images, plus some disconnected sounds, so much that they were overwhelming. Her memory was snapping into place, but it was odd to acquire two years of memories in such a short time. Plus, she was a completely different person from what she'd been thinking in the last few days. Helpless and without magic were not descriptions that applied to her.

*He wants you for your magic.* That thought had been with her all this time, but it didn't match the reality she saw. Now she understood; teleporting. They'd wanted her teleporting. With horror, she realized that she'd been the one to open the portal to Forestglare. How many deaths on her hands? Her hands. Now holding the other person who once had wanted her for her magic. Had he changed, though? At this point it didn't matter much. If he got her out of Forestglare, afterwards she could try to figure him out. For now, her heart was leaping with the knowledge that the super hot guy she'd seen five minutes before was actually her—something.

*This time she would be smarter.* Right, coming from the girl who had been playing into her captors' plans until five minutes before. But that was because they'd taken her memories. She'd been right to feel that her mind had been transplanted into a different body, because, without her last two years, her mind was the mind of a four-teen-year-old.

Holding Sian's hand, she felt safe, which was a little ridiculous because last time he'd been the one to put her in danger. Still, what mattered was getting away from the Luminous. She was curious about one thing. "How did you get here?"

"We'll talk later."

True. Masked and walking, they would be unnoticed by any onlookers, but if there were anyone around them, their talk about teleporting and who knows what else would probably catch attention. There wasn't anyone in that area, though.

Well, there wasn't—until there was. A faint woosh in the distance alarmed her. "We need to run." She realized she had no idea where they were going. "Are we going far?"

Sian obeyed right away striding forward and pulling her hand. "No."

But it was too late. A golden flying capsule passed them and landed on their way.

Sian kissed her face and whispered, "I'll hold them back. Run towards the silent sanctuary, that tall tree, there, yell for Cayla, and go without me."

What a ludicrous idea. "I'm not leaving you."

"Karina." He was almost growling. "Run. Save yourself."

She wasn't afraid of angry voices. "We'll sort it out together."

"Karina," he insisted, his voice dangerous.

Again a warning. Against what? What was he going to do to her?

She turned to him. "No!"

Then she saw who was coming out of the capsule: Satwak, blond curls flowing in the wind.

The blond boy walked towards them with his hands raised. "My name's Satwak. I come in peace. I need your help."

Before Karina had time to process the situation or even say anything, Sian had rushed towards Satwak, dropped him on the floor, punched his face, and had a knife on his neck. "Give me one reason not to kill you."

Aggressive Sian was new and somewhat terrifying. Karina had always thought about him as calm, cool, and collected. She ran towards them. "Sian, no."

Satwak spat blood. "You're scaring her."

Sian glanced towards Karina then back to him.

Sat added, "And you're not a murderer."

"You're wrong," Sian replied.

With all her memory coming back so suddenly, Karina's mind wasn't the sharpest, but she suddenly realized why Sian was beyond himself. She knelt beside him and put her hand on his shoulder. "He never touched me, Sian. We never had anything."

"Why are you queen, then?"

"We pretended to be married. He said it was to protect me." Karina wasn't sure about the protecting part, but she had to calm him down.

"It was," Satwak grunted. "I had to protect her from my uncle. That's why I did all I did. I knew she loved you, though, and I respected that."

Sian glanced at Karina and then stopped pressing his knife on Satwak's neck. "What do you want?"

"I need your help."

"Right. Capture and enchant someone's love, that will certainly get them in a cooperative mode. You win points for creativity, but fail in basic logic."

Sat shook his head. "I didn't capture her, I mean, I did, but I had no choice. She opened a portal to our dimension, the first person in years. My uncle would want the teleporter who did it, so I had to bring her. He would have put her in the stasis room, from where he'd suck her magic. I prevented it by telling my uncle I wanted her for a wife. Lumina hasn't had teleporters in generations, it would be to our advantage if I had children with her. And plus, she'd help us conquer other cities. Forestglare was just a sample of what Karina can do. I did this so that he'd keep her conscious. Firis agreed and he thinks we're in love."

Sian turned to Karina. "Is that true?"

"The pretending part, yes, but this is the first time I'm hearing his reasons."

Sat again spit some blood. "My uncle is a strong telepath. I had to keep her mind safe from him. I also needed to convince him she'd cooperate with us. I couldn't tell her any of this or let her know about her past. She was learning to block her mind, though. Once I knew she was strong enough, I'd let her have her memories back and help me. I had to get to you."

"Me?" Sian sounded incredulous. "What can you want with me?"

"I have to depose Firis."

Karina knew that part, she just didn't understand how Sat planned on doing that.

Sian shrugged. "Yeah. Why should I care?"

"Because you should be in his place."

He rolled his eyes. "Yeah, yeah, yeah. Been there, done that. I'm not deposing any king for anyone anymore. I know I did it once, but that doesn't mean I wanted to become a professional usurper. Do your own dirty work."

What was he talking about?

Satwak shook his head. "It's different. Firis is too strong, and we can't organize any counter movement or he'd find out. The stasis room, it's horrible, he keeps most of the strong magicians there and sucks their magic. Of course, he only gets part of the original magic, but it's enough to make him quite invincible. My sister is in that room!"

He glanced at Karina. "My youngest sister, not Faizana. There's more. Once Lumina killed all the teenagers who didn't manifest any magic. That's how everyone in the city is so strong. Nowadays everyone has at least a little bit, but the weaker ones are silenced and taken as slaves."

He turned to Karina. "Like the attendants who helped you get dressed. You thought they were creepy. A little worse than creepy. I need to do something, but I can't. If I were to try to talk to anyone about what to do against Firis, they'd be caught the next day—and so would I. What am I to do?"

Karina felt pity for the city, for Sat's sister, but she still didn't understand what Satwak hoped to accomplish and why, of all people, he was singling out Sian, whose magic wouldn't do much against Luminous.

Karina crouched. "We could get the Guardians to help you, Sat." Sian gave her a horrified glance, probably annoyed at the use of the nickname. Karina pretended she didn't notice. "We can do that for you. Just tell us what you need."

"I saw Sian in your mind, Karina, I saw him, and then I knew all my prayers had been answered. Firis is not the real royal line, I told you so."

He had *sort of* told her so.

Sat turned to Sian. "You have a spiral on your chest, don't you?"

Sian tensed, glared at Karina, then shrugged. "Not sure. I have a bunch of scars."

That didn't make sense. "You couldn't have seen it in my mind. I never saw his chest." She had to make it clear before Sian started to think she'd peeked while he slept or something.

Satwak closed his eyes for a moment, then said, "No. I saw the scar in a dream, then I saw Sian in your mind. I connected the dots. You're the royal line, Sian, and should be our overseer."

He raised an eyebrow. "Because of a scar you don't even know if I have?"

"It's a birthmark, and it means you can manipulate electricity. Can't you?"

Sian was surprised, or perhaps even shook, but for a second only. "I bet lots of people can."

Sat shook his head. "It's unique, and it can defeat Firis."

"Great. I'll think about your city and your needs. Right now, if you don't mind, I'm taking Karina back. Try to stop us and you'll find out whether I can be a murderer or not."

"I'm alone here. If I wanted to stop you I could have called more people. Just give me your word you'll help me."

Karina didn't like that. "Lumina is invincible, Satwak. I saw you guys training. We'll talk to the guardians, but still... Even if Sian is your lost royal, and if he has special magical powers, what can he do?"

"His power, if he uses it, he could defeat the entire Lumina army."

"How?" Sian asked.

"I didn't find out that part."

Sian snorted. "Awesome."

Karina was quite relieved at seeing no signs of greedy Sian. He wasn't the least interested in an opportunity to be king, or overseer, of the most powerful ethereal city. Perhaps he had changed, or perhaps it had always been Whyland that he wanted.

And he was right that they had to leave. Karina turned to Sat. "We'll do our best to help you. It's in our interest too. Now we need to go."

"Right. After all I risked for you, you'll just take off, without even a word that you'll help me."

Sian turned Sat's face to him. "Hey, hey. You said you wanted *my* help. Now leave her out of it. I'll do my best. That's my word and I don't lie. I'm not going to promise the impossible and I'm not going to die for your dysfunctional city."

Sat shrugged. "Fine. Go. I won't stop you."

Sian got up and released Satwak, who got up as well. Karina wondered if he was going to try anything, but he seemed resigned. As far as she knew, other than his impressive mental abilities, all he could do was cast shields, so he wouldn't overpower them with magic. Sian took her hand.

"Wait," Satwak said. "How did you get here?"

Sian glared at him. "What does it matter to you?"

"It's just... some guards caught an intruder. A girl. Black hair."

"Cayla?" Karina was surprised, but she shouldn't. Sian needed help to teleport.

Sian walked towards Sat. "It's to your best interest to get her out."

Sat raised his hands. "It is. It is. But I'll need to break her out. I need help."

Sian sighed, then whispered to Karina, "The tallest tree in the sanctuary, it's our portal. Go there and teleport to the Light Gardens."

Whispering was stupid because Sat was a telepath, but this was not the time to explain that. Karina nodded.

Sat sighed "Yeah, go. Save yourself." He then put his hand on his head. "No. Wait. Firis is coming. He should be here at any second."

"And?" Sian asked.

"He can feel a strong teleporter. If Karina isn't here, he'll know where your friend, Cayla, where she is. If Karina gets back to the ball... it will confuse him. He'll be near a strong teleporter, so he won't feel your friend, who's further away. Karina can get out later at night. Otherwise you won't have a chance to get out with your friend."

"I'll go back," Karina volunteered. "Sian, get away, get Cayla away. I can teleport later. I could even use the main tower. It's easy now that I know I can do it."

"Not if he wipes your mind."

"You know where Karina is, and you know you can save her. She's been safe for days. A couple more hours won't hurt."

Sian's expression was pained.

"Sian, please," Karina pleaded, "She's my friend."

"I know. She's also my brother's love."

"I'll go back," Karina added. "Sat's right. I've been safe for days. I just need to give you time to escape."

Sian sighed. "Fine. Where do we rescue Cayla?"

"That direction." Sat pointed away from the ball. "The prison."

Sian hugged Karina and leaned his forehead against hers. "Be safe. Be careful."

"I will."

He kissed her briefly on the lips, then turned to Sat. "Let's go."

Karina walked back towards the ball, so many confusing emotions. She hoped Cayla would be all right. As for Karina herself, it would be easy to teleport away after the ball. Her only danger was if Firis inquired into her mind. But Sat didn't seem worried, so there was probably a good reason for that.

THIS WAS TORTURE. For a brief second, Sian almost considered leaving Cayla and taking Karina to safety. But of course, then he'd never be able to face Darian or Karina, so he had to save her, even if the price was way too high. True, Karina had been safe all this time, but every second she remained was a second something horrible could happen.

"Is the prison far?'

"A couple more minutes," blond pretty-face replied.

"Can't we take your flying ball?"

"It only sits one." He sighed. "Listen. I'm sorry. I'm sorry if I had to deceive Karina, but I swear, I do, I always treated her well, and always made it very clear that there was nothing between us. And she loves you."

Dude was trying to get on his good side. "I just want to see her safe."

"I'm protecting her. I'm doing everything I can."

"It better be good enough. For your sake."

"I know. Listen, you should think better about what I told you. Lumina, we're rich. You'd be happy as its overseer. Karina will accept if she knows it's for a good cause."

"Trying to guess my thoughts?"

"Not guess. I'm a telepath."

If that was true, he could be a dangerous opponent. "So you say. Can you prove it?"

"You considered cutting my thing in pieces and feeding it to the birds. Not really, but the thought crossed your mind."

Sian shrugged. "It's a normal reaction, right?"

"Maybe. Not with those details, though. The girl we're going to rescue, Cayla, you don't like her much. You're some kind of childhood enemies or something."

"Point proven. Now leave my thoughts alone."

"But I can't, I need your help. All you want is to go back to your city, but you also want Karina. You need to think about your future. What are you going to offer her?"

"Want another punch? If you were so good at reading my thoughts, or her thoughts, you'd know that offering a usurped kingdom is the last thing she wants."

"But it won't be usurped, that's the thing. And I spent a lot of time reading her mind, Sian."

Sian grabbed pretty-face's throat. "Will you shut up or do I have to make you?"

"Fine. It's weird. You're usually against violence, aren't you?"

This time he took a knife and pointed at the annoying boy. "I'm beyond myself with worry, okay? So don't push me. I'll talk to you once Karina's safe."

"I'm sorry."

Sian released his knife and they kept walking. He hated wasting time with pointless conversation, and blond pretty-face's leaps in logic.

But Satwak didn't seem to want to be quiet. "She thinks you're hotter than me."

Again trying to flatter him. "Well, she's not blind."

Satwak shrugged. "I thought you'd like to know."

Right. So stupid. Since the dude wanted to talk, they'd better talk about something useful. "You know what I want to know? Your plan. You said I could use my magic to defeat Firis. How?"

"I... I'm not sure."

"You're not sure, and you expect me to help you?"

"Hey, I'm desperate. I'm hanging to foolish hope. But from everything I read, if you have the special royal magical skill you'll be invincible in Lumina. That means you can take it, and then free my sister. That's what I'm trying to do. Wouldn't you do that for your brother? Even if you don't get along?"

"I would come up with a decent plan."

"I'm trying my best! Do you believe in destiny?"

"Not really." He then remembered Lylah telling him that she'd had a vision. "But it's true that some people have glimpses of the future."

"Right, but think about it. Destiny brought Karina here, brought you here. What were the odds?"

"Very slim." Which led to the other part that bothered Sian.

"What were you going to do if I hadn't shown up? Would you just keep her forever?"

"I was teaching her to block her mind. Once she was strong enough, she could find you. When I saw you in her mind, I knew something had been set in motion."

"A lot of maybes."

"Things have worked out so far, isn't that a sign?"

"You must be delusional to think that Cayla being caught and Karina staying behind means things are working out."

"They'll be safe."

"They'd better. Or you might have to say goodbye to more than your foolish plan."

15

COMPLICATIONS

Karina walked back to the clearing trying to look natural, as if she'd just walked out to take some air. She tried to keep her mind blank, afraid of Firis. Her bubbling emotions had to quiet down for now. She sat back at the dais. Not much had changed. Some people still danced. Perhaps less. Some were fallen, asleep on the edges of the main clearing. Fantastic. She scanned the crowd. No sign of Firis.

Then she heard steps behind her and her stomach dropped. She focused her mind on the music, on the people dancing.

Firis was beside her. "No idea how glad I am to see you alone."

Karina smiled. "Far from alone. Look at our lovely guests." She gestured to the dancing grounds.

He sat on the chair by her. "True. Where's Satwak?"

Karina scanned the crowd. "He was dancing just now. I don't know. Must be around here somewhere."

"Silly boy, if you ask me." Firis took her hand and caressed it. "Now, this is a lot better, isn't it?"

"What's better?"

He got up. "Let's dance."

"I think they dance in groups."

"Silly apes, these ones. They don't deserve you."

Karina got up, focusing on the music, on the moment.

Firis kept holding one of her hands but put the other around her waist. "I've given a lot of thought to what you asked me."

Karina truly had no idea. "What?"

"You wanted more power. Tell me, beautiful," he whispered in her ear, "how would you like to be the overseer's wife?"

Karina bottled down her feelings. "Why would you want Sat to replace you?"

He laughed and pinched her chin. "Are you a silly girl or a smart girl?"

Her fear was unlikely to go unnoticed. She'd better run with it. "I'm afraid of hoping for more than I can have."

"There's nothing you can't have. You know what you have to do."

"Perhaps I'm silly. I'm not quite following."

Firis smiled. "Be mine."

That was quite direct. "I swore an oath. To Sat."

"You care about your oath? That's not a problem. It was only for one year or until death. I can arrange it."

Karina gulped, shutting her thoughts away. "I don't want him to die."

"Are you telling me you prefer him?"

"No. I just don't want him to die." This was getting creepy and facing him was hard. She looked down. "I'm so afraid, so afraid. And so ashamed of my feelings. What kind of person am I?"

"A smart one."

"Everyone is seeing us. What will they think?"

"They'll think that they'll have to respect you twice as much from now on."

"What if Sat comes back?"

"He'll respect your choice. And mine."

Karina had a nauseous feeling. "I can't help feeling I'm being a bad person."

"Nonsense." He let go of her waist and pulled her hand. "Come. Let's make it official."

"Where are we going?"

"My house."

Panic was taking over Karina. "I'm still sworn to Sat."

"I told you it doesn't matter. And he won't mind. If it bothers you that much, I can do something about it."

Firis could probably feel her pulse pounding. And she had to keep him busy.

Karina stopped and pulled her hand. "No."

Firis' mouth twitched.

She continued, "Romance me, seduce me. Of course I want to be your equal. But you'd better treat me as one."

He smiled. "Forgive my overexcitement. And you misunderstand me. I mean to take it as slowly as you want."

"Tonight, then. I'll come to your room. After Sat is asleep."

He shook his head. "I don't mean to share you with my nephew anymore. Unless you're lying to me. Are you cruel enough to fool me?"

"No. I'm just—overwhelmed."

"Is that it? Or are you stalling? See? I need to be sure. There's only one way to be sure."

"I just need some time."

"I'll give you plenty."

He walked pulling her by the hand. Karina shut her thoughts away. Eventually she'd have to use her mind, though. They came to a tree and Firis opened the door. It was one of those one-room houses.

An idea hit her. She whined, "Here, though? These are not for people, but for animals. I deserve something better, don't I? Can't we go back to Lumina?"

He walked towards her and caressed her hair. "Oh, dear, you deserve all the best in the world. And you have a good point. This is not a place for civilized people. But I'm tired of being civilized, aren't you?"

She was aware of his hand on her head, and her mind went blank. "What do you mean?"

"You know what I mean." He cupped her head and leaned in to kiss her.

Karina turned her head, focusing on the time she swore her oaths to Satwak.

"Still thinking of Satwak? If you're too worried about him, I'll order my men to deal with him right now."

Time to change strategy. "I don't even like him, Firis. I just didn't want you to think poorly of me."

He smiled. "Interesting."

Karina focused on food, imagining a nice plate of sushi, sad they didn't have sushi in Lumina, but still feeling hungry. "I'm starving. Can I eat something first?"

"You could. If I didn't get the feeling you're stalling. Kiss me. Or else, if that's not what you want, just say the word."

Karina pushed him away. "Well, I don't want it. Not like this. Like I said, either you treat me well or no deal."

"No deal, then." He walked towards her, about to put his hand on her head again. He'd probably make her unconscious or try harder to get her thoughts.

Karina stepped back and used her magic, directing an explosion towards him. Firis blocked it with a shield.

"Since when can you do magic?"

"Always." She was going to gag if she had to pretend for another second. "And you're the most disgusting man in the universe."

Perhaps it hadn't been a good idea to offend him. He lifted his other hand, about to shoot some ray. Karina made her explosion and collapsed the tree on them.

～

SIAN AND BLOND pretty-face approached a metal building, which looked like a temporary structure.

"I'll go there and check. Wait here."

"No." Sian realized something. "You are lying." How could he have been so stupid not to notice it before? "Cayla's not here."

Satwak stared at him. "Why? I mean, I can't be sure, but I'm not lying. Do you want to look at the prison?"

"I know when people lie."

Satwak raised his hands. "Fine. But it's true that Firis can sense strong teleporters. He'd also wonder where Karina is. If you want to escape, that's your chance."

"I came here to take Karina back, and that's what I'm doing."

"She can return at any time. You, on the other hand, need someone to teleport you. You'll be a dead man if you walk on that ball now. Go to the Light Gardens, plan something, then come back. Your special power works in Lumina, not here."

Sian moved to punch him, but the prick blocked him. Sian said, "I'll do what you're saying. You'd better hope Karina teleports soon. If anything happens to her, I'll personally make sure your sister never leaves that stasis room. Got it?"

Blond pretty-face nodded. "Perfectly. Now, rush before someone does find out that there are intruders in Forestglare. I'll go back to make sure everything is going well with Karina."

Sian hated that plan, but he also hated rushing senselessly onto something.

A red flare shone in the sky above the clearing.

"Oh, no," Satwak said. "I swear, it's not my fault. You'd better get away fast."

Right. That flare was likely a signal to the Lumina's forces. Sian's chest tightened. "Karina's there."

"She's not an intruder! How many times do I have to tell you she's safe! They'll send sentries. I need you alive. Please teleport away as fast as you can."

The only reason Sian didn't run back to the ball was because he feared for Cayla. Why hadn't she teleported back like he asked? He ran towards the sanctuary.

KARINA'S ENTIRE BODY HURT. She felt exhausted, with her magic depleted, but she had to escape. All she needed to do was run to a teleporting tower, and there was one not far from there. First she had to get all the wood and rubble away from her. She heard the sound of wood being moved and knew Firis was doing something. If he got to her, he could read her thoughts and maybe erase her memory again. Who knows what else he could do? And now, with his talk of *kiss me* and *be mine*, she was more scared than ever.

Depleted as she was, she had to give it one more try. *Boom.* The rubble was pushed away. No sign of Firis. She had to reach the main tree, where their teleporting tower was. She'd run three steps when somebody tackled her. Firis. She could recognize his smell. Ugh. Disgusting.

He put his hand on her head. Karina thought she was going to faint. Instead, images came to her mind as if someone else controlled it. Her meeting with Sian, the conversation with him and Sat. Karina focused on the periodic table, but it was too late. No, no, no, Firis shouldn't be getting that information.

SIAN WAS JUST a few meters from the tree from where they would teleport away when he heard something coming fast in their direction.

"Behind you!" Cayla yelled.

Sian turned. And saw four huge felines, some kind of jaguar, running towards him. They had black fur and were bigger than the animals in Whyland. He had a split second to think. Outrunning them wouldn't be possible. If only he had his magic... He tried doing whatever he'd done in Marisia, but he didn't feel anything. No electricity, no weird magic, nothing. He'd have to fight his way out of this mess.

He yelled, "Teleport away! I'll hold them."

Cayla yelled something that sounded like *my ass*, but he was too focused on the big cats coming towards him.

What a lovely time not to have a sword, a lance, or a pistol. On the floor, he saw something; a long branch. He caught it just in time to swing it against his first attacker. Two more were coming from the sides. He swung the branch and hit one, but as a jaw came to him from the other side, he lunged forward and fell. A feline jumped on him and got stabbed in the neck. First one killed. No time to feel bad for creatures who were likely not aware of what they were doing.

Sian pushed the animal from above him—and saw the three others coming for him. He'd accepted and welcomed death before, but not now when he was leaving Karina in that place. Getting up fast, he picked up the branch, but and a jaguar caught it with its teeth. Sian let it go.

A jaguar came from behind and dropped him face down on the ground, pushing him with his claw. Sian scanned his mind for a solution, an escape. With his back to the animal, he couldn't stab him or try to defend himself in any way. So this was it. He wished he left this world in a more dignified manner. He trusted Cayla to try to save Karina. Perhaps she'd be much happier without Sian. He wished he'd said some kind of goodbye to Malena, Joel, Raja, even Darian.

A hand grabbed his. He no longer felt the weight of the paw on his back, but heard a scream. Crap. Cayla's.

"Get up," she pulled him.

They were in the teleporting tree. Jaguars were entering. Then they were in a completely black place. It felt as if walls were closing in on them, about to suffocate them.

"I can't," she said.

Can't? Teleport to the Light Gardens. Well duh. How could he have been so stupid? "Go somewhere else. Anywhere."

~

STRONG FLASHES of light forced Cayla to close her eyes. When they stopped, she looked—and recognized the tower in Marisia. Other than that, horrible pain on her right arm—and a lot of blood: one of those cats had taken a huge bite of it. What a price to save Darian's stupid brother.

Screeches sounded in the distance. This time there was nobody to shield them. "Will the creatures attack us?"

"They won't." Sian was calm. He'd lived there, so he probably knew something. His forehead was bleeding.

"You're hurt," she said.

"You're worse."

"Did you find Karina?"

He just stared at her as if he wanted to murder her or something. Right. She'd keep that in mind next time she saw him about to become cat food.

Sian looked down and shook his head. "Why didn't you teleport away like I asked you?"

What. The. Freak. "Excuse-me? Sorry but you'd be dead by now if I hadn't stayed."

Sian looked down and shook his head. "No. I turned back because I thought they'd captured you. I wouldn't leave you there. That's what cost Karina's escape."

"But did you get to kiss her?"

He nodded. "I did, and yes, you were right. They'd wiped her memory." He shook his head. "We'd never make it back to the Light Gardens. The portals are being watched, aren't they?"

"I didn't think... that portal. But it makes sense they'd isolate Forestglare."

"It means Karina's stuck there."

Cayla wasn't sure, but a glimmer on his face looked like a tear.

"Quite interesting things in this mind of yours," Firis said, then removed his hand.

Karina was still immobilized, trying to come up with an escape plan, now that she realized Firis couldn't read much of her mind when he wasn't touching her head.

"Uncle." Satwak's voice. "I have a gift for you. I had to be sure, I didn't want to raise false hopes. Now I'm sure. I've found the lost royal."

What was he doing? It was probably too late to try to pretend to be on his uncle's side.

"Is that so?" Firis asked. "Why isn't he here, then?"

"Our magic pumas were sent to kill him. He won't make it out of Forestglare."

"Stupid boy. Who told you to kill him? I'd have more use for him alive."

"But he's too dangerous, isn't he?"

"Stupid legends."

Firis had been immobilizing Karina on the floor but then got up. She sat and was about to get up when the man turned, pointed his hand towards her and shot some kind of blue energy. Too late to block it. But she didn't feel any pain or get hurt. Instead, her body couldn't move. She'd been frozen in place, like some kind of sleep paralysis.

"Well, if he escapes," Sat pointed to Karina, "he'll be back. She's our bait."

"And you're going to tell me that was why you wanted to keep her conscious?'

"Yes. I thought I saw something in her mind, but I wasn't sure. Now I am. And if he brings the guardians with them, even better. We can get rid of them in one swift move."

Firis took out a knife and pressed against Karina's face. "Do you think this... Sian, do you think he'll mind if she has one eye missing?"

"Why take any chances? She's already ugly with two eyes."

"I disagree. She'd make a lovely addition to my collection." He turned to Karina. "Perhaps you'll change your mind." Firis walked to Sat and put a hand on his shoulder. "My beloved, trustworthy nephew, who turned in his sister, sometimes I wonder..." He made a swift movement with his arm, then it sounded like something ripping. Sat fell forward. Firis continued, "Just wondering, I guess, if you'd predict my move. Perhaps I'm wrong. I'll get someone to patch you up—if you survive."

Firis walked away, leaving Karina paralyzed and Sat on the ground bleeding from a wound on his lower back.

She made an effort to speak. "Sat?"

"Alive," he grunted.

She didn't think Sat had been working for Firis, and she didn't think Firis bought it either. "You should have run away."

"Save. You."

Karina didn't see how Sat had saved her, but perhaps he got points for trying. There was a lot of blood and she couldn't do anything for him. "Don't speak, it's a lot of effort. I just wanted you to know that Firis, earlier, he was trying to, uh, kiss me. He threatened to kill you. He said, 'if Sat worries you so much, I'll kill him'. And maybe that's what happened in your past. Maybe she had no choice."

Sat grunted.

"Don't try to speak. I'm just saying."

Karina made an effort to move. No. It was wrong. She was trying with her body. She'd need to try with her mind. Two people came running towards them. Great. Faizana knelt beside Satwak. The other man watched Karina.

"Sat, Sat, wake up," the girl said.

Sat grunted.

Faizana turned to the man. "Go. Get help. Now."

The man said, "I have to—"

"Now!" Faizana roared.

The men ran. The girl turned to Karina and slapped her face. "You. It's your fault. If my brother dies, I'm going to kill you, and I'll do it slowly."

Sat grunted something.

"Firis stabbed him, not me."

"I saw you two dancing. I know what you want."

Karina rolled her eyes, surprised that she could do that much movement. "Yeah, yeah, he's so sexy."

The girl moved to punch her. Karina blocked her—with her mind. It wasn't her body she had to use, but her mind. She focused, and with another mini explosion, got rid of the magic paralysis. She got up and bolted to the nearest hollow tree, hoping to make an improvised teleporting tower and hoping the girl didn't shoot her. Better not hope. Karina turned and saw the girl with her arm raised, palm facing her. "Don't kill me. I'm bait. Ask Sat."

The girl frowned and looked at her brother. Karina turned and got in a tree. She focused on the Light Gardens. But that wasn't easy, because she'd never used a teleporting tower there. Did they even have those? Whyland. No. All the towers she knew were either destroyed or blocked. Her own home. She tried, and felt as if a dark cloud was suffocating her. She couldn't make it. There was only one choice. Karina closed her eyes. When she opened them, she was in the Lumina tower. About twenty guards encircled her.

She moved as if to walk through them, but two guards blocked her.

Karina stared at them in what she hoped was disgust. "Excuse me? Is there a reason you're blocking your representative queen in Forestglare?"

"We block all unauthorized entry."

"From unknown citizens. Simple soldiers. I'm Forestglare's Queen. Now let me go."

The guards spread out and she walked away from the tower. What an impact that saying something with confidence made. She couldn't believe she'd managed it, shook with worry about Sian, worry about Sat, not to mention that since she'd learned what had happened to her she realized her parents must be dying with worry and suffering. So unfair. Perhaps she should have tried to teleport home. Duh. From the Lumina tower, it might have been possible. She was about to return when she heard rushed steps and decided to run and hide. Stupid, stupid, why didn't she block that passage?

Maybe she shouldn't be that harsh on herself. It had only been less than an hour since she regained knowledge about her magic. With all that was happening, it was too much to expect her to know how to use it and to make all the right decisions, and plus she felt depleted. Karina ran downstairs and got in a room, hoping they wouldn't find her.

No. She had to start doing things right. Her chances of escaping these crazy people unscathed were slim already without stupid mistakes. She'd have to get things right from now on. That said, she was probably still too weak to teleport back home. And if Sian's magic was strongest in Lumina, closing the passage wouldn't have been smart. She closed her eyes. If Sian was alive. The thought of losing him right after finding him again was too much. No, she wasn't going to entertain that thought. He was smart, Cayla was smart. Sat wanted him alive. Of course they'd escape.

16

# NEW PLANS

Cayla listened as Sian told her what had happened in Forestglare while wrapping her arm in a piece of cloth. They'd entered a chamber in that tower and closed the door. So far, no Maris had come, but she was still afraid.

"There," he said as he finished tying her arm. "If you don't get proper medical attention in a few hours, you'll lose your arm. Darian will kill me."

He'd said it about ten times now, as if Darian were some kind of murderer. Cayla was sick of replying to that so she just ignored him, thinking about what he'd told her instead. "But if you're the royal line, let's assume it's true, if you died, there would still be Darian."

"Exactly. One reason not to lose an arm to keep me alive."

Ignoring wasn't working and she was losing her patience. "Will you shut up! Of course Darian wants to see you alive and he'll be glad I saved you. Where do you get these freaky ideas?"

"My freaky head."

"Karina, too. I told you she's my friend. How would she feel if you died?"

Sian shrugged. "Didn't you say she should forget me? Perhaps it would be best for her."

"Fine. If I ever see you almost dying again, I won't interfere. Now it's too late to go back, so don't piss me off."

"Well, had you teleported back like I asked you, none of this would be happening."

"Yeah, yeah, yeah. Your thankfulness is touching, Sian."

He crossed his arms and looked away.

Perhaps she should be quiet, but she didn't want to. "And you're being stupid. Didn't you say the guy lied? He could have lied anyway. If it's true he can see your thoughts, he would know what to tell you so that you wouldn't teleport Karina away. Plus, he couldn't claim I had been captured if I'd been with you!"

Sian glared at her, looked away, then looked back. "That's a valid point."

Cayla stared for some time, waiting for the rest of the sentence and some retort, but it didn't come. Being attacked had really affected Sian.

"So... back to our thoughts. The royal line would continue, but there's a special skill only you have, is that right?"

"That's what the guy said. Again, we can't take it for truth. But... Leena also told me not to mention what I can do, so there might be something there."

"I'm assuming Darian doesn't have it, so even if he were to be in the line, he wouldn't be able to take Lumina."

"Well, I'm not taking that stupid city, especially after what Satwak did."

"We just need to get Karina."

Sian nodded. "If we ever get out of here."

Cayla wasn't that worried. "Darian will wake up, he'll see my note, and he'll look for us. They'll find us."

"How are they going to guess we're here?"

"By elimination? I don't know. He'll find me." True that they no longer had the twin necklaces, and more than ever she missed hers, but she trusted Darian. She regretted not having trusted him more, not having talked to him, not having listened to him. Perhaps they could have come up with a better plan than the one that got them stuck in Marisia without rescuing Karina. Too late now.

~

KARINA'S HEART was pounding so hard that she feared it would give her away. There were steps in the hallway and doors being opened. She'd be caught—and have nowhere to run to. Perhaps she should just surrender. They weren't going to kill her —yet.

She opened the door and raised her hands. "I'm here."

Her hope was that they'd try to take her back to Forestglare, and, in the teleporting tower, she'd have her chance to escape.

Five guards approached her, and two of them held her. This was not her day. No. She'd kissed Sian. It would never be a terrible day. She was dragged not to the teleporting tower, but to the throne room. Firis was there. Karina panicked, and in the moment the guards let her go, she used her magic to cast an explosion and ran away to the elevator. When she got out on the first floor, metal balls were circling her. Karina pushed them away and ran outside. All she had to do was hide long enough not to be caught, and hope that the Guardians or Sian would come and save her. Now, hoping Sian would come to the very place where people wanted to kill him was a terrible hope. Karina ran down the stairs, turning and pushing away some flying capsules. Most of the security was around the teleporting tower, so she'd been correct to run away from it.

Even when Karina was exhausted from running, she kept running, until she reached the woods. With the impression they'd quit, she climbed a tree and waited.

After many minutes, she heard someone calling her, "Karina!"

The voice was familiar, and she was glad when she recognized it. Sat. He was alive! But she shouldn't trust him. If he needed Sian to defeat Firis, he'd obviously want Karina caught. That was the truth she should have seen when he faced her and Sian on their way out. Too late, now.

He stopped below her tree. "I know you're there."

*You can pick up my thoughts and find me?* She thought.

"Pretty much."

*How come you can walk and you aren't dead?*

"This is Lumina we're talking about. We don't die from silly wounds."

*Good for you.*

"Come down. I need to talk to you."

*Isn't your medicine super advanced? Climb.*

"Kah, don't be silly. You know they are going to find you soon. Who do you prefer? Me or Firis?"

Karina jumped down. "What do you want?"

"I want to apologize. Truly. But you see, I don't even care about my life. I just want the freedom of my people. My sister's freedom. If you're such a good person as you think you are, you'd help me. You'd understand."

"I told you I'll help you."

He was acting weird and Karina had better escape.

"Im sorry," he said as he raised a hand and shot a yellow flare in the sky.

Karina ran, but it was no good, as soon she was surrounded. Someone paralyzed her, the same way Firis had done. Sat walked towards her and put his hand on her head.

*Asshole,* she managed to think before it all turned black.

SIAN'S HEAD was going to explode if Cayla continued trying to ask him about what blond pretty-face had said, about his powers, about some unfeasible plan, as if they had any way out of that dump. Fine, he also thought someone would figure out where they were, but his estimates weren't nearly as optimistic as hers. And her voice was grating. She had saved his life, though. He would have felt thankful if she stopped annoying him.

He decided it was best to tell her the truth. "Fine. Want to know my power? I can control electricity. No idea how I can do it, no idea how it's done, no idea how to control it. I've only used it twice. Once, when I killed a bunch of Maris like a coward. Twice, in the meeting room, when I collapsed. According to Leena, I would have killed everyone in that room if she hadn't shielded me. How this freaky magic I have no control over can make any difference, I don't know."

She covered her mouth with her hand, as in surprise. "Sian, don't blame yourself. When people can't control their magic, accidents happen."

"In Marisia it wasn't an accident."

"Wasn't it self defense?"

Sian shrugged. "Maybe."

She thought for a moment. "Lumina probably has something that can be affected by your type of magic, or, I don't know, has some affinity. The issue is what. We can research when we get back."

Right. In about a month. What good would it do? But he didn't want to argue. "That's an idea."

He fell silent, hating himself for having been so stupid, incompetent.

"Stop blaming yourself," Cayla said.

"Thinking you're a telepath too?"

She shrugged. "It's in your face."

"I didn't ask you to look."

"I'm not gonna close my eyes just so you can mope without interruption."

Sian got up. "There's a window, you know? You could look outside."

He took a look at the valley. Amidst so much disappointment, one thing lifted his spirits; the vegetation was growing back. Sian would have smiled if he didn't feel he was about to drown in an ocean of sadness.

So far no Maris had come to the tower. Perhaps they were both invisible, unafraid. Not true, though. Sian was terrified about what could happen to Karina. Powerlessness was one of the worst feelings in the world. No wonder his father, and so many more people, coveted power over all things. As much as it had a dark side, it could also mean being able to do something for the people he loved.

Cayla stood beside him. "You still hate me, don't you?"

Seriously? She thought he had any room in his mind for her? He tried not to be rude, though, for Darian's sake. "Of course not. I'm just worried."

"Sian, maybe there's a reason we're here."

"There is. We rushed into Forestglare with a lame plan and I was an idiot. So?"

"Not that." She looked down, bit her lip, then looked back at him. "I want to apologize for how I treated you. When we were kids. It was horrible and I have no excuses."

He waved his hand. "Oh, please. You think I care about some stupid stuff from years ago?"

"Maybe you don't. I do. If it helps, the whole plan to shame you—"

"I don't want to hear about it." Trying to be polite with Cayla didn't work.

"It wasn't my idea. The girls, it was them, which doesn't excuse me—"

"I asked you to stop. I'm not interested in helping you feel better about yourself. You did it, own it."

"I am owning it. And I was wrong. It was cruel, it was stupid, and I hate the person I was. I know it doesn't change anything, but I really wanted to say I'm sorry. I've always been sorry."

"You're delusional. I'd rather you hate me than feel sorry for me."

"Sorry for me. For *my* actions. People died because of a stupid game."

That didn't make any sense. "What do you mean?"

Cayla was startled. "You don't know? Anna and her sister, and their family. They were sent away—and had an accident."

Was she accusing him of what he thought? "I never told this to anyone. Not a single person knows about what you did. I wasn't aware they died in an accident. I think it's sad, but I have nothing to do with it."

She had tears in her eyes. "I do. I told my father."

He snorted. "You know who to blame, then."

Cayla started bawling, and it was awkward because Sian wanted it to stop but didn't know what to do.

She spoke between sobs. "I know I'm a horrible person. Nobody should be my friend."

What? "I didn't mean you. I meant your father."

She shook her head. "Karina's in danger. Alessa's hurt. I don't even know if she's alive or not."

"Alessa? The same Alessa?"

Cayla nodded. "We almost died together." She dried her eyes with the back of her left hand. The right arm looked terrible and that worried Sian more than anything. But worry wouldn't fix it.

"Blaming yourself is not going to help anyone," he said.

She still wept.

Sian added, "And for the record, I never had any resentment against you. I just thought you were a little snob and self-centered, that's why I wasn't very friendly, but no resentment. And I might have been wrong."

"When I met Darian, you tried to separate us."

Now she was getting to a real reason he didn't like her, and hoped she didn't push it because it wasn't proper to upset someone already crying. He had to be honest, though. "Well, of course. I wanted my brother alive. Unlike you." He shouldn't have added this last part, but then, he wasn't in a very hypocrite mood.

"How could I have known my father would want to kill him if he saw us together?" At least she stopped crying.

"Oh, really? Why didn't you present him to your father, then? Why meet in secret?"

"We were just starting. We were just friends."

"I'll take it. You had no idea he could have died. Fine. I warned you, though. I warned you and you didn't listen."

"I didn't think it was true."

"You could have checked."

"I was fourteen. I was in love."

"Selfish love, Cayla, because Darian almost died because of that."

"Right. You're going to tell me you weren't the one who betrayed us?"

"Are you out of your mind? I was fifteen. I had to duel and kill a man. You think it's easy? You think it's fun? You think I didn't have nightmares about it for years? How do you think I felt, learning that I was about to lose the brother that I had just found? The only decent family I had? The brother I'd been trying to protect?"

"It didn't look like you cared about him."

"Well, because *he* didn't care. What was I supposed to do? It takes two to be friends. That didn't mean I couldn't watch his back."

Cayla watched him for a moment, then said, "You two need to talk. Darian loves you, Sian, despite everything."

Sian snorted. "Despite everything. Cause I'm obviously not worthy of my virtuous brother's love."

"That's not what I said. Plus, I saved you. I teleported you from outside a tower. It's not normal magic. You know how I did it? Love. Love for your brother, because I knew he would be devastated if something happened to you."

"He'll be upset about your arm."

"Well, I'm pretty sure he thinks your life is worth more than my arm. And so does Karina. That's two people already, even if you disagree."

"Fine. Fine. I don't hate you, I don't hate my brother, I don't hate anyone. You do have good reasons to dislike me, though, after you almost died and saw your friend almost dying—because of me. I accept that."

"True. But still, you're Darian's brother. We can't hate each other."

"Hate is a waste of time and energy. I don't entertain such stupid notions."

"Great. I also think you like Karina, and she likes you. I just hope you find better ways to show your feelings than deceiving and manipulating."

"Yeah, I was totally planning on doing that, since it worked so well last time." Again Cayla was poking his wounds.

"You can't say it didn't, though."

"Yeah, I almost destroyed Whyland, almost got her killed, almost got you killed, plus I ended up in this place for months, and almost got killed. I kind of noticed I made some mistakes, you know?"

Cayla shrugged. "Perhaps that was the only way you knew how to love."

"Yeah, sure." Again he looked at her arm, and more than feeling worried, he welcomed the opportunity to leave that conversation. "Listen, the Maris have a type of medicine. It could help your arm. It might be scary, though."

Cayla rolled her eyes. "Right. I'm going to be terrified of a medicine."

Sian smirked. Just because of her attitude he decided not to explain to her what he was going to do. He opened the door, went to the middle of the tower, climbed the steps to the top and rang the bell.

A few minutes passed when he heard a familiar set of wings. Komiak. Sian realized that it hadn't all been awful when he lived in the mountain with that tribe. The terrible days had been when he'd come to this tower, hurt, guilty, and alone.

Sian walked towards the giant bird and hugged his chest. "Thank you for being my friend."

Komiak had brought the stone. "Are you back to assume the throne?"

"No. I'm leaving. I might never come back. You have many tribes, though, you don't need a king, do you?"

"There's already a lot of infighting."

This wasn't Sian's problem. "Hopefully things will settle down. Is there an official way for me to quit?" He was wondering if he'd have to sign something, which was ridiculous, as they didn't have paper.

"No," the stone replied. "If you're not here to claim it, you'll lose it."

Sian nodded. That was good. "What happened to the others? No Maris tried to attack us since we got here."

"We have rain, plants, more animals. Less hungry. Less desperate. Humans taste horrible."

Sian chuckled, wondering if they would be half as bad as those terrible worms. "That was fast."

"Three moon cycles."

That was a lot more than the time he'd passed in the Light Gardens. Perhaps there was a time difference. There was something Sian had to say.

"I'm sorry. For the killings."

"They were cowards to attack you like that and deserved to die."

Maris had a more brutal view of the world. Perhaps living among them for so long had affected him. He still felt bad. Sian got to the part that mattered. "I need a favor. My sister is here. She's hurt."

THEY OPENED the door to the room where Cayla was sitting. She saw Komiak and opened her mouth as if to scream, but perhaps decided against it. "What, what, what's this, Sian?"

She was terrified, and Sian was a terrible person because he had to suppress his laughter. "A friend. He'll help your arm heal."

Komiak approached Cayla while she let out a deafening scream.

KARINA WOKE UP IN FORESTGLARE, tied to a chair with some brilliant rope. She was by their well, a transparent blue energy ball around her. Her muscles were still paralyzed. Sat watched her. He'd been responsible for bringing her in. Instead of upset, she felt relieved, as she realized she still had her memories. Memories she didn't want to access right now, otherwise she'd be giving them to Satwak.

He had a pleading look.

*Are you sorry or something?* She thought.

He looked away and called someone, "She's awake."

Karina heard steps approaching her chair. Firis, with a relief sigh. "Finally we can get this over with." He turned to Karina. "So sad. You'd have made a lovely consort. Alas. You chose otherwise."

"We'd better do the transmission soon," Satwak said.

Firis stepped in the bubble and stood beside her chair running his fingers through her hair, but she couldn't move away. A light shone in front of her.

The old man said, "This is a message not for the Guardians, but for those of you who dare defy us. Here we are, in Forestglare, where the population received us gladly and has participated enthusiastically in all the festivities. We came in peace and mean to harm nobody.

"Still, there are some of you who have threatened our appointed queen; my betrothed. We plead with you not to disturb our peace and happiness nor our upcoming nuptials. As you can see, she's very scared and very shaken. She hasn't been hurt, hasn't been tortured, and we plead that it may continue so. As a peaceful city, we ask for understanding, for a truce, at least until all the nuptials are completed."

The light faded. It wasn't hard to understand the man's twisted words; he was basically saying, "Come and get her or else..."

Karina still couldn't talk. She didn't think the man really wanted to marry her or anything similar, not after what she'd told him, but he could hurt her.

"He'll come, uncle, and he'll be so upset he'll be an easy prey. You'll never have to worry about anyone defying your true claim or disrupting the peace in Lumina."

"I still wish we had caught him when you first lured him here. Your secrecy had a high price, Satwak."

"I didn't want to raise false hopes." He lowered his head. "But I was wrong."

Karina would need to escape before anyone else risked their lives for her. But she couldn't try to come up with an escape plan with Satwak beside her. She wasn't even sure what he wanted anymore.

"Uncle, I still think you should have caused her some pain."

"Right. And alert all the Guardians. My message was for one person only, and only that person should react to it."

"He might bring reinforcements."

Firis' smile could only be described as evil. "Let's hope he does."

17

## A NOTE

The sun still hadn't risen when Darian opened his eyes. Cayla wasn't in his room. Well, she also had her room, not that she used it much. He closed his eyes again. No. She wouldn't be there. There was something else happening. Their last encounter flashed through his mind. True, he'd been very close to connecting with his magic, but that should never have been at the price of ignoring her.

He checked her bedroom. Empty. No, there was something; a note on the bed. Only after reading it three times the meaning dawned on him.

*Gone to Forestglare with Sian to rescue Karina.* He hadn't seen Cayla's friend in the transmission, and neither had Leena. But Cayla had certainly seen something—and so had Sian. His brother's indisposition gained another meaning. How could Darian have been so dumb? So focused on himself, on waking up his magic, when the people closest to him were suffering. He crumpled the paper, the proof of his shame.

The sun was rising when Darian knocked on Leena's door. She took a couple minutes and came out wearing a dress, eyes half closed. "What's wrong?"

"I don't want to disturb you. I mean, of course I'm disturbing you. I have a question. Is it possible to teleport to the Light Gardens using a different, unknown portal?"

"Everything's possible. From where do you think people are going to teleport?"

"Forestglare."

She shook her head. "It's the second most isolated ethereal city, right after Lumina, and it's obvious why."

"True, but, could one *go* to Forestglare?"

The woman thought for a moment. "Well, yes. All the efforts are into blocking people from going out." She frowned. "You didn't wake me up at this time for a theoretical conversation, did you?"

"No. I—"

"Come in."

Darian entered and she closed the door after him. "Just tell me what's happening."

Should he tell her? Well, he'd need as much help as possible. "Cayla and Sian went to Forestglare."

"Sian?" She had a horrified expression.

"Well, yes. Cayla says the queen she saw was Karina. If my brother went with her, and if he collapsed when he saw the transmission, he probably saw the same thing."

She put her hand on her forehead and shook her head. "Not him, not him."

Neat how she just ignored Cayla, but it didn't matter. "I think they'll be stuck there. Or they already are."

She touched his chin and lifted his face. "You're different."

"Yeah, I spent three days meditating."

Her eyes pierced him. "Well, use it, then."

"Use what?"

"What you've awoken."

Darian sucked in a breath.

Would they just leave Karina sitting there, in the blue bubble? Satwak was still sitting near her, and it was super annoying because she'd never be able to escape if someone were to predict her movements.

He seemed lost in thought.

Karina wanted to bring him back to reality. She tried to speak but she couldn't. What a horrible feeling. She wondered if that was what they did to the attendants in the Lumina castle. She decided to project a thought. *Hey, I'm hungry. Is that how you treat your prisoners?*

Satwak looked at her. "Count yourself lucky. The treatment our prisoners get is usually ten times worse."

*Yay, thanks for the unusual hospitality.*

He just shrugged.

How could Satwak be so dumb? Yeah, dumb, and she hoped he heard it. Firis had almost killed him and didn't look like he was too interested in his nephew's survival.

"Can you hear me?" Sat asked. She looked at him, but he was looking away, his mouth closed. "I'm projecting my thoughts," he added. This time she knew he wasn't speaking. Not out loud, at least. Quite weird.

*Yeah, I can hear you,* she thought.

"This has been my life; not knowing if I'll survive until the next day."

*You could have hidden, you could have let me escape.*

"They would have found you. By catching you, I got a little goodwill from my uncle. That's my game, to stay alive and free for as long as possible, until my work is done."

*But how can you do your work? If Sian comes here, what chances does he have against all these people?*

"He's smart, isn't he? That's what I saw in your mind; someone who plans things well. Let's count on that."

*That's a huge risk. What about me? You swore an oath to protect me, Sat.*

"I haven't broken it." He looked elsewhere and it was quite creepy to hear his voice like that. "You're still safe and unharmed."

*Not thanks to you, who suggested your uncle torture me.*

"Suspicious of my motives as he is, he did the opposite I suggested. You should thank me. Anyway, projecting thoughts like this is tiring. I'll stop it now, but please be on the watch. I might do it again, when the need comes."

This mental talk left Karina with a nauseous feeling in her stomach. "Hoping for the best" was a recipe for disaster as far as a plan went.

Sian was upset at himself, feeling the time passing by while he remained in this place, unable to do anything.

"I'm getting hungry," Cayla said.

"Well, trust me on this one, you'll want to be the hungriest hungry before tasting the local food."

Cayla shrugged. "I guess I'll trust you."

She was quiet for a while, then said, "You're still upset."

"Me? Upset? You think? Outrageous. Why would that be?"

She sighed. "I gave it some thought. The guy, Satwak, he won't let them hurt Karina. If he has a sister that he wants to protect, he'll make sure Karina's safe."

"Not really. Do I look like someone who'd leave an innocent... Fine. Scratch that. I might *look* like someone who'd leave an innocent person vegetating forever. But that guy saw my mind. He knows I'm not like that. I'm no hero, though. I'm not going to risk my life to fix a problem that's not mine."

"He'll want to make sure you care about their problems, then."

Sian waved a finger. "And that's the issue, he won't want us to rescue Karina until his city is free, and he doesn't understand we have no clue how to do it and perhaps no power to do it. And there's another possibility. Maybe he was lying. Maybe he wanted to lure me there, to kill the royal line, whatever they think I am."

"Didn't he go talk to you alone, though? He would have gotten you killed or imprisoned, not allowed you to escape."

"I almost got killed, didn't I? That's the thing. Plus, regardless of what exactly he wants, we have no reason to believe anyone there cares about her well-being."

"He does. If he expects you to go back there."

"Maybe. But I bet he has no idea I'm stranded in another dimension."

"I told you. We'll get back soon."

Her optimism was unnerving. But then, Sian took another look at her arm and felt bad for getting annoyed at her cheerfulness. He'd seen people with a lot less serious injuries lying down, moaning, crying, and thinking they were dying. If he hadn't seen it with his own eyes, he'd think she wasn't hurt at all, and only his knowledge of anatomy allowed him to realize that his sister-in-law was probably in horrible pain. One more reason to worry.

Cayla smiled and got up. "Hear that?"

Sian had a pretty good ear, but he heard nothing. "What?"

"Darian!"

Cayla ran out of the chamber to the main hall. There were no Maris around, but still Sian didn't think it was a good idea. Plus, perhaps the girl was hallucinating. He got up and followed her.

He'd never been so happy to see his brother. Not that he could see his face, which was about to blend into Cayla's in a kiss that should have been left for a more private moment. Sian looked away, and saw a blond woman. Slightly familiar. His brother was still almost crushing Cayla's bones—which was not a good idea.

"Darian," Sian yelled. "She's hurt."

Darian stepped away from Cayla and said, "We'll take care of it."

Sian looked down. Regret and shame were stupid, and yet, he barely had words to apologize or explain. Then he felt Darian in front of him, and his brother's arms around him. "I'm sorry," Darian said. "I shouldn't have ignored you."

The hug felt awkward. Sian pushed Darian's arms. "Nothing to be sorry. Take care of Cayla." He then whispered. "It's serious."

Darian nodded, not half as worried as he should. Had it been Karina hurt like that, Sian would be freaking out. Maybe worse, maybe he'd be killing everyone around him with his bizarre magic. A great thing Darian wasn't like him.

Cayla approached Darian. "How did you find us?"

"I can always find you."

"I thought it was the necklace."

"So did I. We were wrong."

Sian looked away and recognized the blond woman; she had been the previous king's wife. Sian bowed. "Nia. Good to see you."

"Same here," she said, then added. "I'll teleport you one by one."

"I can teleport," Cayla said.

Nia shook her head. "Not where we're going, and you're too hurt to try anything."

The woman held Sian's hand. He saw flashes of light, then opened his eyes and found himself in a tall circular structure, a teleporting tower, with white sparkly stone. The woman disappeared, then brought Darian, then Cayla. She was quite a fast teleporter, and it was odd, because Sian had never known she could do any magic.

"Where are we?" Cayla asked.

"Brighteria," the woman replied.

That was the ethereal city with a portal leading to South Whyland.

She continued, "We didn't want to take risks and open a passage to the Light Gardens, since they're being so closely watched. You'll have to stay here for a while."

No way Sian would sit idly while Karina was in danger. "I have things to do."

"I've heard," Nia said. "And you'll be able to do them."

They walked outside the tower to a hallway with the same kind of material on its walls which soon gave way to windows on both sides from where Sian saw the depths of a cliff they were crossing.

"I thought you were overseas," Cayla said.

Nia shook her head. "My mother was from here. I came to visit—and stayed."

"Is my little brother here?" she asked.

True, Nia had been pregnant before she disappeared. That would have been Cayla's half sibling.

Nia smiled. "He is."

"I want to see him."

"Sure." She pointed to Cayla's arm. "After we fix this."

Finally. A sensible person. The girl had her arm half-chewed and here they were talking pleasantries. Perhaps better than Sian, who hadn't bitten back his tongue when they were in Marisia. But he'd been a pile of nerves. Silly excuse.

They came to a patio, then Nia took a side door and went down narrow stairs. "We don't want a lot of people knowing you're here," she said with an apologetic look.

The stairs led to a door, then to a valley, where they walked for a few minutes. Sian was reconsidering his opinion that they were sensible, if they were going to spend so much time walking. He took a look back. It was a large castle, its white walls glistening in the moonlight, with high towers. This city looked more like a kingdom, like Whyland, than just a city.

Eventually they reached a small stone house.

Nia opened its door. "Just Cayla. You two can't go in."

"For what?" Cayla protested.

"They'll heal you. Come."

Darian kissed the top of her head. "Go. Brighteria healers are among the best."

Nia took her inside and came out alone a few seconds later. "She'll heal. Don't worry." Her words were directed to Sian.

"I'm sorry," he muttered to Darian.

"It's fine. Come. We have a lot to discuss."

They walked away from the house, but not back to the castle, and then came to another house. Not a house, as it consisted of one single room with a large table. It was more like a meeting room. Leena was sitting there. Nia left.

Sian took a deep breath. This was the part where he had to tell them what had happened. Now, if it was hard for himself to accept how stupid he'd been, it was horrible to have to admit it. Twice. Plus he'd have to explain how he'd agreed to help Cayla without telling Darian and how she'd gotten hurt saving him. But he needed the help and didn't know who else to ask.

Darian didn't take it half as badly as Sian expected, though. He listened in silence, without any protest.

After Sian finished, Darian was silent for a while, then said, "Sian, anyone in your place would have done the same."

Sian snorted. "Really? Like believing in some nonsense the guy told me? Letting Karina go back?"

Darian shook his head. "You're looking at it the wrong way. Aren't you the strategist? From an intel-collecting perspective, there was no failure. With information, you can take the right action, which you couldn't before."

Sian stared at his brother, wondering if he was all right.

Darian turned to Leena. "Do you know more? About Sian's magic and the possibility he's some kind of lost royal?"

"Well, yes," the woman sounded cautious. "I'm one of the only people who knew Sian's secret." She turned to Sian. "I thought you knew it too, and that was why you were so worried that I saw the symbol on your chest."

Sian hated that talk, and hated that she'd seen him. "No. I had no idea. Just... for some odd reason I feel uncomfortable when people see me without my shirt, so I don't like it." Perhaps because of the dozens of scars bringing back lovely childhood memories, but he didn't want to talk about them.

"It's possible your mother told you not to show it. She was a powerful spell speaker, and if she's given you a suggestion when you were still a small child, it would stick in your mind."

Sian wanted to change the subject. "Can the Guardians or people from the ethereal cities help us?"

"That's what's tricky," the woman said. "And dangerous. Nobody can know about you, Sian. There was a time when Lumina conquered every single ethereal city. People were killed, enslaved. The memory is still raw even if that hasn't happened for generations. Some of the guardians could want to kill you."

That made no sense. "Aren't the guardians the good guys?"

The woman tilted her head. "Good is relative. They'd be doing it to get rid of a bigger evil."

Quite ridiculous. Sian wasn't the nicest person in the world, but he certainly wasn't worse than those people who killed teenagers.

Before Sian could point that out, Darian spoke, "They believe Lumina will go back to its full power if their royal line is reestablished."

Leena nodded. "Exactly. And that was why Sian had to be hidden as a child."

That made no sense. "In the castle? In plain sight?"

"Ethereal people aren't too concerned with what happens elsewhere. If Bianca said her son was dead, they wouldn't go and investigate it. They had no reason to suspect anything. Nobody had any reason, in fact. The Lumina special skill hasn't shown up for years, and we have no idea from where it comes in your lineage, just that it's there. Now that you're old enough, you can hide your powers."

"Like when they exploded in that room?"

Leena shook her head. "I had no idea you were so unstable. I was going to talk to you and suggest you stay away from the Light Gardens, I just didn't have the time."

Sian shrugged. "I'm not even interested in your ethereal city. I was forced to stay there, remember?"

"What would you do in my place? You hear about a breach in

Lumina, and that they came to Whyland. Who do you suspect they are looking for?"

Whatever. Those things didn't matter. "Fair enough. What I want to know is what I can do, how my magic manifests in Lumina."

"Nobody knows. I searched for it. It's been erased from all archives."

"Excellent. And the good guys could have killed me just because in theory I have a power they have no clue what it is."

"People fear the unknown," Darian said. He had gotten weird in these last few days. Too calm and philosophical.

Sian sighed. "I just want to get Karina back. I feel pity for Lumina, but it's not for me to fix it."

Leena fixed her eyes on Sian. "You'll need to go to Lumina, find your magic, overpower their army, and then you'll be able to get her back."

"Just that?"

"Exactly," the woman agreed.

Sian didn't understand how she could say all that with a straight face.

Darian reached out his arm and touched Sian's shoulder. "I'll help you."

"Wow, thanks, that multiplies my odds for two. Now let's see... zero times two..."

"You're forgetting your magic," Darian insisted.

"Right. The magic I have no clue how to control and nobody has any idea how it works in Lumina. Now, really. I do accept your help, but I'm not overpowering an army on my own. That's just absurd." He turned to Leena. "Maybe, if the Guardians loosen the hold on the portals, maybe Karina can teleport away."

Leena shook her head. "Too risky. She could be mind-controlled or brainwashed again and bring the Lumina forces with her."

"I thought I could overpower them. Have no fear. Super me will be around."

"You need to go to Lumina for your power."

Sian sighed.

Darian then said, "I'll tell you what I propose to do: we can open a passage to Lumina from here. We can get old diagrams and maps from the city and find a way in, an improvised tower. You go there, try to find your magic, see if you can do something. If you can, you teleport to Forestglare with your new power and get Karina back. If you can't, you come back and we try something else."

Sian would hate to return empty-handed again. Everything about this plan sounded even worse than Cayla's plan, and look where it had gotten them into. And there was another problem.

He turned to Leena. "Isn't my magic depleted, though?"

"I don't know. How do you feel?"

"I sure don't feel magical."

"It's been a day, and you recovered well," Leena said. "While you might not be able to explode and kill everyone around you, you should be able to do something."

*Should. Maybe. I don't know.* This wasn't a way to plan things. Sian closed his eyes. He recalled his fight against the Maris, and how his magic had saved him. If he could connect to that power again, he had good odds. He didn't know if he had to go to Lumina, though. But maybe it would be good to find out about that place.

"So the suggestion is just to get to Lumina, check it out, see if I find my magic, and then go to Forestglare?"

"Pretty much," Darian confirmed.

Sian tapped his fingers on the table. "Right. So, meanwhile, aren't these Guardians supposed to take care of interdimensional stuff? What are they doing?"

Leena shook her head. "Caught in some debate. Lumina got Forestglare to sign as if the occupation hadn't been an invasion, so the Guardians have no legal grounds for a retaliation. The other issue is that they fear Lumina, so most of them are strengthening their own city protections."

"Why is Brighteria helping?" Sian asked.

"Not all of Brighteria," Darian replied. "We got Nia to help because she likes Cayla. We'll be doing some illegal portals. But it helps that Brighteria doesn't get along with the Guardians much, so they won't be paying attention here."

Leena got up. "Come. You'll have to regain your strength."

Sian kind of agreed with that despite his anxiety. They went to another house, close by, this time. It was a family house, with a young man with dark brown hair and a blond toddler. The young man was setting the table. "Welcome. Nia and Cayla should join us soon."

His voice was familiar. "Do I know you?" Sian asked.

He reached out his hand. "My name's Talon. I'm Lylah's brother."

Another hidden brother. Interesting. "What are you doing in Brighteria?"

He smiled. "Came to visit and stayed."

Sian still felt he knew the man, but he didn't know from where, which was odd, since he was good at remembering people's faces and names—a great trick to get more allies.

THERE WAS a thrill going through Darian. He still hadn't told anyone about the magic he'd found. He'd been upset that connecting with it had led him to neglect Cayla and his brother, but now he felt that it had been the right decision.

Someone knocked at the door. Nia opened it and entered with Cayla, who had changed into a light blue dress. Other than a bandage on her arm, she seemed fine. Darian glanced at his brother's funny expression then rushed to hug her.

"How are you?"

Cayla smiled. "Much better." She then whispered, "Can we come outside for a moment?"

They left the house. Darian looked at her arm. "Once I had an accident and Brighteria healers also gave me a miracle recovery. We have that in common now."

She smiled. "Yeah... I'm glad it's fixed."

"You were very brave. Thank you for saving my brother."

Cayla squinted. "Have you told him that? Because he annoyed me to no end, complaining you'd prefer my arm to his life."

Darian just closed his eyes. "That's Sian." He was going to make some other joke when it suddenly hit him that it was exactly like his brother to think Darian valued so little his life. The thought stung, not that he felt offended, but rather sorry—or guilty.

"What?" Cayla asked.

Darian shrugged. "Maybe I failed to show him how much I value him."

She rolled her eyes. "Oh, my. Could it be because he disappeared and conspired against you? He never reached out to you other than when he needed, Darian. I'm not saying he's a horrible person, I'm just saying that it goes both ways."

"Both ways. And perhaps I should consider mine."

"You're here. You're helping him. That's what matters." She sighed. "There's something I wanted to tell you."

"Yes?"

"The Luminous sent another transmission. It's a veiled threat against Karina. She's in Forestglare, and the Lumina overseer wants Sian there before the end of the day. He's threatening to hurt her or... other stuff."

"How long do we have?"

It was Nia who spoke, "A couple hours."

It felt weird to realize their conversation was being overheard, but that wasn't the worst.

Darian rested his forehead on his palm. "We lost so much time..." He then looked at Nia. "We need to show Sian the transmission."

"No." Cayla held his wrist. "I thought about it. I don't think it's a good idea. He's... he's not well, Darian. If he sees that, he'll do something stupid."

"Should we just lie to him?'

"You say it as if you didn't enjoy lying."

More than she knew, and than even he had known until recently.

Darian nodded. "Fine. Cayla, I just need you to teleport Sian to Lumina. Can you do that?"

"Of course."

"Wait a second," Nia said. "I agreed to help, but I'm not helping with a suicide mission. This is just insane."

"But it's not—" Cayla started to protest.

Darian cut her. "No, no, Nia might have a point. Come inside and we'll discuss this. We won't do anything you don't agree with, Nia."

Cayla squinted at him. She was so lovely when she was angry, Darian wanted to kiss her, but instead he just whispered in her ear, "Trust me."

18

ILLUSIONS

Sian noticed that there was something slightly off about Darian when he came back with Nia and Cayla. And there was something definitely off with her arm. He wasn't crazy; he knew about injuries. That recovery was impossible. Great news, though. One less worry in Sian's mind.

Cayla embraced the little boy and Lylah's brother. So this was Nia's house. Some shared looks between Nia and Talon revealed a little more. Sian felt as if he was invading something quite intimate. A happy home. This was something he'd never seen before. Perhaps with Malena and Raja, but that had been after the woman had been through so much pain. Here, there was something almost sacred about the quietness and peace, the love that was palpable in the air. It just gave Sian sadness and longing, since he didn't know if he'd ever have any of that.

Darian came to him and whispered, "I'll need you to convince Nia to help us."

Strange. "Why me?"

"I think you're the real spell speaker between the two of us."

Great. "How many magical powers I don't know how to use am I going to have to try today?"

"Forget magic, just try to convince her the way you convince people when you want to. She says she won't help with a suicide mission."

Sian sighed. "Well, that's a tricky one. You know I hate to lie. How am I going to tell her it's anything but what she's thinking?"

Darian shrugged. "Don't know. You're the spell speaker, Sian."

Right. Sian was everything.

Darian added, "I have to do something with Cayla, I'll be right back."

CAYLA DIDN'T UNDERSTAND why Darian had to watch the transmission so many times.

"Trying to come up with a plan?"

Darian stroked his chin as if thinking. "I think I *have* a plan."

"Care to share?"

"It's what I told you. Just teleport Sian to Lumina. From there, the passage is open to Forestglare and he'll be able to teleport without help."

"And if he isn't?"

"You're the backup."

That still sounded like a very lame plan. "Fine, but he made me promise I'd not save his ass again."

"I don't think you'll have to do anything, Cayla. I'd never make you risk your life. I'm sorry it came to it earlier. It was my fault. Maybe if I had helped..."

Cayla disagreed. "I should have insisted. Talked to you more."

Darian shook his head. "You tried." He embraced her in a tight hug. Tugged in his arms, there was no place for fear or worry. He then whispered, "And you're the bravest person I know. That's only one of the million reasons why I love you."

She broke the hug to look him in the eyes. "Really?"

He ran his hand through her face, ending at her lips. "More than I can put into words, and when I do they sound all wrong. 'I love you' doesn't quite convey what you mean to me. But I guess it's the closest I have, and I should have said it more often."

Cayla's heart was beating fast and she was at a loss for words. She closed her eyes, enjoying the sensation, his touch, then his lips against hers, as they dissolved into a kiss.

KARINA WAS STARVING and was almost glad for it because at least she wasn't focusing on her fear. She'd spent so long wondering what would be like to see Sian again. It had been better than in her dreams—but so short, and now she risked never seeing him again. Not only him, her family, her friends, everything. She had no idea what was going to happen to her but she doubted Firis would just allow her to live normally in Lumina after what had happened. She took a deep breath. The fault had been hers, trusting the wrong people, trying to open a teleporting tower where there shouldn't be any. A tear ran down her eyes. Was ignorance a decent excuse for anything?

Satwak hadn't moved from his chair. He was probably starving too. He hadn't tried to communicate since earlier, and neither had Karina. There were guards all over the clearing with the well. Funny that Forestglare should have everything outdoors like that. Didn't it rain? It should rain if it was a forest.

A flash of lightning, then a low rumbling came as a response. Right. Because nothing could get worse. Well, rain would affect their visibility, so perhaps it wasn't so bad. Thick droplets hit the ground, but Karina didn't feel wet. The water was running on the circular ball shield around her, and she was dry. After a couple minutes, a girl was brought to the clearing and cast a shield, protecting all the area from the water. So that was Karina's answer.

With dark clouds in the sky, the day was turning into night. The wind was shaking the trees. A lightning bolt illuminated the area.

When it was gone, Karina couldn't believe her eyes, and couldn't drown her horror.

Sian was there, on the opposite side of the well. He glanced at her. There was something wrong about his glance, though. It lacked Sian's intensity. This was more like a curious glance. He walked forward and raised his bare hands.

"I come in peace. Let her go, and you can have me."

This was unlike Sian. Couldn't he see all the guards among the trees? Couldn't he see that if he was giving himself away there would be nothing left to negotiate? No. Sian was smarter than that.

"Kill him!" Firis voice came from beside Karina.

Satwak got up. "Uncle, no! This is your chance to prove that you're the true ruler of Lumina. They're all watching."

Sian pointed to Firis. "That is not your true overseer. It's me. Here's your chance to lay down your arms. You have a prophecy, don't you? The Royal line keeps the prosperity in Lumina. Well, that's me."

"I'm going to repeat once." Firis' voice was fierce and certain. "Whoever dares defy me will pay the price. Kill him."

Metal balls and energy rays were directed at Sian. They hit a shield. Karina's heart was thumping on her chest. She wanted to scream and yell so many things. Sian was not casting the shield, though, because he had a look of surprise.

"Keep firing!" Firis yelled. "Whoever is shielding him won't be able to hold for long."

Thunder roared in the sky. Karina glanced at Sat. He looked elsewhere, but seemed focused. Was he the one shielding Sian? Firis walked towards his nephew. This wasn't good. He was about to put his hand on Sat's head when the young man got up, turned, and tried to stab his uncle. With a wave of a hand, Firis sent Satwak far from where he was. The shield around Sian disappeared, and all the rays and balls hit him at once. This was like sleep paralysis. Karina was unable to move, unable to scream, as her worst nightmare took form in front of her.

~

SIAN TOOK a deep breath as he stood in the Brighteria teleporting tower. He'd gotten his brother's promise that he would rescue Karina if Sian failed, and that made it easy to walk into what could be certain death.

It felt odd to repeat his failed experience and teleport with Cayla again, but it was different with Darian having encouraged them. Nia had taken some convincing. Sian still wasn't sure about his so-called spell-speaker ability, but he knew how to charm when he wanted to. Of course, he had to tell his secret, but she didn't strike him as the murderous type. Hopefully she wouldn't babble, but he wasn't thinking far ahead anyway. His goal now was to get Karina and make up for his previous mistake. Hopefully he'd never set foot in an ethereal city again.

Cayla held his hand and soon he had to close his eyes due to the strong flashes of light. He opened his eyes when he felt his body submerged. They were in a tall tower all right, but it was a water reservoir. Sian swam up until his head emerged and he caught a long breath.

Cayla emerged a few seconds after him. "I guess it's wetter than we thought."

"Aren't we glad it's water, not grains?"

Cayla chuckled, then got serious. "Sure you want to go alone?"

"It's my destiny, isn't it?"

She nodded. "Good luck." Then she swam down and disappeared.

He felt a lot more at ease without having to worry about an additional person.

The tube was open on top and he swam to the edge. It wasn't simple, because the tower ended in an opening, like a funnel. Made with smooth metal, it was a hard climb. Sian removed his shoes, and only then, with the grip of his feet, he was able to make it to the border. Bare feet. Perhaps it could make a difference.

From the edge, he saw a glistening city under the dawning sun. Far away, on the top of a hill, a high tower, which was the main castle. From the top of it he should be able to get to the portal to Forestglare. Before that, he'd need to figure out how to get down from that water reservoir. He had an inkling that his special skill didn't allow him to fly. The tower was too tall for him to jump, and he was far from its outer wall to find a way to climb down.

He went to the edge, lay belly down and turned his body to see what was below. The outside of the tower wasn't smooth metal as he'd imagined. He dangled from the edge of the opening, then jumped in the direction of the reservoir—and slipped—until he found a groove for his feet, then hands, slowing his descent.

No alarm, no pursuers. It meant Lumina didn't have a system against intruders, or else he'd come up in such a weird place that whatever system they had didn't catch him.

Now all he had to do was walk to the main tower... and what? Declare himself the new king or whatever they called it? Sit somewhere and wait for his magical abilities to manifest? Well, at least he wasn't feeling weak, and if he had to fry some people, he'd hate it but he'd be able to do it. Hopefully that would be enough against the legendary Lumina might.

HER HEART TIGHT, Karina dared look at the place where Sian had been. Instead of his body, she found empty ground. But they didn't have time to remove his body. Her thoughts weren't making sense. Were her eyes betraying her?

"Find him!" Firis roared.

So Sian had disappeared. She didn't understand how, but cherished the idea that he'd be alive, hidden somewhere. Karina still couldn't move, though, and it was a problem.

Firis ran to her. "Show up or I'll cut her hands off."

He was about to touch her hand when she decided to make one last effort. *Push. Explode.*

"Don't." It was Sat's voice, inside her head. Karina gave up, but she wasn't sure she should listen to him. He added, "I released the magic binding you, but he'd better not know it yet. Use it when he's distracted."

That made sense. At the same time, if she didn't move away, the man's threat would make Sian show himself.

"He escaped once, he'll escape again." Sat's voice echoed in her head.

And she took too long to think because at this point her hand was being raised.

Sian's voice came from behind her. "I'm here."

Firis turned and shot a ray from his hand. Sian disappeared before the ray got him. Was he teleporting? This was Karina's chance. *Boom.* Firis fell down and she ran away.

"Take her," Firis yelled.

At this point the guards had dispersed, looking for Sian, who appeared somewhere else, because Firis yelled another set of instructions, which allowed Karina to run and find a tree to climb. She knew that staying close to Firis was dangerous, but she doubted she'd be able to run very far. She needed to get to the teleporting portal, but that was the place with the most security in Forestglare.

Firis then dragged Satwak to the middle.

"Karina," he called in a singsong voice. "If you don't show yourself I'll kill him."

Satwak wasn't really her friend. His goal was honorable, though, and he'd tried to help her. Karina felt torn.

Sian walked unopposed and reached the heart of the city, in front of the main tower. His feet hurt from the prickling of rocks and sticks.

That said, being barefoot had worked once, and he wasn't sure what he was going to face.

He found himself in a square with strange metal statues surrounding it. The tower stood above it, just a few steps away. Of course walking in the city would be completely different from entering a type of government building, though. He wondered if he should climb it. No, he'd be an easy target if someone spotted him from the outside. He closed his eyes. Did he feel different? Any special magic? Not that he knew.

"Halt!" a man yelled behind him.

Of course. Sian turned. The man had no visible weapons, but that shouldn't fool anyone, since at least in theory, everyone in Lumina had strong magic.

Sian raised his hands.

"Who are you?" the man asked.

A couple different answers went through Sian's head, like saying he was taking a stroll, just walking, whatever, but the man probably knew he didn't belong there.

"My name's Sian Keen. I'm your true overseer." He still thought the word was funny. "I'm here to take back what's mine." Just take. He wasn't planning on keeping it.

The man stared at him for a moment, then asked. "Can you prove it?"

That was interesting. Sian had expected a laugh or something else. Could he prove it, though? "If you know the symbol of the Royal line, I could—"

"Nobody knows it, and it could be forged. Regardless, if you are the lost royal, your powers should be unmatched. Show me."

The man didn't move, but some whooshing in the air attracted Sian's attention. Some ten metal balls were flying towards him, from all directions. With no idea how to fight against inanimate objects, Sian waited for them to get close and jumped down, dodging them. It didn't work, though, as the balls fell over him then floated again. Think, Sian. No, not think. If it was about magic, what he had to do was feel and react. Sian sent a current of electricity to the man, but it met a shield and dissipated. This wasn't good. If people from Lumina could cast shields against him, there was no way he could do anything with his power. The man sent an orange flair from his arm.

Sian took the opportunity to run away from the square, but before he could get far he was surrounded by about eight people.

"State your purpose and surrender!" a woman yelled.

Sian raised his hands again. "Firis is not very nice, is he? I'm here to depose him."

This time he did get some laughs. Perhaps he was attuning his sense of humor. Should Sian try again to use his magic against all these people? Would they block him? Before he made his mind, something hit him from behind and he collapsed. This wasn't going well.

# 19

# EMBRACING MAGIC

Karina pondered if she should try to help Sat, when she heard his voice, "Leave me. Firis is going to kill me anyway. Just try to save my sister."

No. This wasn't going to end this way. One smart argument to save Satwak was that he could see in people's minds, and therefore was a good ally.

Karina jumped down and walked towards the clearing. "I'm here."

Firis stabbed Satwalk's shoulder then grabbed Karina's hair. "Now it's time to hurt you."

"Impostor!" Firis yelled from the other side of the clearing. "Arrest him and protect the Forestglare queen!"

How could there be two Firis?

The guards were confused. Well, of course. While Karina had no doubts that the real Firis was the one holding her by the hair, Karina had been crowned in that place, and it wasn't logical that Firis would be threatening her so.

A couple guards approached the real Firis. He turned to attack them, and it was Karina's chance to run away.

While the two Firis had a shouting match, Karina came to Satwak. "Can you walk?"

"He paralyzed me," came his voice.

She grabbed him from beneath his arms and dragged him, meaning to hide them both. Satwak was bleeding too much, though. As she was away from Firis, she crossed Faizana. In silence, the girl put Satwak on her shoulder and carried him away. Hopefully what he had was just a silly wound for Lumina standards.

Karina came to the tree they'd been using to teleport. There was indeed confusion, as all that was left were two guards.

Before they could do anything, Karina pushed them away with her magic. She got in, hoping to teleport somewhere else, but it was like trying to go through a wall—unless...

Karina opened her eyes and recognized Lumina. That wasn't a lot of progress, but she just wanted to be away from Firis. Plus, if Sian's powers were bigger in Lumina, this was better. Sian. The more she thought about it, the less convinced she was that it was Sian who'd shown up in Forestglare a few minutes before.

Whoever had done it was the same person as the fake Firis, either casting illusions, teleporting fast, or both. Hopefully he'd be safe, whoever he was, and Satwak too. As much as she disliked "shoot first, ask questions later" Faizana, the girl cared about her brother.

There were about five guards around the tower.

Karina nodded and walked through them, trying to exude the confidence that wouldn't make them suspicious.

"Where are you going?" one of them asked just as she was about to cross the door.

She frowned. "Excuse-me? Since when do I answer to you? I'm under Firis orders. Now let me pass before he comes here and unleashes his fury."

She kept walking, aware of her steps reverberating in the hall. Despite everything that had happened, she still had her black dress and tiara. *Dress the part and act the part.* The castle was less guarded, probably because so many people had been sent to Forestglare. For some reason, she went to the window overlooking the square.

*There* she saw him. Unconscious and being carried inside. Sian.

This time she knew it was him, even if he was unable to pierce her with his intense stare. Four people surrounded him. Karina rushed to the elevator and went downstairs. She was about to meet the group head on, perhaps talk them into releasing Sian, but then she got the feeling it wouldn't work, and if it didn't, the price would be too high.

Karina hid and observed where they were going, following from a distance. They took the elevator to the second floor. Karina went up the stairs. Those people didn't try to muffle their steps, so she knew in which direction they had gone. The issue was that they weren't coming back.

Karina came to a poorly illuminated hallway and heard voices from its end, where there was a double door. She waited. Eventually, two of them passed by, and Karina saw her chance of going in. The place had innumerable horizontal glass containers where people lay suspended in a pink liquid. Sian lay at a table.

"We don't know if that's what we need to do with him," a young man said.

"No, but that way Firis can decide. Remember we're on high alert for an overseer impostor," the woman replied.

"What if he's telling the truth?"

She chuckled. "He'd be a tad bit more powerful, don't you think? It's not as if he gave us any fight. Disappointing."

Karina knelt behind a table, considering her options. She could fight them, perhaps by exploding some of those containers. No. She'd better wait.

SIAN WALKED BESIDE A RIVER, with no memory of how he'd gotten there. A woman with half her face hooded approached him.

When she removed her hood, Sian recognized that face. The face in the glass ball he'd broken, the face whose words he didn't want to hear. He turned and ran, but his legs were short and he couldn't run far. The woman scooped him up with one arm. His body was a child's.

"My love," she said. "Stay close."

Her other arm held a little bundle. No. A baby.

"Can you walk?" she asked.

Sian had to walk. Since the baby had come, he was always second. He was struggling behind when someone else scooped him up. His father. His mother turned back but instead of smiling she turned around and ran. Was she running from him? From his father? He yelled for his mother to return, and yelled, and yelled, and yelled, as she disappeared.

"Sian." Bianca's voice came from behind him.

Sian was alone, and turned. "I wasn't worth saving, was I?"

She shook her head. "It was the hardest decision in my life. Every day I remembered you, every day I thought about you, but I figured you were safe with your father. The Light Gardens protected me, but not you."

Sian snorted. "Very safe with my father."

"I did my best. I had people watching you. All I heard was that you were growing up to be a very strong and capable young man, happy, good-looking, popular. How was I to know?"

Sian was crying and he hated it. She didn't deserve his tears. "Yeah, I mean, it's not like people miss their mothers or anything."

"It was a mistake and I'm sorry."

She moved in to hug him and somehow he lacked the strength to push her away. It didn't feel good, it didn't feel bad. It just felt odd. She ran her fingers through his hair.

Sian then was on Malena's establishment, eating cake for the first time in his life. It wasn't that the castle didn't have cake, just that his father didn't let him eat it. And yet, his father had sent him there.

Even though he suspected that he hadn't been sent to eat cake, he pretended to believe it. For the first time, he heard what a good boy he was. Was he? Even though he failed and failed and failed? But Malena didn't care if Sian won or lost his fights, if Sian did or didn't do the tasks he was assigned. Somehow, just existing was enough for her. Despite no blood ties, she treated him well just because he was good. And Sian almost believed it, until he came back to the academy just to hear what a failure he was.

He was back by the river. Bianca said, "I always loved you, Sian. You were my firstborn and the light of my life."

"But duty was more important."

She shook her head. "Protecting you was more important."

Protecting him. Sian then found himself in the castle, where, by accident, he overheard his father. "Sian is the brightest jewel in Whyland."

It turned out that General Keen, far from hating Sian, was quite proud of his son's achievements. Achievements. Fighting. Sian's real achievements were in Siphoria, with Malena, when he learned as much as he could about handling a business, when he started to invest, when he realized he could change lives. All of this so far away.

Sian was then in the Light Gardens, outside his room. His mother walked to him. "Keeping you alive was more important than keeping you happy. I thought if you were away from the ethereal cities, you'd be able to lead a normal life, that destiny wouldn't catch up with you. But I was wrong. Now you have to find your magic. There's no escape, Sian, you'll have to face who you are."

Someone touched his face, held his neck. He felt lips on his. Strange. Children shouldn't kiss. But he wasn't one. He jolted awake and saw a familiar face in front of him. More than familiar, it was the face that washed away all the pain. "Karina?"

She smiled although her face had tears.

He felt as if he'd been unconscious for days. "How long has it been?"

"A few minutes."

He remembered then. They were in Lumina. How was Karina there? But the most important was being with her. "Can you teleport us away?"

"Look around you."

Sian realized his body was submersed in a weird glass tub. At least they hadn't undressed him. He looked around. Those people were undressed. Hundreds of them, in tubs like Sian's. "This is the stasis room."

Karina nodded.

"We could set them free," Sian said.

"I wouldn't know how to, uh, get them back to normal. You've just been put here and I already had a lot of trouble." She choked a sob. "I thought you were gone."

He reached out his hand and caressed her face. "I'm here. There's something I need to ask. Do you forgive me?"

"For your stupid decisions last time I came to Whyland?"

Sian nodded.

"Well," Karina started. "My decisions are not brilliant either. It's my fault Lumina had a portal to Forestglare."

He smiled. "I'm not going to complain. I was stranded in Marisia. They rescued me because of the Lumina breach. So I guess I have to thank you."

Karina looked horrified. "Marisia? How did you survive?"

"Lots of raw worms. But you saved me."

"I was having nightmares about you."

"Oh, c' mon, I'm not that ugly."

She laughed. "I thought you didn't lie. You know you're good looking."

"That was a joke, it didn't count." He took a deep breath. "I also dreamed about you." He looked around. "So, what should we do?"

"I used to think I didn't care about Lumina, but this..."

"I know. And I do have to wonder why life has brought me here, if it wasn't to do something. But I haven't found any special magic. My magic can't defeat them. Maybe they're wrong."

"I don't want you to get hurt."

Her eyes were so kind and calming. He realized she'd always look at him like that, regardless of what he did—within certain limits of course. Limits he almost crossed. He looked at her. "Do you love me?"

She was startled, then laughed. "Sian, usually people first declare their love, then wait to see if the other person says the same."

"Is there like a rule book or something? What's wrong with asking?"

"Loving is putting your heart out there, knowing it might be torn to pieces."

He sat up and straightened. "And willing to have your whole body torn to pieces? Does that count? Because I've done it for you. And I'd do it again if I had to."

"And yet you won't tell me what you feel."

"Do I have to? To the girl who won't answer my question?"

Karina laughed and shook her head. "Sian." He perked up his ears, glad she'd finally decided to give him an answer. "Someone was pretending to be you. In Forestglare. Who was it?"

That wasn't what he'd been expecting, and it was surprising. "I have no idea. What did they do?"

"It was good, created a distraction. That's how I escaped and ended up here. They also pretended to be Firis. I thought you were working together."

Sian was puzzled, confused, surprised. "No." He sighed. "They are probably distracting Firis so that I..." He looked down, then chuckled. "Do whatever magic I don't know how to do."

"It's fine. We can teleport away. This is not your responsibility."

By this she meant Lumina and that horrible room. Because she probably thought Sian wasn't this lost royal after all. Perhaps he should feel relieved that someone finally agreed with him, but he felt just a bit disappointed that she didn't trust him.

"I don't know. I don't know Karina. You know what the problem is? I lived an entire life away from magic. As much as I tried to learn about it, can reading for one year replace a lifetime?"

She touched his shirt, over the place where his heart was. "You don't need to know it. You feel it."

"Do you think I'm this Lumina person they think I am?"

"You are you, Sian, and whoever you are, you're here to find out. And we'll find a way regardless."

This was better. It wasn't that she didn't think he was in the royal line, it was that she just didn't care. Not because she didn't care about him, but because whatever role he had didn't matter.

He held her hand. "This time, promise, whatever happens, let's not break apart. Let's find another way. There's always another way."

He almost added *don't leave me*, but then decided it was perhaps too much.

Karina smiled. "We'll stick together."

Just then she turned. The door opened. Two people were thrown backward and fell on the floor. Karina had done it, with a burst of energy coming from nowhere. Sian was surprised. He knew she was powerful. He'd always known it, but he thought it was just teleporting. Dressed like a queen, with her mighty magic, Karina looked like a born ruler.

She pulled his hand. "Stop staring and let's run."

They went out of the room. The hall was empty other than the two people unconscious on the floor. "You have magic."

"No kidding."

He stopped. "No. It's serious. *You* can defeat them."

"I can't. This is nothing. The only reason I got these two was because they were caught by surprise. Had they fought, I'd have no chance."

She started running again and Sian followed. It felt weird not to have a plan. "Where are you going?"

"To the portal. We can go to Forestglare and then from there, teleport away."

"It's not that easy, Karina."

"It's our only shot."

Was it? Or could Sian try to do whatever he was supposed to do? His mind was getting clearer. It was as if being by Karina cast away all the shadows in his mind, the anguish, the pain, the anxiety. Such a powerful magician that she was, she looked at him as if he was so special. Special just for existing.

He had to ask again. "Karina, do you love me?"

"What's with the stupid questions?" Her voice had raised an octave to the point of being shrill. She was upset. But it was unfair. This was the most serious question he'd ever asked anyone. She stopped and turned, still looking annoyed. "Of course I do. I mean, within my understanding of—"

He silenced her with a kiss, which wasn't as well received as his kisses normally were, either because she was upset or because she was worried about escaping, but after a few seconds she softened, but just for a short while, as she eventually pushed him away.

"We can't do this here. We're in enemy territory, Sian."

He smirked. "Are we?"

Images flashed through his mind. The square. The statues. The balls. The walls. Once he stopped feeling like an intruder, once he stopped seeing everything as separated from him, the truth opened up to him. The floor rumbled.

Karina was startled.

"Don't worry. That's me." He kissed her forehead. "Just trust me. And stay close. Ah, I might get a little weird. Try not to worry, all right?"

Karina wasn't sure if she should feel glad or worried that Sian was finally finding some magic. She'd thought that they'd have a much better chance of survival by simply escaping. The floor kept rumbling beneath her, and now the walls shook. Sian had his eyes closed. Karina didn't ask what was happening from fear of disturbing his concentration.

Sian opened his eyes. "Good. Let's go to Forestglare. We have an army."

Was he all right? Again, she didn't want to say anything because he sounded so confident. If his army idea didn't work, they could try to teleport away. They came to the main hall with the elevators. No. The main hall. The elevators were broken on the bottom.

Sian looked. "Oops, that wasn't on purpose." His face then got serious, focused, almost distant.

The floor kept rumbling.

She was about to ask, "What..." Then Karina saw. The metal statues from the square, and more statues, moving up the stairs at incredible speeds, three or five steps at a time.

Sian was calm, focused. That probably meant those things weren't going to attack them. One of the giant statues grabbed Karina and then went back to the stairs, where it climbed.

They came across guards who were too shocked to do anything. One or two tried to shoot something towards the statues, but they paralyzed whoever tried to stop them.

At the portal, the thing dropped Karina on the floor. A hand pulled her. Sian's. But he didn't look at her, eyes focused on something in the distance. Would these things work outside Lumina, though? This was an open portal and anyone—or anything—could go through it.

Soon light consumed them and they were in Forestglare, followed by the moving metal statues. They came to the clearing by the well. Someone sat in the chair Karina had occupied. Darian.

And about ten guards charged towards them. That's when she understood what the statues could do; they reflected the person's magic. Some guards were immobilized, some were hit. Firis was soon pinned on the ground

Sian walked towards him. There was none of the sweet Sian, or even the sarcastic Sian. His face showed only ruthless determination. If she weren't on his side, she'd be scared. Oh, to be fair, right now, he was scary regardless.

Firis laughed. "Make one move, and your brother dies."

"Tell them all, tell them you accept me as your true overseer, and I'll give you a quick death."

"I'm not afraid of pain."

Sian crouched near him. "Aren't you? I guess we'll find out."

Karina then heard a shaky voice, "Kill him. Fast." Satwak.

She yelled, "He's dangerous and powerful!"

The statue holding Firis in place burst into many pieces. He got up and directed a ball of energy at Sian. It stopped midway.

"Pathetic effort," Sian sneered. "I could do this all day. But it's boring."

The ball returned to Firis, who shielded it. "I can say the same. You can't kill me. I have the magic of more than a hundred people flowing through me."

"Boring. You're not mine to kill, though."

Satwak came behind Firis and stabbed his back. The man turned and sent Sat flying away with a ray of energy. A stronger ray hit Firis. Faizana's.

"Leave my brother! And for my sister" she yelled.

Firis fell. His eyes were open, glassy, staring nowhere. Dead.

Sian blinked as if coming out of a trance, but just for a second. His angry face returned and he yelled, "I'm your new overseer. If anyone disagrees, please step forward and pledge your cause."

Of course nobody did.

"Karina, Karina." A desperate plea. Satwak.

Karina ran to where he lay. His head was bleeding.

He opened his eyes and spoke with difficulty. "Please. Please promise you'll free my sister, you'll restore order in Lumina. Promise."

A hand touched her shoulder. Sian's. "A deathbed promise is binding, Karina." His voice was soft.

"Promise," Sat insisted.

She turned to Sian. "We can't leave those people there, can we?"

"It's a hard decision, Karina, but if you want to help Lumina, I'll back you up."

She turned to Sat. "I promise."

Sat exhaled.

2 0

# SETTLING DOWN

Karina went through her clothes, trying to figure out what to bring and what to leave, but nothing seemed appropriate. Clash of styles. Karina got up and put them back in her wardrobe.

Zoe stood by her. "Yeah, I bet they're not the latest style over there, are they?"

Karina laughed. "No."

"Take just a couple, just so that when you come to visit you don't look like an alien."

"They don't dress like aliens."

Zoe shrugged, then sat on the bed. "You know what part I find most impressive?"

"The moving statues?"

"No. You playing femme-fatale with sexy evil uncle."

Ugh. "Trust me, he was not sexy."

She had a teasing face. "Aaaah. But you do agree you were being a femme fatale."

"Oh, no. I don't think he ever liked me. It was just weird."

Zoe looked up as if thinking. "Hum, didn't you say you had to project a thought about sexy times?"

Karina was regretting having told Zoe so much. "Yeah, so?"

"So?" She rolled her eyes. "Isn't it obvious, Karina? I bet even Satwak got a little different, didn't he?"

Karina shrugged. "He was always weird and distant. No wonder, he had to gain my trust but didn't want me to fall for him or anything."

"You didn't tell me how he survived."

Karina also sat. "I have no clue. Those people have some impressive doctors."

Zoe was thoughtful. "If only we could learn from them…"

"Yeah, but I've heard that was how it started. Lumina went to other places to spread their superiority and ended up taking over the other cities."

"Still, it's a shame. And they're still going to be isolated?"

Karina nodded. "Yes. The Guardians don't know who the new overseer is. For Sian's safety."

Zoe was twisting a lock of hair on her finger. "Do you think it would make any difference if they knew it was Sian? I mean, would they say: 'all right, Lumina is being led by the guy who took over a kingdom less than a year ago. Nah. What are the chances he'll go after any ethereal city?'"

"Very funny, Zoe. Anyway, Lumina is still isolated, other than a special portal to Brighteria. Another portal was made from Brighteria to Siphoria. There's one from there to the Light Gardens."

Her friend stared at her. "And you really want to be a guardian? The jerks who could kill Sian and didn't lift a finger to save you?"

Yeah, it didn't make sense, but at the same time… "I'll get magical training. And teleporters like me are rare."

"Maybe there are a bunch of teleporters in our dimension."

That made sense. "Maybe. But teleporting is not in their destiny."

Zoe sighed. "I guess. I wish I could figure out *my* destiny."

"You will. It can take some time. You could come visit one day, you know? I think Sat finds you cute."

Zoe rolled her eyes. "Sounds tempting. A guy who can read your mind. What's the fun in that? And you know I'm already taken. Plus, I saw that magic, and... I won't lie and say I'm not afraid."

"I'll still come and visit."

"How often?'

"I don't know."

Zoe pointed a finger towards Karina. "Well, figure out something. If you guys are that advanced, find a way to email or text me."

"It's magic, not technology, Zoe."

She shrugged. "Doesn't sound that different to me." Zoe then looked up again. "I'm thinking something. How did Darian pretend to be his brother?"

"I'm not sure exactly how. Cayla told me. Darian's magic is the magic of illusion. He found it I think sitting down and waiting for it to hit him. Incredible, right? I wish inspiration would hit me like that when I had to write essays."

Zoe rolled her eyes. "You have to meditate, not browse the internet."

Karina nodded. "True. Now back to Darian, his illusion clashes with his spell-speaking. He had to choose one."

"He chose the lies."

Karina shrugged. "Well, it is more useful."

Zoe looked at Karina. "And how does Sian disguise himself? Because you said he's talking to the other cities."

"Just a cloak, plus some manipulation in the message."

"Um, cloak. Sounds sexy."

Her friend was into teasing her, but Karina decided to play along and smiled. "He's always sexy."

"True. I bet you prefer him without a cloak. Speaking of which, did you ever see him without his shirt?"

Oh, this was getting worse. "Yeah..."

"What does he look like?"

Desire, sunshine, perfection, tenderness, openness, vulnerability, strength, love. "Uh... Someone who's exercised all his life."

"You can say hot, Karina."

"You asked what he looks like, not what I think about him. I'd think he was hot even if he had a flabby belly."

"But flabby bellies are super hot." They laughed. Zoe then got serious. "And did you guys... already..."

Karina got an empty feeling in her stomach. She knew what her friend was asking but decided to steer the conversation away. "Pacify Lumina? It's a long process."

Zoe nodded. "Long process. I see. And how did you convince your mother to let you go?"

"I brought Sian to talk to them."

Zoe chuckled. "Since when he's an ideal son-in-law?"

"Spell speaker."

"Lucky for you." She then hugged Karina. "I'm going to miss you, my nerdy, kind, supersmart, reading-challenged friend."

"I'll miss you too."

Not only her friend. It was an entire life she was walking away from. It wasn't for a guy. It wasn't for curiosity. It was just that she'd finally found where to make a difference.

Tears ran down Sian's face as he hugged Malena. He'd been to Siphoria to make sure things were settled down and to say goodbye to his friends. Leaving that city was like ripping out a piece of him, especially now, when he finally understood what Malena had been for him.

"Thank you," he said, "for loving me like a mother. Like my mother never did."

"Sian, darling." She broke his hug and took his hand. "There's one thing you need to understand. People don't love like you want them to, or like sometimes you even need them to. They love the way they can. Our lives are screwed up and we love in screwed up ways. Your father loved you. Your mother loved you. I'm sure your brother loves you. Don't shun his love just because it's not the way you think it should be."

"But yours is perfect. Karina's is perfect."

"It might not always be. But don't judge them. Your love is not perfect either."

He remembered everything he'd done to Karina. "Far from perfect. But I'm trying to be better."

"I'm sure you'll do whatever you have to do wonderfully. I've always known you were a good boy."

Tears ran down his face again. She could never know where he was going, what he was going to do. It felt lonely and strange. "I'll come and visit."

"You better!"

CAYLA HAD to come to terms with quite a few things. She should have noticed that Leena had been too eager to show everything to Sian and Darian. Well, she wanted to retire. The Light Gardens also had a lineage system of leadership, and it was quite silly that she hadn't realized what it meant.

Leena's role was temporary. Darian decided to take the seat. Cayla could have decided to stay between Whyland and the Light Gardens, but in the end, she knew that Whyland was changing. Plus, she'd always dreamed of being queen just because she had no idea what else was out there in the world.

Now she wanted to improve her magic. Cayla, like her mother, was a descendent of Gleam Fortress. That meant she would probably take longer to age, and she'd be more powerful than most, but it also meant her magic bloomed later.

Cayla had yet another dream. The Guardians had proven to be the most incompetent interdimensional force. The world needed something better. She thought that perhaps with Nia, Darian, Karina, and a few more, she could start something new. She hadn't told anyone yet, but that was her plan.

The most shocking thing was that Darian had proposed and she'd said yes. But for real, not in some unspecified future. Well, she figured that getting married wouldn't change her life much, and since he insisted...

But the butterflies in her belly told another story. The image staring at her in the mirror had a very complex hairdo with a crown of braids. Her eyes had been lined with dark blue ink. She thought it was weird at first, but now, looking at her image, she liked it.

If they were to do this right, they should be getting married in the Light Gardens, but Sian had been avoiding the ethereal cities, so they did it in Whyland, in the castle, in their garden.

She walked in and saw Darian wearing a red suit, just like he'd done in the first ball they had together. Tears ran down her eyes, and she hoped that the ink was truly waterproof. Her loved ones sat in a circle on the grass. Her mother smiled when she saw Cayla, even if she'd been against this wedding claiming Cayla was too young. Nia held an unwilling Leo, and Talon—it was weird to get used to his new name—tried to distract the boy.

Ayanna was near them. Alessa was there too, looking fierce and amazing as always. Leena looked more emotional than Cayla would have expected. Sian held Karina tight, whispering something in her ear. Karina gestured for him to turn and look, but he kissed her cheek instead.

Karina whispered, "You have to look at the bride!"

"I'm trying to make a point."

Cayla and Darian sat in the middle of the circle. This was similar to Lumina that the couple chose their words.

Cayla said, "I promise to love you, respect you, cherish you, and look at you, at the real you, today, and to renew this promise and this intent with each sunrise."

Darian then repeated that. Those were beautiful words.

"This is nonsense," Sian whispered.

"I think it's beautiful."

"They're promising just for today. I mean, why get married?"

"I think the idea is that every day they have to start again and bring their best."

He had a face. "What if you wake up in a bad mood?"

"You try to remember your vows and treat the other person well, despite the bad mood."

Sian shook his head. "I don't know how it's like where you're from, but in Whyland we promise to love each other forever."

"It doesn't make a difference. People break up all the time." She thought about her parents and tons of other parents. That wasn't a good thought at a wedding.

"Maybe. But when you promise, you mean it." He held her hand. "We'll do it Whyland style."

Uh? And when had he proposed that she didn't remember? When had she ever said yes? She could have asked these questions, she could have teased him, but the truth is that he'd just given her a love declaration.

She smiled. "Whyland style, then."

"Sooner rather than later. Think about it. I'm taking care of that dysfunctional city where more than half the people want to kill me, and I'm doing it for a promise you made for a dude that ended up not dying."

"Hasn't Sat been helpful?"

"Satwak. Say his full name." He was frowning, and she wasn't sure how much of it was teasing.

"It's a complicated name."

Sian widened his eyes. "It's two syllables. You don't call me See."

"Is that what you want?"

"Of course not." He had a playful smirk. "I'm more into Dearest Eternal Love of my Life, Light of the Universe, Owner of My Heart."

"Can I shorten it to Sian?"

Sian waved a hand. "Yeah, ignore my wishes."

She rolled her eyes.

He pointed his finger at her. "But you are. You had no issues marrying him."

How many times would she have to explain it? "I was being threatened."

"Right." He made a high-pitched voice. "Oh, no, you could have upset the Lumina overseer." He stared at her, his voice back to normal. "Well, you are upsetting the Lumina overseer."

Karina scrunched her face. She'd been between there and the Light Gardens, and Sian didn't like it. Too bad, she had her life too.

Darian and Cayla were hugging everybody and it came to Sian and Karina's turn, so they got up. Cayla stopped in front of Sian and extended her hand. "Friends?"

"No way."

Cayla stepped back.

But then, Sian hugged her. "You're my sister now."

"You're my new brother," she replied.

From Cayla's previous dislike of Sian, this was a huge step. Heartwarming. Just not as heartwarming as hugging her friend.

"We'll see each other," Cayla said.

"For sure."

Karina looked at Sian and Darian. They shared a strong embrace.

Sian said, "I love you, little brother. You're one of the best things that happened in my life, and the best brother anyone could ever ask for. Sorry I never told you that before."

Karina looked away because she got the feeling Darian was crying. Maybe Sian was too. Her eyes met Cayla's and they shared a smile.

KARINA DIDN'T REGRET SPLITTING her time between the Light Gardens and Lumina, even if it was uncomfortable having to keep her mouth shut about Sian and her teleporting into the city of light. After one month of training with Anika, she felt that her magic was getting stronger.

In Lumina, things were getting better. The people who'd been in the stasis room were getting medical treatment. Some of them had lost their memories and it had been so long that they were having trouble getting them back.

The attendants were no longer mute, even if it was hard to notice, since most of them were still afraid of speaking. Everyone was terrified of Sian, which made him quite uncomfortable. Slowly he was making friends, but his role was a burden. But if he hadn't been meant to take it, why had he been born with the Lumina affinity magic?

Karina went to the training grounds. Even if Lumina wouldn't take any military action against anyone, Sian didn't want to get rid of their training. It was part of their traditions.

They were still powerful and magnificent. The woman with short purple hair approached Karina. "Want to give it a try?"

Karina felt embarrassed, since her magic was so inferior to everyone there. She was even more embarrassed about her lack of manners. "What's your name?"

"Gia."

"I'm—"

The woman had a half bow. "I know who you are."

Of course. Everyone did. Karina smiled. "Nice to meet you."

"Come give it a try. There's always something to improve."

A lot to improve, in Karina's case, and plus she was already training... But then... why not?

Karina stepped in the grounds. "What do you want me to do?"

She'd been doing a lot of physical preparation with Anika. The girl said that the body had to be ready for the mind. Karina imagined Gia would give her an exercise like that.

But instead of instructions, the woman sent a gigantic metal ball flying in Karina's direction. By pure reflex, she pushed it away. That had been close. Had the woman meant to attack her?

"See?" Gia pointed. "You're doing it wrong."

Well, no kidding, genius. She hadn't even warned Karina. But she decided to be polite. "Why?"

"The problem is that you think you have to use your energy to push the ball. That will get you tired in no time, you could even faint."

Well, yeah, Karina always felt depleted after using her magic. But it was normal, wasn't it? "What energy should I use?"

"Don't feel that it's coming from you, feel as if you were just manipulating the energy around you. Can we try again?"

"All right." Another gigantic ball in her direction, and Karina tried to do what the woman had told her. It was like ten times easier.

"That's a little better. There are a few tricks you still need to learn. You're using less than one percent of your magic, girl."

"How do you know?"

"I can see it."

"Can you tell me some tricks?"

"Sure thing, but it won't do you no good if you don't practice correctly. You need to come here every day if you want to reach even one-third of your potential."

Karina didn't like hyperbolical math statements. If you want to exaggerate, use something less specific than math. "You said I'm using only one percent of my potential. If I were to be thirty-three times stronger, I'd be more powerful than Sian."

"He, he. Sure thing. But he can harness the power of the city. That's a tough one to counter." She laughed. "Like that, eh? Come in the morning. From nine to ten. You need consistency, not long hours."

This was so, so much better than the crappy training Karina had been getting. Of course Anika—and sometimes Leena—did their best. But still, this was a whole different kind of best. She turned around, thoughtful.

"We start tomorrow!" Gia said—or ordered—because she was the scary teacher type. The kind that pushed you to your best.

This was the day Karina decided to move to Lumina and stop her here-and-there nonsense.

SIAN STILL SOMETIMES HAD TROUBLED DREAMS. He now understood what Lylah had meant when she'd told him she didn't enjoy being queen. Having power was also responsibility, selflessness.

At least he started to enjoy the city. Slowly they were getting more arts, music, and Sian was getting a hint of normality—if it weren't for the fact that everyone was scared of him. They should be scared of Karina, but she trained alone in the morning so they probably hadn't seen what she could do. He hoped she'd never need any of that. Hoped, but at the same time kept talks with his brother about a new type of Guardians.

The issue was that Lumina had better not get involved in any of that. They were too powerful. He'd listened to the historical records. Lumina conquering and domination had started hundreds of years before with good intentions. They had the best magicians, the best teachers, the best doctors. Perhaps they'd failed because they considered the other cities inferior.

Sian didn't know what to do. Sharing wisdom with the world was a noble goal, unless it became imposing. If they were to get involved in a society for interdimensional security... Darian said it would be just Karina and him, and still, they had no idea what they were becoming. He and Karina could take an army if they wanted. It was good but at the same time scary.

His other bothersome thoughts were about all the unhappy upper-class citizens now that the attendants had to receive fair wages. The working class now was free, and there was talk about resistance.

The only good thing was that he could threaten to unleash the city on them and then they'd all shut up. But this wasn't the right way to do politics. He wasn't sure what the right way was. It was a process. Sian's strategy had always been to make as many allies as possible, but he was just beginning to understand the Luminous, so it was hard. He didn't regret having become Lumina overseer. To refuse it would have been to run from his destiny and from who he was. Plus he was lucky that he had Karina with him, helping him take care of the city.

She rested her head on his bare chest, her presence so calming. His scars no longer made him uncomfortable. They were part of who he was. A sign he'd gone through pain and suffering and had healed. Not that anyone other than Karina ever saw them.

But then, other issues sometimes haunted him. He'd never told anyone, but there was something quite dark and dangerous about his magic. He suspected Karina had felt it, but she, more than anyone, understood he had to use it. If Sian could, he'd never use it again.

Then there was Darloom. It had left Marisia. Perhaps blocking the cave had worked, perhaps no longer having a king serving it made it go away. Who knew? Still, it had gone somewhere. Sian couldn't forget that he'd made a deal with Darloom once; to be king beside Karina. Fine, he was now overseer, but it was pretty much the same. And he got it.

A chill ran down his spine; a reminder that peace was something he'd need to fight constantly to maintain. At least it wasn't boring.

Day Leitao lets her characters take her to new, incredible places, and she hopes to bring readers with her.

She's originally from Brazil and lives in Montreal, Canada.

To learn more about her books, visit her at dayleitao.com

Don't forget to sign up for news, updates, and a free novella at dayleitao.com/sign-up/ You'll get *The Spell Speakers*, a prequel novella where you'll learn more about Darian, Cayla, and Sian's past.